I0687290

6 Mile Chronicles

The Birth of a Hustler

A novel by
Mi'Kiel Los

6 Mile Chronicles is a So Real Publishing book published by arrangement with the author.

Printing History First Printing 1/17/2013
Copyright 2013 by Mi'Kiel Los

Cover Design and production by Melissa Talbot

For information www.sorealpublishing.com
Authormikiellos@gmail.com

ISBN: 978-0-9840216-3-5
Printed in the United States of America

Aknowledgments

This is the 6th time that God has rewarded me for my efforts by blessing me with a complete body of work and I would like to thank him for showing me that he is whom he says he is! He has blessed me and my family and has always provided a way when the world said that it was impossible.

This book was a little more challenging than my others because I have been losing so many friends and family members throughout the time that I've spent working on it. RIP to all of my people who have lost their lives over senseless violence as hazards of the game.

Back in the day, when I was coming up, getting my feet wet in the blood of the streets, the hustlers use to have a saying "THE GAME AIN'T TO BE TOLD IT'S TO BE SOLD!" And that's exactly what I'm doing now! I'm writing about it and entertaining people with my intelligence; instead of ignorance!

I dedicate this one to all my fallen 6mile soldiers RIP Lil Yo, Big Dion, Bokie Mac, Eddie, lil Bobby, RayRay, Chip, Pig, and therest of the fallen soldiers everywhere!   SALUTE

CHAPTER 1

Fox lay across his bed livid, while speaking to Antoine on the phone. He'd had to move to the eastside of Detroit. Fox had grown up running the streets of his neighborhood, so the transition to a new area was an unwanted experience for him.

"I'm telling you, my nigga," Fox said into the telephone. These niggaz over here are corny as hell! I can't wait to get back to the west. This shit shakin a nigga up."

I feel you, dawg." Antoine felt him, but he had ulterior motives. "I need yo slick talkin ass back over here so you can talk Keisha into given me some of that pussy." He chuckled before going silent. "Aw shit! My moms callin me. Hold up." The telephone went silent after Antoine set it down.

Fox held the phone to his ear for a while, but it went dead. He was sure that Antoine was in a fucked up situation after that. He felt bad for his boy because Antoine had been catching it bad, from his mother, lately. The beating started about six months ago or shortly after his father vanished from their lives. Fox knew about the beatings and the abuse because he and Antoine were best friends and they shared everything, especially secrets. After Antoine's father left their household, his mother went into a vicious state of alcoholism. She would get drunk and take all of her misplaced frustration out on Antoine. He looked identical to his father, so it was

4

evident that he was getting everything that she wanted to put on his old man.

Antoine's father, diamond, was an extremely abusive type of nigga. He would savagely beat Antoine's mother religiously, so naturally after his pops left the cycle continued only his mother was the abuser, and Antoine was the victim. He was getting the repercussion of his father's action. For him, this was the beginning of his birth into the streets.

****

After putting Fox on hold Antoine went into the living room where his mother was waiting for him. He was sure that she had heard his and Fox's conversation, but he tried to play it smooth by asking her what she wanted. There wasn't any sense in initiating a situation that didn't have to happen.   "What's up?" his guilt written look said more than his mother needed to hear. She went into a cursing tirade before slapping him across his mouth and making him hang up the telephone. This had become a frequent occurrence for him and he was becoming fed up with it.

Now, Antoine lay across his bedroom floor, holding his swollen mouth, and mumbling profanities. He was sure that Fox knew what was going on because they talked about everything that went on within their lives, including the abuse that he'd been receiving from his mother. It was an embarrassing ordeal, but Fox was his nigga and he felt at liberty to share that type of shit with him. Antoine angrily kicked the bed post.

"I gotta get the fuck outta this muthafuckin house!" He mumbled to his self trying not to fuel his mother's rage any further. He considered himself to be a man, at the age of fourteen, so being slapped across his face by his mother was unacceptable. He'd been putting suckers to sleep, with his hand, since he was a youngster, and now he was being bullied by his mother. What part of the game was that? Although he loved his mom deeply it was time. He was ready to leave the nest before he continued to be beaten for no reason other than someone's drunken rage. This was the type of shit that happen on television and now it was in his own life happening to him. Fuck this shit! He thought.

His mother had always been an authoritarian, but the shit she'd been putting down lately was on another level. The drinking that had become lush was herself medication for the mental wounds that diamond had left her with. And it eventually caused a negative whirlwind that intensified everything about her, including her anger. Fox had assured Antoine that he was receiving the backlash of the years of abuse that his father had given his mother, and he was starting to take his word as the truth.

Antoine peeked out of his room and saw his mother sprawled across the living room sofa in a drunken sleep. She looked horrible. He shook his head with empathy. His mother was at her worst. Although his parents were a solid couple on the outside, he knew that his dad had taken a lot out of his mother mentally, emotionally, and especially physically because his mother was an unbelievably attractive broad.

She was a light skinned sister with deep dimples, and a head full of cinnamon brown hair. It fell across her back like a cape, and her thin waist was followed by a mountainous ass. She was the envy of plenty of woman in their neighborhood. Antoine had seen his mother's naked body when he was eight and the thought always popped into his head when he thought about what she used to be.

That day, he was awakening by a loud thumping sound followed by a muffled panting and moaning. After coming to, he realized the voice was his mother's. She was screaming and violently panting.

"Ooooo…...please! Diamond, don't do me like this. Ooooh!" something was crashing against the wall causing the thunderous pounding that had woken him. At eight years old Antoine was terrified. He thought his father was putting another cruel beating on his mother. This was something that had awakened him on several occasions and he was fed up. How could his pops treat his mother like that? It was time for him to defend her. He reached into his closet and came out with a baseball bat. It was on. He slowly crept down the hallway, leading to his parent's bedroom, fearful that his father would hear him before he could get a swing off. The closer he got, the more violent the screams became. He wanted to turn around and run back to the safety of his bedroom closet, but he was afraid that Diamond would kill his mother. Once he reached their bedroom, he pushed the door opened and rushed in swinging the slugger wildly. He stopped and stood by the bedroom entrance wide eyed after realizing what he'd stumbled onto. His father had his mother in the doggy style position, pounding her deeply, with his foot glued to the back of her head pressing her face into the bed.

Antoine chuckled and shook his head at the thought of the night. Man, I miss my pops, he thought while taking another peep into the living room at his mom. He shook his head again, but this time it was in disappointment. "I miss my mom too." He said softly. Because that drunk out there on the couch ain't her. I gotta get some paper so I can get mom dukes some help." He slipped back into his room and stared out the window.

****

Fox threw his television remote to the floor. He was angry because he knew Antoine was catching hell at home. Fox loved his mother, but he'd sworn to himself that he'd never let anyone treat him like Antoine was being treated. He shook his head defiantly. ***Ain't no muhfuckin way***, he thought. He was facing some of the same plights that Antoine was. His father had been killed around the same time that Antoine's father had disappeared so his situation at the crib was fucked up too, but his mother wasn't wilding out like Antoine's.

Fox's father Alfredo was a majority breadwinner in the household. He was a great provider. Alfredo was a true to life four corner hustle. He shot craps, sold heroin and cocaine, and would even put a bitch on the track. If there was a dollar to be made Alfredo wanted in on it, and his family benefited swell. Fox was spoiled rotten until tragedy struck. After his father got smoked, things got real tight for his family. They were forced to leave there middle class life style because his mother could no longer afford the mortgage on their home moderate pay rate. Fox put on a strong façade, but he was affected by his father death.

Alfredo was supposedly killed during a drug deal gone bad. He was usually a skeptical and alert type of cat, but this was one that he never saw coming. The police detective, who was overseeing murder, claimed that Alfredo was sitting inside of his car, with two kilos of cocaine, waiting on the buyer when someone jumped into the passenger's side and blew the top of his head through the driver's side window. Since the person who committed the murder didn't take the drugs, the detectives assumed the killing was drug deal gone bad rather than a robbery. In addition, there were no witnesses to the murder, so the details were still speculative.

The Thought of Alfredo's death haunted Fox from time to time, but he kept it bottled up. His pops had raised a gangster and there was no way that he'd show the streets any signs of weakness. He shook his head.

"Hell nah!" he whispered to himself while looking around his current living conditions. "A nigga gotta man up 'cause being broke ain't hittin on shit!"

He knew it was time to do what he had to because his mother's clerk job couldn't afford him the luxuries that he'd became accustomed to while his father was alive. It was his own responsibility now. He had to make sure that he had. His sister, Sherry, had escaped what he was facing. She'd married, Rone, a major nigga from their father clique. They had chips and helped out his mother's request, but that black pride prevented her from asking, and Fox didn't blame her. He was sure that it was hard for a broad to fall from the top of the world only to become a begger.

Sherry did the right thing by latching on to Rone. She was a piece of eye candy that no nigga could resist. She stood five foot ten inches, dark skinned. Her jet black hair was that silky looking shit, and she had thick lashes and perfectly sculpted eyebrows to compliment them. Her toned and bowed legs carried a heart shaped ass that made niggaz eyes pop out their heads. So when she spun her web, Rone fell in willingly.

Sherry and Fox were tight to death too. Of course, she was his older sister so it was natural that they vibed, but their relationship had an even powerful synergy than DNA alone. Fox would lie down or lay ten men down for his sister and he was sure that she would do the same for him. That's just how they got down for one another.

The night was closing in on the city as Fox lay on his bed thinking about a way to get at that gwap. He knew that there was something he could do to get his feet wet before jumping all the way in. it hadn't come to him yet, but he was sure that it would. The hustle was in his bloodline so getting rich was his destiny.

CHAPTER 2

Fox lounged around the house waiting on his aunt to return his call. He'd racked his brain for days trying to figure out a way to stack some paper up. He'd considered jumping off the porch and head first into the game, but he quickly changed his mind. He knew selling dope was a hard grind which eventually led him to the next best thing. While he waited he mapped out a few moves that he could make to put a lock on shit. He was sure that he'd have to make a way for Antoine too because his boy could use some bread also. They looked out for one another like that, but their friendship wasn't always as solid as it is now. In fact they started off as enemies.

Fox had just started at his new school and him and Antoine immediately set the tone of their dislike for one another. "Get your bitch ass outta my face," Antoine said and looked around to see who was watching. Fox just chuckled.

Although Fox had parents that would beat all the hell out of him at any sign of fucking up in school, he was still down to put hands on any youngster, on the playground, who wanted it with him. Just so happened Antoine really wanted it. He didn't know that the little time that Alfredo was able to spend at home, with his family, was usually spent teaching Fox to use his hands. Alfredo was the truth with his knuckle game. He'd learned from the best in the game, and had passed what he knew on to his son. So dropping a nigga on his knees was effortless for Fox.

"Yo momma's a bitch, hustlah." Fox replied nastily and stepped back into a standard southpaw position. As Antoine rushed him swinging a windmill of wild punches, fox stepped aside and tripped him. The entire playground erupted into an earsplitting laughter after seeing Antoine go down to the gravel. His Pants were ripped in the crotch area and he looked defeated, but Fox wasn't finished with him. Fox knelt to the ground and punched Antoine in the face repeatedly. He'd really humiliated him with that one, but things changed. It took some time, but they did.

A new youngster named Jackson moved into their school district and was placed into their class. Fox had animosity against the young cat instantly. Jackson was true to life down south stereotype. He was dark skinned with a thick build, and heavy southern drawl. He tried to intimidate everyone in their school, but fox wasn't buying into his bully tactics. One day after class, Fox was busy chasing some little mami's around when he saw Jackson shaking Antoine down for his candy. Although he didn't like Antoine too much either, he'd grown to detest Jackson and this was his way to check the water. You know how it is in the ghetto, a nigga always want to know if the hype is gospel. He ran over to them and pushed Jackson away. "Hold up, dawg!" Fox stood between him and Antoine, who was visibly shaken. He'd chosen sides and he wanted it to be clear. Wuzzup, bwoy?" Jackson threw his hand in the air, like he wanted trouble; Fox shot a quick left hand to his throat, he chocked and gagged for air while grabbing for his throat. Fox tugged at Antoine's arm. "Come on, hustlah!" Fox said while running off. Antoine quickly followed behind him. That was the first of many acts of violence for them because after that day they were inseparable.

The telephone rang disturbing Fox's thoughts. He rushed over and answered it. "Hello?" he spoke into the phone knowing it was his aunt Stacey. "Did your mother call me?" Stacey asked after hearing Fox's voice. "Nah auntie. I did. I need a favor from you." Stacey chuckled. "You must not need it too bad because I told you about calling me auntie." She said sassily. She was a dime piece too. A light skinned honey with an ass and thighs like Beyonce. "If someone hears you say that shit...... I'm fuckin you up." She teased knowing she couldn't do anything to hurt her little man. She loved Fox just like everyone else did. Fox was more cunning at fourteen than most full grown men. He'd picked up a lot of game from his old man and he wasn't shy about using it.

"No doubt aun... I mean Stacey." He caught himself because he was sure that Stacey would pull back on the help he needed. "I need some of those syringes you be bringin home from work sometimes?" Stacey was a home health care nurse. She visited outpatients at their homes to make sure they were being properly cared for. She brought them medical supplies and other things they needed and sometimes she'd bring things home.

"What do you need with syringes?" her cut nature attitude quickly became evil. Don't have me come over there, boy! I have a forty-five minute lunch break coming up and I'll spend it beating the shit outta you!" she was livid and hoped that Fox wasn't doing what she thought. Fox chuckled lightly. He wanted to break the stench of anger that had fallen into their conversation. Stacey always overreacted to anything concerning Fox, but he quickly defused the situation.

"Stacey, you trippin. Tee's mom got laid off from work a few months ago and they cut her insurance last week. She can't afford her syringes to take her insulin shots." He lied without any signs of dishonestly.

"Oh, Okay." She calmed into a soft giggle. "Yeah, I can do that, but I thought I was gonna have to fuck you up. Y'all just moved to the east side, but I've been here all my life. So I know ghetto." Her snicker continued. Soon after hanging up with Stacey, Fox's manipulative mind continued working. He dialed number after number setting things up. He'd done a lot of odd jobs for the gangsters and shot callers in the city during his childhood. He'd clean up a few bars, looked out for a couple of drugs houses, and help out around some juke joints. He was sure that he'd have a welcome reception back into those establishments, but it wouldn't be as a worker, instead it would be as an entrepreneur. After getting the okay from his old bosses, he called Antoine,

"What up wit it, hustlah?" Fox asked gaily after hearing Antoine voice come through the phone.

"Shit, what it do?" Antoine replied. He was nonchalant with his greeting, but Fox was sure that

Antoine mood was about to change after hearing what he had to say.

"We 'bout to get paid, my nigga! That's what's up!"Fox was expecting to hear some enthusiasm in Antoine response, but it didn't happen. Although those were words that Antoine had desperately wanted to hear, he replied with a doubtful. "How?"

"You ask too many question, hustlah. If I wanted an interview I would've gotten us a job instead of a hustle." Fox teased and Antoine chuckled. "Fuck you."

"On some real shit though. Do you still have your bus pass?" "Yeah, I got it. Now, what's up?" Antoine questioned. He wanted to know what type of shit Fox had come up with because he needed to get it cracking immediately because shit was getting uglier and uglier around his parts. "Meet me at the burger king inside the greyhound station downtown. Be there at ten in the morning." He demanded. Punctuation meant everything to Fox, especially knowing that his father's life had been taken because a nigga was late for the buy. "A'ight then! It's a bet."

"Bet it up." Fox hung up the phone and began putting the details together inside the privacy of his mischievous mind.

****

After hanging up the phone Antoine sat around his bedroom trying to figure out what Fox was up to. He was aware of Fox's urgency to get some paper, but he was skeptical about the whole situation. He wonders why Fox was being too secretive about what he planned for their come up. Antoine knew how ambitious his nigga was. That's what type of guy his boy was, but sometime he'd push it to the edge to get something accomplished. During their childhood they'd gotten into all kinds of shit, and Fox would always have an out for them. One time, they'd gotten suspended from school for putting a stumping on a nigga from across the tracks. Neither of them had been into any trouble in their junior high school, at that point, so their parents hadn't been to the school. Right after they got their suspension slips, Fox started running a con.

"Dang," Fox said with despair as the principal walked away. Auntie is gonna kill us for getting in trouble at school." He made sure his statement was loud enough for the principal to hear it as they walked off into the other direction.

"What the fuck was that about?" Antoine asked after they got into the hallway. He was confused and didn't know what Fox was putting down. "My pops said a nigga s'pose to plant seeds at the beginning of the season." He nodded like he'd just dropped a jewel on Antoine. "Just roll with me, hustlah." He smiled sinisterly knowing that he could pull it off.

During their walk home Antoine pestered Fox about what they were going to do. He was scared out of his mind because he knew his mother was looking for a reason to put a whipping on his ass. Fox assured him his parents wouldn't find out that they'd been suspended and to meet him out front of the school the following day. The next morning Antoine reluctantly walked up to the building knowing that his ass was cooked if Fox's plan failed.

He saw Fox standing to a scrawny looking woman and rushed over to them. He gave Fox pound and waited to here the play. Fox wanted him to stand silent and look regretful while the older woman did the talking. Antoine looked over to her and shook his head. He was sure that he had an ass whipping coming because she looked smoked out of her mind. How could she help them do anything? Her mind was far away from some kiddie disco shit! She was thinking about her next blow. He just dropped his head and followed them into the building.

Luckily, just as Fox had planned, they were let back into school and their parents never found out. Fox paid a basehead hoe ten dollars to act like their aunt, and she earned it because her performance was Oscar winning.

Antoine laughed at the memory. Fox's juvenile display of manipulation was one of the reasons why he was so skeptical about what his boy was up to.

****

Fox's eyes roamed the room looking for Antoine immediately after he arrived to the bus depot. He briefly sat in the terminal before hearing the sound of Antoine's voice near the arcade area. He saw his boy at the millipede game and walked over to him. He gave Antoine a pound.

"What up doe?" Fox greeted. "How long you been here?" "Since nine-thirty. You said on time, so here I is, nigga." He chuckled.

"I'm on time too." He knew that Fox would be tripping if he was late, which was understandable to him because of what had went down with Alfredo

Fox was impressed. Being on time was usually a problem for Antoine, so seeing him there let Fox know that Antoine was just as serious as him about getting money. He knew Antoine wanted to help his mother out, which was motivation enough, but he was impressed nonetheless.

"Peep it hustlah." Fox began. I got three boxes of syringes wit a hundred in each box!" he was excited. Fox knew it wasn't like a ton of blow getting dropped off in the port of Miami, but he did expect to hear some type of cheer in Antoine. Instead, Antoine's eyes squinted into an evil stare. "What?" he asked nastily. "I know you ain't got me downtown at nine o'clock in the muhfuckin mornin talkin 'bout no hospital equipment! I ain't no muhfuckin surgeon!" he was fervid, especially after seeing Fox's nonchalant head shake.

"Is you finish!" Fox patronized him. He was disappointed in Antoine's quickness to shoot him down.

Yeah, I'm finish."I should raise up outta this muhfucka! He thought while staring toward the exit of the building.

"Look nigga...." Fox's tone was stern. He meant business and whether Antoine was with it or not, he was going to make that scratch. "We fixed to get paid. I got these from the lady down the street from me. She's a basehead that works at the pharmacy. She gets the five finger discount and we get the basehead discount. Nigga.... I sold my mimi bike for these muthafuckas. Each one goes for four dollars on the streets all day. We gon cut it in half and push'em fo two since we gettin'em so cheap. That's two hundred a box." Fox leaned back in his seat and smiled. He was sure that Antoine would be with it now.

Antoine looked dumbfounded. He'd placed his foot into his mouth before hearing Fox out. After briefly sitting silent he rubbed his head and chuckled.

"My bad fo doubtin you, my nigga." He gave Fox a pound with his apology. "I was trippin."

"Tee, you my peoples. Don't trip 'cause I appreciate our little differences. If you agreed with me about everything I wouldn't trust you. So what's up? You at this cake or what?"

"Hell yeah!"

"Aw'ight then. You remember that after hour I use to be the lookout for on Plymouth?" "Yeah, I know which one you talkin 'bout." "Good..." Fox nodded his head before continuing, "I already hollered at Big Rock. He said it was cool if you posted up over there. I got this little pool hall I've been working on. You know… sweeping around and taking out the trash and shit. I can move there too."

"I appreciate this, man." Antoine tone was sincere. He needed this break, and although he knew it wasn't much, he was grateful nonetheless. "What's up with the hulk bag though…" he chuckled, "You done had that muhfucka since third grade?" "While Antoine doubled over laughing, Fox flashed his bald fist at him.

"Fuck you nigga. You remember what happen to you back then about crackin jokes," he teased.

Antoine quickly became defensive. "That was yesterday, muhfucka." He stared at Fox letting him know that he meant what he said. He was much more experienced in life and would never let anyone punish him like that again. At least, not and live afterwards.

"Whatevah, hustlah." Fox replied. He'd seen the seriousness in Antoine's stared, but didn't acknowledge it. Antoine was his boy and didn't pose a threat to him. "Besides, the bag goes with you." He pushed the bag over to his partner and gave him a pound before he walked off. He really admired his and Antoine's deep camaraderie. Not to mention, he'd gotten the ok from his mother to hang out with him which didn't happened too often. She didn't believe in true friendship. She would always tell Fox, "If you get one good friend you're a lucky motherfucker!" but if you claim to have two, you're a lying motherfucker!" And that was the real about frien'emies. Friends usually become enemies because those types of relationships were very conditional.

After that day, the two youngsters wasted no time becoming the niggaz to see if you wanted to cop some clean work. Antoine solidly held down his hood while Fox was shaking it up on the eastside of the motor city. They were pushing needles like it was dog food itself. Having storefronts and pool halls crowds with friends trying to stay AID's and hepatitis free. For the next couple of years, the two of them put in shrewd grinds. They eventually branched off into other hustles. Running cons, gambling, and selling heroin on a petty level. This was the beginning of a thorough street partnership, and it was a good one because Antoine's situation at the crib had turned him into a calloused nigga, which always came in handy when it was time to bust a head or two, and Fox's thirst for that paper and his foresight insured their future prosperity in the game.

CHAPTER 3

TWO YEARS LATER

Fox jumped out of his Chevy and ran up to Sherry's front door. She opened and let her little brother comes in. there weren't many people who knew where she and Rone lived let alone be welcomed in, but Fox was her brother, furthermore, Rone felt him too. It was the go getter quality he had that drew the major niggaz in the city to him, but he stayed humble in his own lane. "What up, lil brah?" Sherry asked happily while following him into the house.

"Nothing, what's been up with you?" Fox laughed. "I see you lookin good for a change." He shot a quick one at her because he knew she was ready to spray him. That's what they usually did when they saw one another—talk shit. Sherry laughed.

"Fuck you, boy." She pushed the back of his shoulder. "I called you over here because Rone wants to talk to you.' Her eyes shifted sneakily. It was something that told Fox bullshit was on the way. He glanced over to her with a confused look on his face.

"What he wanna talk to me 'bout?" he asked and Sherry looked away before shrugging her shoulders.

"I don't know. He probably wanna give you a job at one of the companies since your ass ain't in school," she rolled her eyes at him. He's in the din waiting on you too."

23

Fox sighed after hearing the mention of school. He'd dropped out a few months ago because his grind had gotten so intense, but he always planned to return one day soon. He gave Sherry the middle finger and walked off toward the den. "I've heard it all before, so go ahead with the lecture. I hope Rone ain't on that ho shit either," as much shit as he be off into on these streets, he thought while walking down the hall. Although Fox liked Rone personally, he was skeptical about having a conversation with him about business—any kind of business.

Rone had been a suspect in string of unsolved murders during the late eighties and early nineties. Word on the streets was "Rone's way of trigger play," and Fox definitely didn't want to be in that arena with him. Especially after hearing some of the gruesome tails of the murders and mayhems that he'd put down over the years. As Fox approached the door to the den, he rubbed his head from curiosity. Damn, he thought, I wonder what this weirdo ass nigga wants with me? I ain't even tryna fuck with this nigga! Sherry had told Fox about Rone sitting in the dark and how distant he got at times. She believed he was hunted by those street demons that a trail of murders brought him about, but Fox didn't give a fuck what it was. His hustles was with limited muscle and he was tryna keep it that way. He'd seen cats get too big for their bridges, have to smoke a nigga for respect, and spend the rest of their life in the joint being disrespected by bitch ass CO's. He shook his head, fuck that shit. Fox knocked on the door before going I'm. Surprising Rone had the lights on. He was leaned back in his recliner reading the newspaper. "Big brah!" Fox said when Rone looked over to him. Rone gave him a once over, and smiled. "What up, young trap? You good, my nigga?" his demeanor was welcoming. Unlike the seriousness he usually aired while a nigga was in his presence. Fox's apprehension began settling. "Yeah, I'm good." He walked over and gave Rone dap. It was a quick pound on the hand that spoke volumes between two players. "What up? You got something good to tell little brah?" he played interested, although, he would ultimately turn whatever Rone shot at him down. Fox's eyes canvassed the room between statements. "I see you and sis doin some remodeling." Rone chuckled. Rone recognized small talk and bullshit when he saw it. That's what he did for a living. He small talked and bullshited niggaz all the way to the top of the game. It was all regatta to him, but he respected the rules, so he played alone because he needed him and didn't want to scare him away. "Yeah, we're trying to put it together the way we want it. I couldn't live any other way and, sure you feel the same." He kept a steady eye on Fox that made him a little uneasy.

"No doubt."

"Dig it, trap. I called you over here because I needed a favor. I'm going to Georgia tomorrow to take care of some business and I want you to come with me. My man ain't my mans no more, so you my new mans." He appointed Fox the position without so much as questioning his resistance. Rone wasn't use to being told no. people usually fell in from one or two things—his

25

charisma or his force. Whichever had to be used, he didn't give a fuck, but he wasn't one to accept no for an answer. Fox knew that, and although Rone was a fearful cat, he wasn't laying down his principles for no one. Fox was anti job. Legal or illegal, it didn't matter because he refused to work for another man another day in his life. He had his own mind and his own hustle. He knew that his bankroll wasn't the size of Rone's, but it was nonetheless and he'd earned it at his own pace. "I know you been moving heroin for them petty ass niggaz from yo way, but it's time for you to start making some real paper." "I appreciate the opportunity… I do, but if you ain't talkin 'bout letting me do my own thing on my own terms, I'm good." Fox was candid about how he felt. He needed to make his own mark in the streets if he planned to stay in them, and couldn't do that in another cat's shadow. Rone chuckled. He liked Fox's heart. There weren't many niggaz out there willing to turn a spot on his team down, but Fox had done it. He didn't know what he was turning down, but he had and that was an admirable trait in the game filled with lackeys and goons. He'd watched Fox grow into a man, and he was impressed.

"Listen lil nigga. Come through tomorrow morning at ten. At least check this shit out before you shoot it down."

Fox nodded. Aw'ight. I can do that." He agreed although he was still apprehensive about the whole ordeal. He didn't know what Rone had planned for him but he was no one's sycophant. Rone pointed to the cocktail table. "Pick those keys up on your way out." He chuckled because he was sure that Fox's surprise would change his mind all together. You can park the Chevy in the garage until you're ready to put some money into that raggedly muthafucka. I'ont think you're gonna be needing it too soon." He teased as Fox grabbed the keys from the table and walked off. After parking his caprice classic in the garage he rushed over to the truck that was parked in the backyard next to the garage. He knew that a gift like that came with some obligations. Obligations that he wasn't sure he was willing to commit to. He wanted to return to the house and return the keys, but the twenty inch Dayton spokes that the ford expedition was squatting on distracted his thoughts. The truck was candy blue-purple with peanut butter guts. The paint looked like it was sliding off the truck it was so wet. He opened the doors and nearly shitted in his briefs. The headrests were embroidered with his name. Daaaamn! He thought to himself while getting inside. He'd been hustling in the streets, doing hand to hands in the frosty winter months, for two years straight. Sun up until sun down and didn't have shit, but a Chevy and a couple of grand stashed at his mother's house. Now, after being in Rone's presence for all of thirty minutes he was sitting behind the wheel of a thirty thousand dollar truck. Next to the brick city niggaz, a set of dope boys in his neighborhood, he'd came up with the coldest whip in the hood. Quake, and Erk where the man's out in the brick city niggaz. They'd always smash down on Fox sitting high in their whips and looking down on him. Quake had that new Lexus LX 470 cinnamon brown with the double moon roofs, and Erk was pushing an H1 with luxury package. They were both average hustles with an extraordinary plug. Second generation dope boys who inherited the connect from their uncle, Wheat. Wheat was a nigga who had watched Fox grow up, over the past couples of years, in the game. From the youngsters with the work into the niggaz pushing the hardest blow in their hood. And wheat knew, unlike his nephew, Fox was the real deal. This is a different season, Fox thought while driving off. The smell of new leather filled his lungs and he hoped that he'd be able to cover the ticket because he wasn't about to fold for no one—not even Rone. He wondered if Rone wanted to use him as a teenage mule. He'd heard of all kinds of odd shit like that. Restavecs, from Haiti and other countries, being used to traffic narcotics for cartels. Niggaz getting chained to radiators inside dope houses and being forced to sell rocks. He'd heard it all and hopes that Rone wasn't going to try to get at him like that. He wasn't buying it, furthermore, at seventeen there was no more juvenile hall for him if he was caught, instead he'd be on the snow bird up interstate 75, and he prayed that prison wouldn't be his fate.

****

Fox was awaken from a deep sleep. His mother was yelling for him. Her voice was menacing and angry.

"What's up, ma?" Fox rushed out of his bedroom while wiping sleep from his eyes. His mother met him in the hallway. "Who's truck is that in my driveway...." She asked angrily, "I told you about borrowing people's shit, boy!" Her upsetting demeanor was visibly undeniable. Fox had pissed her off. She stood with her arms folded across her chest defensively while waiting on an answer. "It's mines, mom dukes." He replied coolly as not to upset her further. He knew that she'd already lost hope after he dropped out of school, so he didn't want to stress her any further. "Rone and Sherry bought it for me, so I can get back and forth to work. I start working for Rone Monday." He lied swiftly. His mother stared at him disapprovingly. She was sure that he was lying, and she told him as much.

"Work?" her lips curled into doubtful snarl. "Boy, who in the fuck do you think you're talking to?" all ends meet at some point. If you don't know what I mean, keep on doing what you're doing, and you'll find out. Now get that truck out of my driveway so I can get to my real job." She stormed out of the house and Fox follow behind her. He was disappointment in himself. After all his mother had been through with his father getting smoked, he'd turned into the same type of nigga---a hustler.

After moving the Expedition, Fox rushed back to the house, and took a short shower before picking Rone up. He called Antoine to let him know that he'd be leaving town for a few days. He didn't give him any details about what was going down because he didn't know too much himself. He didn't tell him what to do concerning what they had popping off because he knew his boy was a bad decision maker. Antoine had turned into a hot tempered head buster over the last couple of years. It was good for some shit, and hadn't gotten out of hands, so Fox didn't dwell on it too much, however, he did keep a close eye on him.

Fox drove through Palmer Woods, the area that Sherry and Rone had moved to. Damn, he thought. For the first time, since his sister had been living in Palmer Woods, he payed attention to the scenery. Large exotic looking homes aligned the streets. Each of them had perfectly manicured lawns and shrubbery surrounded them. Trees were scattered throughout the blocks hiding the homes from the city that surrounded them. The Woods was a refuge from urban Detroit life. As he pulled into the circular driveway of Rone's home, he smiled. The thirty –one square foot home that she roamed through daily was a long way from the modest two bedroom "bungalow that he'd just left. His sister had made it. She'd beat the odds, and know it was his turn to get a piece of the American dream. Fox pressed the doorbell and Sherry quickly came to the door smiling.

"What're selling, little boy?" she teased while opening the door for him. She couldn't contain her snickers and Fox smiled. It was a conniving smile that warned her of what was coming.

"Muzzles!" He snapped and brushed pass her and into the house. They both burst into laughter.

"Ah'ight! Ah'ight! You got me with that one." She continued laughing and so did Fox while looking around taking in the upgrades they'd done to their home. They'd add a gourmet kitchen, which was a waste because Sherry wasn't cooking shit! Granite counter tops aligned the kitchen and the door trimming were lined with Brazilian cherry wood. Fox knew that Rone had shelled out some major paper into their spot. And Sherry walked around with an air that she'd become accustomed to those type of luxuries. Rone walked into the room and gave Fox a pound. "What's up, young trap?"

"Shit!" he replied with a laid back demeanor. He didn't want to seem anxious and neither did he want to appear too skeptical. After all, Rone was his brother-in-law so he wanted to give him some trust. "What it do, hustlah?"

Rone chuckled. He knew where Fox had picked up the term hustlah, it was from Alfredo, his father, and it was wild to Rone that Fox stilled carried it, after all the years that his old man had been dead. Rone really missed Alfredo.

"Everything is everything." Rone said after coming out of his brief haze. "Sheeit, you ready to bounce?" Fox nodded his head. "Yeah the truck out front you ready?" Rone laughed.

Fox never seemed to amaze Rone. He was sure that Fox thought they were going to drive to Georgia, but that was a ten hour trip that wasn't going to happen.

"What?" Rone asked, but it was more of a statement of bewilderment. "Nigga you gotta be

31

bullshitting me! I ain't getting in that hot ass truck…." He shook his head defiantly. "I'ont sit my ass in nothing that cost less than a hundred thousand. All you're gonna need outta there is your shit." he teased, but he was serious because he knew the attention that a truck like Fox's would bring. That was the young boy swag and he respected that, but be wasn't falling into that type of trap.

Fox was puzzled. "I thought we were drivin, brah." He shrugged his shoulders "Sheeit, I ain't know." Rone chuckled and tossed Fox the keys to his CL600 Mercedes. "We are." He continued his friendly chuckle. "Right down to the metropolitan airport." When Rone said that, Fox's eyes bulged from his head."We flying?" Fox asked in shock. He was sure that the uneasiness in his voice was noticeable, but he didn't care. He'd never flown anywhere and didn't want to now. That alone would have been a deal breaker if he didn't have a quick flash back of the look he'd gotten, from some neighborhood bopper, while he was on his way to Rone's pad. Damn, he thought to himself while contemplating.

"What, lil nigga? Yo little tummy got butterflies?" Rone teased because he'd heard the flight fright in Fox's voice. "Nah, brah brah." Fox lied because he was nervous as hell. This would be his first time flying, and it wasn't something that he wanted to get used to. After a little more teasing Fox walked out to his truck and got his bags. He threw them into the trunk of Rone's Mercedes and waited for him to come out. Fox sat in the driver's seat rubbing the Italian leather that aligned the steering wheel. Damn, he casually thought to himself while taking

32

in all the luxurious amenities in the CL600. Last week he was cascading through the city's east side in a beat up Chevy. Now he had a truck of his own and was chauffeuring Rone around in a CL600. He couldn't imagine life getting any better for him, that it was at that point, but he was sure, with the assistance of Rone, what his life was set to be like was unfathomable. After Rone got into the car, they drove off. Fox whipped the Mercedes in and out of traffic like he'd been driving one throughout his entire life. The potholes that usually shook the medal off of his caprice weren't even noticeable as they floated across 94 west. The conversation between them was heavy during their drive to the airport.

Rone explained what it was like being a major player in a game that was filled with snakes. And what it took to get to the top. Fox was surprised to find out that Rone was a genuine businessman. He'd heard so many foul and savage stories about Rone, over the years, that he'd started seeing him as an animal. That's how the psychology of the streets tricked weak minded niggaz by painting horrid pictures of cats that were only trying to eat or feed their families, but Fox was escaping that trend because he was learning about Rone straight up. Although they were from two different generation and they had two different backgrounds that shared some of the same values and conviction. They developed an understanding. It was that they both intended to be successful at whatever they did in life because they were both willing to go to the extreme extents, just short of compromising their integrity. "It's about the four gets." Rone explained.

A nigga had to get the four get in order to get it. Get over to get yours, and get out before you get caught up! You know how cats in the hood who seem to have it all, but they keep cracking the whip at the paper until it turns on them. Rone elaborated on the four gets for a while before allowing Fox to share his juvenile view of the game. By the time they reach the airport a bond had formed between them. The butterflies that were fluttering in his stomach had settled and he was ready to get it.

Although Fox had never flown before he was impressed with the luxury of a first class flight. Balling out was beginning to look real attractive to him. He could tell that Rone was a frequent flier because he slept throughout the entire flight. Once they arrived, Fox was introduced to the hot southern weather. He'd heard the term hotlanta, and now he knew what it meant. Georgia weather was a still breeze of heat and the sunshine was blinding as Fox stood out front waiting on Rone. "Damn!" he complained to himself, before seeing Rone hustling toward him.

"Come on, trap." Rone yelled and waved him over. "Our car is ready." Fox followed Rone to a Lincoln Town car and got inside. "Damn," Fox complained, "You can smell the heat out this muhfucka." He and Rone laughed. This was a strange new relationship to Fox. He'd never seen Rone so relaxed and welcoming. He wondered if this was a façade to pull him into some gangster shit only to turn on him later, but Rome seemed so genuine. Throughout their ride to the hotel the conversation was limited. Fox stared out of the window taking in the

34

scenery and Rone read a book. After getting settled into his room, Fox jumped onto the elevator and went up to Rone's suite. The elevator doors opened and Rone stood in the hallway in front of his suite door. He walked down to the elevator and gave the elevator attendant a nice tip. Fox laughed and followed Rone toward his suite.

"Nigga, you movin on up to a deluxe apartment." Fox joked and Rone chuckled lightly.

"T'ont do apartments, my nigga." He opened the room door and they walked in. "This a presidential suite, youngstah." Fox's mouth hung opened. He stood near the entrance of the suite. Daaamn! He thought while looking around. He couldn't hide his enthusiasm.

"Damn, my nigga! This muthfucka look like some shit off the Robin Leach special." His eyes roamed around the opened space of the suite. The room was surrounded with unabashed luxury and quality. The lavish marble entry set the tone for the other plush interior finishes. This was the coldest piece of living he'd seen in the short breath of life.

Rone looked over to Fox and laughed. "Close yo muhfuckin mouth, nigga." He teased Fox "You drooling and shit. Plus we got shit to do." His teasing quickly turned into seriousness, and Fox swiftly straightened himself up.

"Aw'ight, brah brah." Fox nodded. I'm ready." Rone gave him an intense stare. For the first time since they'd left Detroit, Rone wondered if Fox was ready.

35

What they were going to do would change his life forever. And he wanted to be sure that the youngster can handle it.

"I can trust you right?" Rone asked Fox while holding the intensity of his stare on him. It was a test of will, and he wanted to know if Fox believed he should be in the position that he was in. Fox nodded. He didn't know what Rone was looking for, but he was sure that if it was some coward or snitch shit, he wouldn't find it in him. He'd grown up around the game and knew the rules, and he wouldn't violate them because they were him.

"Yeah, you can trust me. We fam'ly." Fox's reply was confident. Of course, he was nervous because he knew what Rone was capable of doing. Faces of the men who Rone was suspected of murdering blew through Fox's mind, but he wasn't going to show Rone any sign of fear.

"We're not family right now." Rone corrected him immediately. He wanted to set precedence early between them because there was no turning back after today. "We're business partners, but I'm glad I can trust you because I've got something up after we're finished taking care of this business." Rone turned to walk out and Fox followed behind him.

After getting inside the elevator, Fox noticed Rone passing the attendant a small piece of folded paper. He found that odd, but he brushed it off. Once they walked out of the lobby they were once again greeted by the scorching hot weather. A young white man pulled up to the entrance in a Tang colored Ferrari. He jumped out and passed the keys to Rone. "Your keys, Mr. Swinney." The valet said while holding the driver's door open for him. Rone tipped him before getting inside the car. He looked up and saw Fox looking dazed. ***This nigga***, he thought before closing the door. Fox had seen this type of luxury on television plenty of times, but he'd never experienced it in reality. He knew that Rone had money, but he had no idea it stretched like elastic because he was balling out at all cost. Rone waved him into the car.

"Come on, nigga." Rone seemed inpatient.

Fox got in the car and shook his head in amazement. "My bad, brah. Let's bounce." He looked around admiring the Ferrari's mechanics and the grade of Italian leather that hugged his body.

Rone glanced over to Fox while driving off. "What's up, young trap? You cool? I know you ain't use to this type of weather, my nigga. It's hotter than a muthafucka, but what is just is." Fox shook his head and chuckled.

"Nah, hustlah. The weather's cool. It's this type of stuntin that I ain't used to!" They both burst into laughter and suddenly the mood between them had lighten again. While on their way to link up with Rone's people, Rone popped game at Fox while he attentively listened. His ear was stiff because he didn't want to miss shit. It wasn't like changes like this one fell on niggaz like him everyday.

"This here is how we're s'pose to live, my nigga. When I say we, I don't mean black people or hustlers. I'm talkin 'bout real niggaz!" His voice went up a few octaves because he wanted to emphasize his point. "Muthafuckaz always talkin 'bout real niggaz do real thangz and 'bout getting down how they live." He chuckled. "All that shit sounds good and all, but these niggaz out here really don't understand what the fuck they be spittin off they gums. It's strength in those words that these niggaz don't even possess. But ….." He glanced over to Fox to make sure he was listening and he was, so Rone continued. "I see something in you that you don't see and damn sure don't understand. You and me….we one in the same. This getting money shit comes natural to us. Real niggaz ain't made they're born!" he was getting hype, like a preacher in a pulpit, but he wasn't holding church about Jesus. He was telling the gospel of that all mighty dollar. "But that's only twenty-five percent of it. Add that with thinking, which is twenty-five percent. And listening, which is twenty-five percent, and you got what?" he asked Fox, and Fox laughed.

That was simple mathematics, but somehow Fox knew that there was a jewel behind what Rone was popping at him. It was like the science that those east coast rappers be talking about.

"Seventy-five percent." Fox answered. He wanted to say *son, in a New York accent,* to mock Rone afterwards because this seemed like the appropriate time since they were kicking knowledge and all, but he held on to it. A devious smile swept across Rone's face.

"Right, my nigga. See real niggaz know the math! They know that seventy-five percent is a perfect man." He nodded as if he'd just given Fox the word of life.

Fox couldn't believe what he was hearing. Not only couldn't Rone count, but he was starting to sound like one of those niggaz who had done a stretch in the joint, came home and opened up a health food store, and pushed ecstasy and hydro out the back.

"Fuck is you talkin 'bout?" Fox was offended. He felt like Rone was playing him for a Shorty. Of course, he was young, but he wasn't the type of cat you could just shoot anything at. "Nigga, seventy-five percent of a hundred is average."

"See, Fox. You're talking school arithmetic and I'm talking real life shit. The other twenty-five is for growth. It's part of evolution. Anything that isn't growing or evolving is dead. And anything that's a hundred percent is perfected, and ain't shit perfected 'cept for GOD! Feel me?" he asked while pulling into a driveway of a newer style home. "Yeah, I feel you." He nonchalantly agreed. He'd conceded for the sake of arguing, but in truth he still didn't understand. Rone reached into the glove box and pressed a button. He turned the windshield wiper and hit the gas pedal. When he lifted his foot off the pedal the floor shifter flipped over revealing two semi automatic handguns in clip-on holsters. Rone passed one to Fox and clipped the other onto his belt and pulled his shirt over it. Fox looked at the pistol and back to Rone.

"What we need these for?" Fox asked curiously and Rone laughed. "For protection, nigga. If anything goes wrong, let off at everybody but me. You know how to use it don't you?" Fox clipped the thumper onto his shorts and pulled his jersey over it.

"Yeah, brah."

"When we leave this car you go wherever I go. And don't speak unless you're spoken to. Oh, and if anything goes down." He chuckled, put two fingers to his head, and made a gunshot sound. "Anybody but me." Fox nodded in agreement.

Damn! Fox thought as they walked toward the house. He'd wondered what type of shit he'd signed up for. Maybe it was a robbery murder or some shit like that? He was sure that niggaz couldn't make boss status without a body or two, but he wasn't sure if he was ready for that type of action. *Damn, that's heavy for the first day on the job!* They reach the porch and walked through the opened entrance door. As they walked in they were greeted by a huge dark skinned cat. He looked like someone from a blacksploitation flick. His bloodshot red eyes were sunk deep into his face and he looked felonious until he smiled. His teeth were pristine white surrounded by a soft pink gum line. Fox was sure that he'd had years of expensive dentistry.

"Roney Rone!" He clasped hands with Rone while peering over his shoulder and at Fox. Rone chuckled and waved his fist at the man teasingly.

"Nigga, I done told yo ass 'bout that Roney Rone shit, muhfucka."

The large man laughed."Yeah, whatevah, nigga. Ain't you the one that gave me the nickname that I can't shake?" Rone laughed.

"Yeah, but yours fits you. Black muthafucka." They both burst into laughter. Fox wanted to fall right in because Black was a perfect handle for the guy, but he held it. Black turned to walk away and Rone followed him with Fox in tow as well.

"Come on, nigga. You got these uppidy as negroes back here waiting on you."

Fox's eyes wondered through the house as they walked through. He was impressed with how it was laid out. The hard wood floors and antique furniture was brought to life by the expensive art work that lined the hallway wall leading to the three season sun room. Black led them through two large sliding doors and onto a cement patio. There was a modest size swimming pool and three lounge sets surrounding the deck. Two middle aged black men set at one of the patio sets talking. Fox was startled by a large splash in the pool while trailing behind Black and Rone. He swiftly reached for the street cannon that rested in his waistline, but settled after seeing the most beautiful woman that he'd ever seem in his life ascend from the water. Fox was motionless; his hand was still resting on the handle of his throttle, as her almost naked body came out of the pool. Her cocaine white

41

thong bikini didn't leave shit to the imagination because it was all hanging out. She was phenomenal and he was captivated by her 36-22-40 measurements.

She walked over to Rone and gave him a hug and kiss on the cheek. It wasn't a tender passionate kiss; it was more of a hello kiss. Rone took her hand and pulled her aside to have a personal conversation with her. Fox stood back and watched. He was sure that the broad was Rone's southern bitch. That's how cake boys did it. A bad bitch in every State. Like Lil Wayne said "It ain't trickin if you got it" and it was evident that Rone had it when he slapped her on the ass sending her on her way. Rone gave Fox a swinging head gesture to join him as he walked over to the men who was sitting at the patio table.

Each of the men rose and greeted Rone with a hand shake before sitting back down. They looked like the mafia--- only they were niggaz. One of them turned to Fox and pointed.

"You must be Fox?" he assumed, but formed it as a question and Fox nodded. "I'm Cadillac," he introduced himself, this is Ray..." he pointed to one of the other men. He was well groomed and could pass as a politician. A real professional looking type of cat. "And I assumed you've already met Black?" he pointed to the guy who'd walked them out to the patio. Fox looked each of them over thoroughly. He heard Alfredo's words, "Look a man in the eyes. Read them, judge them, and prepare to be judged." Fox could tell that Cadillac was a nigga that had came from a humble beginning. The type who had struggled for everything he had and would kill to protect it. Ray looked like the complete opposite. He reminded Fox of Hill Harper or a cat like that. Someone who kept an impeccable appearance, but was hiding something diabolical. And Black confused him, although, he had an intimidating appearance his personality was kind natured and laid back. After being properly introduced to everyone and categorizing them, he felt more comfortable. Like he belonged with the group of men.

Fox listened as the group bounced a lot of meaningful conversation around to one another. Black and I were discussing the weather earlier today." Ray said and pointed to the lawn. "He believes that the heat is causing the grass to become a darker shade. That's a problem for him, but I know that the darker shade still holds the same quality and volume that it has in the spring." He chuckled lightly. The crazy thing is that the price of upkeep is ridiculously high because no one wants to work in two hundred degree weather." Rone smiled at Black before looking back over to Ray. I hear you, but you have to pay for what you want. How much are you paying them anyway?"

"It depends, but I'd say at least a thousand biweekly." Cadillac nodded assuring Ray that he was right on the money.

"Sheeit!" Rone laughed. "That's a nice piece of change. Who do you have working for you these days anyway? The Mexicans or the Cubans?" Ray giggled and took a sip from his glass before answering. "The

Mexicans." Ray answered. "The Cubans prefer working during the winter time. Their productive too. A friend of mines has a thousand of them working in orange fields in Florida. He only paid them seventy-five hundred dollars a year."

"Damn!" Rone sounded surprised. "That's damn near slavery. Does he get them back home after harvest?"

Fox looked over to Rone wondering why he was so concerned about some Cubans working in orange orchards. Niggaz had picked cotton and all other types of shit in America and he didn't have any compassion for them. He'd sent at least ten cats from the west side of Detroit to their essence and now he was playing a self righteous civil rights activist. At that point, Fox knew for sure that this new swagger that Rone had all of a sudden developed was some bullshit. He was running game on these old cats a mile long, and Fox was sure that he'd been duped as well. Cadillac joined into the conversation.

"Oh yeah, he got them home." Cadillac assured Rone and Black nodded in agreement.

"Yeah, definitely." Black Reiterated and spit into the grass. Rone laughed.

"That's real of him." Rone rose from his seat. "I've got plans, but I'll be in touch before I leave town." He shook hands with them and walked off. Fox shook hands with the men too before following behind Rone. As they walked back through the house Fox scanned every room hoping to get another peek at the broad, who came out of the pool, but she was nowhere to be seen. They put their pistols back into the safe after getting back into the Ferrari. Rone looked over to Fox and nodded.

"You did good my nigga." Fox nodded coolly.

"Thanks." Yo people livin it up, big Rone. It seems like y'all real close too." Rone's look turned serious as he drove off. "Those ain't my peoples and we ain't close. We're all business acquaintance not Friends. And if you're referring to that house or that female, neither of them belongs to them." "Oh, I feel you." Fox replied knowing that he'd offended Rone. Maybe that was his hoe's crib. Rone smiled and looked over to Fox throwing him off balance a little. He was starting to wonder if Rone was bipolar or something. "You never answered." Rone said. "Which of them you talking about? The house or the broad?" Fox laughed. As much as he wanted to lie to Rone he couldn't.

"Sheeit, to be honest I was talking 'bout that bitch with all that ass." His laughter continued and Rone fell in with him.

"Nigga stop it. Her name is Egypt and you can't handle all that action, lil nigga. Did you see the body on her, boy?" Fox nodded. "Definitely, brah. She cold! Girl was built like my third grade teacher." He continued laughing. "I use to call her Ms. Ass." "She must've been cold because you mesmerized." They both laughed heavily. They talked throughout the drive back to the hotel. During the ride, Rone finally concluded that he

45

made the right choice with Fox. The youngster was all the way game tight, but the trust factor was still out for a verdict.

The elevator attendant seemed a little more upbeat when Fox and Rone walked into the shaft. Rone gave the young man a pound.

"What's up? Is everything ready?" Rone casually questioned him and he nodded.

"Yes! Everything!"

Rone chuckled. "What time do you get off?"

"In ten minutes." He replied instantly.

"Come up when you're finished." Rone invited him up to his suite, and Fox dropped his head to the floor.

Ain't this 'bout a bitch! Fox thought, while shaking his head disappointedly. ***Rone's a muhfuckin punk!*** He hoped this wasn't the shit that he need kept a secret because it wasn't going to happen. Fox knew all about those down low wanna be thug niggaz who sold dope, popped pistols, and oh, occasionally took it up the ass. ***Nah***, he shook his head once more. He couldn't allow this nigga to give his sister a living death sentence. He had to put it out there. Him having another family would have been nothing to keep quiet, but a sordid homosexual relationship was something completely fucked up. The anticipation that had swelled within Fox over the last couple of days had deflated. He wanted to go straight to his room and pack, but Rone had something to show him in the suite. Rone opened the door to the suite and revealed heaven.

"Damn!" Fox yelped. There was a room full of dimes. This was what any sane minded nigga would consider heaven minus the ten virgins because the females that were in there were boss whores, including Egypt. She walked up to the door and grabbed Fox's hand pulled him inside. She was wearing a soft pink bikini top, some Dolce capri's that hugged that soft looking ass she carried around, and some spiked Manolo Blahanik strappy sandals that matched her top. Damn, Fox thought while giving her a once over, this bitch's feet are even cute! She pulled Rone aside and briefly spoke to him. Fox's eyes canvassed the room checking out the exotic looking group of broads. They were all suggestively clothed. Some wore lingerie, while others wore nothing at all. There was a redbone with some huge titties and thick thighs lying across the couch with a cheerleaders outfit on. Her legs were spread wide enough to see the auburn color pubic hair that lined the top of her pussy. She looked directly at him and opened her legs wider. "You must be Fox?" she asked, but he didn't reply. He'd heard her, but his mind wasn't on kicking it. He wanted to tap that ass. Rone snuck up behind Fox and startled him. "She asked you a question, pimp." Rone tapped Fox on the back. "Young trap?"

"Oh," Fox came back to, "Yeah, I'm Fox." He walked toward her. It was on. He was ready to put his bid in right then. He may not have known about moving pounds of cocaine, but he was surgical with a bitch.

Rone rushed over to the sofa before Fox could get there. He grabbed her and two others. Fox watched as he walked them into the master suite. "Hatin ass nigga." Fox whispered. Although he wanted to pound the freaky cheerleader out, it was revealing to see Rone snatch her up. A least his assumption about Rone's sexuality wasn't true because that would have been one he couldn't G-Code. His eyes search the room for Egypt and her body must have heard his because she pulled up behind him kissing him across his neckline. It felt odd because they were sluts, and she was giving him tender kisses.

His body stiffened. This hoe was kissing him and he was ready to put in work, but he didn't have any condoms. He thought that they were coming for business only, so he didn't bring any. Damn! He thought while rushing down the hall and into the room that Rone had taken the cheerleader into. He wanted to fuck, but he wasn't so thirsty that he was willing to put his life on the crap table for it! After opening the door, his semi swollen dick sprouted into a massive erection.

Rone lay sprawled across the king size bed with a slim broad gyrated her pussy in his face while she tickled another's clitoris with her tongue. He'd wasted no time getting to it once they entered the bedroom. The cheerleader was giving Rone a raunchy blow job. When she saw Fox, she spit on Rone's bellhead and caught it with her tongue as it dripped from it. All the while she was eyeballing Fox libidinously implying that he could be in Rone's position. She deep throated his member without gagging, and messaged it seductively before repeating.

"Rone?" Fox called out. I need a magnum." The cheerleader smiled at him. She'd heard him asked for the magnums and wondered if he could fill his request. Rone pointed to his luggage that sat in the corner.

They're over there. Now gone out there and handle your business, nigga! All this free pussy 'round here." Rone demanded and grabbed the slim woman's ass roughly pulling her toward him. Fox grabbed the condoms and rushed out of the room. After seeing what Rone had going on his excitement had risen.

Egypt met him while on his way down the hallway. She had a sensual strut and swing of her hips that seized Fox. She aggressively pushed him into the wall and fell to her knees. While looking up to him she unbuckled his belt and pulled his shorts and briefs to his ankles. Egypt licked her heavily glossed lips while stroking his pulsating dick. She'd dreamed of this moment, but she didn't imagine him being so well endowed. She breathed lustfully before leaning in and sucking his sack. She worked her way to his crown giving him the type of brain that was told in stories.

While leaning against the wall receiving his piece of heaven, Fox saw another one of the woman approaching them. She seductively undressed while sauntering up the hallway; she passionately kissed Fox's mouth before her and Egypt led him back down the hallway.

Earthly moans rode the melody of the music that played in the front room, while the other two women pleasured each other. They were entangled in a sixty-nine position. Fox had pounded a few freaks out with Antoine before. They had all the young rats in the hood begging to double up on them, but he'd never experienced a fuck fest until now. His erection throbbed and he vulgarly palmed Egypt's voluptuous boy toy. Damn, this muhfucka soft." He said before being interrupted by someone knocking on the door. Ah shit, some mo hoes! He thought while opening the room door.

The elevator attendant stood outside the door grinning and peaking into the room. Now Fox understood what all the note passing and smiling was about. He let him inside, grabbed Egypt and the sexy cocoa complexioned mami that had joined them in the hallway, and went into the other bedroom leaving the attendant with the other two horny broads.

Egypt and the other woman immediately started making out. They kissed each other passionately while unclothing one another. Egypt's body was even colder than he originally thought. Her dark brown skin was flawless. She had a Brazilian body wax and a tattoo above her pussy that said "CAUTION! SLIPPERY WHEN WET!" shit! Fox thought after sliding inside of her from the back, what a watery ride. "Oooo!" Egypt moaned softly. Her fuck face was pornographic and her hips

50

rolled to the same rhythm as his. He'd forgotten about the condoms that he'd grabbed from Rone's suitcase. The cocoa complexioned mami lay on the bed pleasuring herself.

"Ahh…oooohoh!" the sound of a self induced climax poured from her mouth energizing Fox's stroke.

"Oh….ooh..oooooh!" Egypt panted while Fox pounded her deep and hard. The moans became louder with every thrust. Fox was silent. His mission was to set precedence with the Georgia peaches. Egypt's body stiffened and convulsed.

"Aaah..oh!" her climax billowed. One following another as her, the cocoa complexioned mami, and Fox continued their lewd sexual romp throughout the night. A night that Fox would never forget.

****

Fox woke into a brief reminisce of the night before. He left the bedroom searching for his clothes and the woman that he'd shared the night with. His clothes weren't in the hallway where he left them so he walked toward the kitchen area of the suite where he was greeted by the smell of breakfast. His erection swelled as he walked in the kitchen full of butt naked woman. His youthful hormones were ready to put in work. Egypt was the first to take notice of his phallic nature and although she was impressed, she took advantage of the opportunity to tease the man who had soothed her appetite for raunchy sex the night before.

51

"Whoa, cowboy!" she teased while holding up her hands and taking in every inch of his manhood. "There's a time for everything...." She smiled girlishly. "Even breakfast," the cheerleader laughed before joining in on the teasing.

"We are impressed though." She smiled and the other girls giggled, and cried cat calls teasingly. Rone walked into the kitchen amongst the laughing.

"Is there something amusing that you ladies didn't include me in?" Rone asked flirting with them. He turned to Fox and chuckled. "Oh, my bad. I see what's up now. What it do, young trap?" He fumbled with his tie. "I see you're a real party animal, huh?" Fox threw his hands into the air and laughed.

"Man..." Fox started, "I'm seventeen in a room full of naked ass dimes! How is a nigga s'pose to act?" Everyone, including Rone burst into laughter. Fox checked Rone's gear out while walking off to get some underwear.

Rone was pimp boy sharp. Wearing a soft cream Brooks Brothers suit with a wine burgundy tie accented with cream diagonal stripes. His Rolex made the 24kt white gold and diamond cufflinks piercing his shirt sleeves stand out. Fox was impressed and he wondered why Rone was so dressed up. When he came back into the room he saw Egypt and Rone talking privately in the corner of the kitchen.

"Why're you so dressed up?" Fox causally asked while wondering why him and Egypt kept having private talks. He wasn't jealous because he didn't even know the broad, furthermore, he was sure that Rone had loaned him Egypt for a night only, but he was still curious about their relationship.

"I'm making an appearance before the lord, baby." Rone replied with a laugh. "I'll be back though so…" he suggestively looked around the room to the women, "Enjoy yourself and I'll see you later." Fox gave Rone a look of disbelief. Rone was the biggest drug dealer in Michigan and questionably one of the most barbaric one's at that, so why would he be going to church. Fox was sure that Rone would be expedited straight to hell's inferno if there was one, so it was useless for him to repent.

"To church?" Fox questioned with a doubtful smirk. "I know you're not going to church?" he couldn't believe Rone was actually serious. The truth always came forward and Rone's truth had surfaced. He was a larger con-artist than anything. Church! Fox thought in disbelief. Rone nodded and chuckled while walking toward Fox. His wine burgundy alligator shoes cascaded across the kitchen tile.

"I'ont give a fuck where I'm at, how much dough I'm getting, or how many hoes I fuck my Sunday's belong to Jesus." He said calmly while fidgeting with his cufflinks. He looked over to Egypt and back to Fox. There's a car at the valet for you if you need to go

53

somewhere or wanna kick it, but you have to take Egypt with you." Fox nodded and watched as Rone walked out leaving him with the harem of groupies.

Fox put the rest of the woman out so he and Egypt could get a little one on one. He'd enjoyed himself the previous night, but he had to have a go at her all alone. After they finished their brief bout of ecstasy they lounged around playing video games and talked about who they were outside of last night.

Fox was surprised to find out that Egypt was her real name and that she was in college. He'd put her into a lot of categories, but college student wasn't one of them. She danced on the side because she had an expensive appetite for nice things. He thought she was cool, but when she started getting too personal he shied away. He wasn't interested in her life story. She was a tramp and all she'd ever be to him was a good time in Atlanta. After hours of meaningful conversation, Fox decided to step out. Egypt wanted to show him her city. After they showered and got dressed they left the suite. When they got outside the valet drove up in an emerald green convertible corvette with the top already down showcasing the dark tan interior. He jumped out and tossed the keys to Fox. "Your keys, Mr. Fox." He smiled and tried walking away. Fox dug into his pocket and peeled off a few tens, but the valet didn't except them. He assured Fox that he'd already been taking care of and thanked him for his generosity. Fox figured Rone had already taken care of everything so him and Egypt jumped in and mashed off.

Egypt gave him directions. She wanted to hit the mall first. While they waited at a traffic light she reached into her purse and tossed a huge bankroll, that she'd pulled from inside, onto Fox's lap. He reached into his lap and grabbed the wad of money. Damn, Fox thought while sizing the roll of cash up. This bitch wants me to pimp her. He'd slayed her and now she wanted to break him off. Fox had heard a lot about hoes like her. Southern bells who had slipped off the porch and fell into a life of pandering. Although he was flattered, he was uninterested because he was riding another money train.

He glanced over to her while holding the money outwards. Damn this bitch fine! He couldn't believe a woman as beautiful as she was would be so loose. "What's this for?" he asked coolly. Egypt smiled almost as if she'd known what he was thinking.

"Rone gave it to me and told me to give it to you if we left the hotel." She reclined her seat and giggled.

"Ah'ight, it's on." He tucked the knot of scrilla inside of his briefs and sped off. Egypt looked over to him and smiled naughtily.

"Is there any room in there for that?" she asked implying that his cock wouldn't be able to breathe with the company of the bankroll he'd just tucked into his underwear. They both burst into laughter.

Fox liked Egypt. This bitch is aw'ight. He thought while cruising up 285. Egypt wasn't like the young teeny boppers that he'd been dealing with in Detroit. She was

55

subtle and knew what it was between them. Back home he pounded a broad and then the bitch would think that they were in a committed relationship. He glanced over to her. Egypt couldn't have been too much older than he was. Her skin hadn't started showing the signs of heavy partying yet, but he was sure that it would soon. He was sure that she could smoke and drink him under the bar any night. That was just the reality of what hoes like her did.

They shopped and did some sightseeing before having an early dinner. Fox was careful to only spend the money he'd brought with him. He didn't know how shit would get between him and Rone and he wanted to have some scratch just in case shit got ill. He'd grown to trust Rone a little, but he trusted his intuition more. He knew that the voice who spoke to niggaz telling them to be cautious was far more smarter than he was. After they ate, Egypt took him to her school. She was a sophomore and although she had a double life, she was well respected on campus. No one seemed to be bothered by what she did on the side and that seemed unusual to Fox. Unlike Egypt, people judged him about being a dope boy all the time. Whether it was the females around the way assessing his cash flow or the Christian family on the corner assessing his sins, someone was always judging him. Fox saw a familiar face as they walked into the registration building.

"Hey, Fox!" Ray greeted him with enthusiasm.

"Hey, Ray!" I thought that was you." Fox greeted Ray with a handshake. He wondered what Ray was doing at Egypt's school. Ray reached into his pocket and passed Fox some car keys. He looked at the keys while they loosely dangled from his hands.

What're these for?" Fox asked curiously. *Maybe Rone done blessed me with a whip for down here*! Fox thought excitedly.

"Egypt will explain." Ray replied and nodded politely before walking away. Egypt took Fox's hand and led him through the building and into the parking lot. Fox felt like he was being toyed with. Egypt will explain? He thought curiously while following her through the lot. She stopped and leaned against a Cadillac STS chromed out with vogue tires.

"Guess which one we're riding in?" She played a girlish naïve role and Fox laughed at the terrible acting. He knew that the bitch was playing him and trying to keep his mind off what she was suppose to tell him, but he was hip to her. The jig was up, but he played along only with better acting.

"Sheeit!" He continued his laughter. "It better be this 'lac 'cause if you scratch it a nigga ain't got enough bread to pay for it." Egypt laughed and waved him off before getting into the passenger's side.

"Boy, let's go." She laughed and giggled while closing the door.

Fox got in and they drove off. He tried to figure out what he'd unknowingly just been part of. Something had taken place, but he didn't have an idea what it was. On his way out of the parking lot he drove pass the corvette and glanced at the license plates. They were from Michigan. Maybe it was someone else's whip? Fox thought. Egypt gave him direction to her place. She had an apartment tucked off near the Peachtree airport. The drive there was short and quiet. Fox was upset about being played and wanted some answers, but he tried to play it smooth. He walked in and looked around Egypt's pad. She had a nice size apartment. Two bedrooms with an open space layout. It looked New York loftish. The exotic green leather sofa set was lavish. Matching aquatic colored marble end and cocktail tables sounded the sofa, and the panoramic view of the kitchen was trump. Although Fox was impressed he pretended to be unfazed by her life style. She looked over to him and smiled.

"Do you like it?" Egypt asked and led him to the couch. Fox smiled impishly.

"Yeah, this nice." Egypt smiled weakly. She could tell that something was bothering Fox. She pursed her lips.

"Fox can I tell you something?" Fox nodded and she continued. "I'm nineteen. My mom is a dope fiend, and my dad could be any nigga in the nation, so don't judge me." Fox shook his head. He was unsympathetic. He had a story of his own and didn't give a fuck about her enough to tell it. All he wanted to know was what she was suppose to explain to him. She'd turned out to be just like the shifty hoes in the motor city. Fox looked over to her with an insidious smile and chuckled.

"I feel you and all, but I'ont even want to hear yo testimony, ma. You could've went to church with Rone for that. His tone was cold. Egypt's face cringed.

"Because I like you, Fox." She seemed to be offended. "And have for a while now!" her tone had changed. Her causal demeanor had became emotional and Fox wasn't having it. He laughed.

"Look, hoe." He said sharply trying to cause her pain. Egypt was running game a mile a minute on him, but he wasn't going to let her get another word out before putting her back into a hoe's place. I was born at night...." He chuckled, "maybe even late at night, but it wasn't late last night! Who in the fuck do you think you foolin?" bitch! You's a tramp." He expected Egypt to become irate, but to his surprise she remained calm. Usually the word hoe bitch put fire under a broad's ass, but she seemed unfazed by what he said.

She sighed. It was a sigh that said, nigga, you just don't get it" and he didn't. Two days in Atlanta wouldn't be enough time to prepare him for the shit she broke him off with."

"Fox! Sherry and Rone got married four years ago. Their fifth anniversary and, the fifth year since we met is February 6th." She ran her fingers through the long silky hair that fell across her back and sighed heavily. "I can't believe we've been kicking it for two days and you still haven't recognized me!" Now she seemed to be getting upset.

Fox chuckled. "Recognize what? That you's a lying ass school girl who freaks for dollars?" He was still taking shots trying to enrage her. He was giving the bitch a hood interrogation. He did it to females all the time. He'd say anything that came to mind and eventually they'd tell him what was really on their minds.

"No, boy! I was the bald headed flower girl in the wedding. The one you wouldn't escort down the aisle." She laughed and playfully threw a couch pillow at him. She was sure that what she'd just laid on him would get his self absorbed attention.

Fox's face went flush. He was clueless to what was happening. Ain't this 'bout a bitch! He thought while taking a closer look at Egypt. It was her--- the girl from the wedding.

"What type of shit is y'all on?" Fox asked inquisitively. He'd seen Rone smack her across the ass while they were out with Rone's friends. "He told me that you were his sister and he slapped that ass out at Cadillac's house. I love Sherry to death, but I ain't touching my sister's butt naked ass booty! That's some Jerry Springer type shit!" Egypt rolled her eyes at Fox.

"First of all! I ain't never been to Cadillac's house. That's Rone's house and he slapped me across the butt and told me to put some clothes on before he had to bury one of them niggaz." She threw her hands into the air. She'd became frustrated. "You know what? I don't even know why I'm even explaining myself to you."

"Oh, so now you mad when y'all the muthafucka's been runnin game on me since I got here! Playin a nigga like a pass around dildo!" he angrily jumped to his feet. He wanted to go upside Egypt's head, but he didn't. After all, she was Rone sister which made them family. Bitch, take me back to my muhfuckin room!" He demanded. Egypt folded her arms across her chest in a childish manner.

"Nope." She said and poked her bottom lip out.

Fox tilted his head sideways while staring at her. He could tell that she was used to getting her way, but she hadn't ran across a thoroughbred like himself because he wasn't buying into the fat rump and a smile jig. This hoe think I'm some trick ass nigga or something! He thought while staring at her. Bitch, I ain't tryna hear no more of that bullshit you pushin off yo muhfuckin tongue! Get me back to my suite." He demanded, but she shook her head defiantly.

"Nope," she said in a girlish tone and Fox chuckled. She'd broken through his angry façade."I wanna talk. After I'm finished you can leave, but I'm saying what I have to say." She was adamant about getting out what she wanted to tell him. Fox nodded. He was defeated because none of his tricks worked. Egypt was too stubborn.

61

"Aw'ight," Fox conceded, "But you gotta tell me what Ray meant by you'll explain. You muhfucka's runnin 'round on some real secretive bullshit." "That was Ray's corvette and Rone felt more comfortable with you driving one of his cars so we switched. That's all."

"Yeah, Aw'ight." although Egypt's story seemed authentic Fox remained cautious. He knew how deceptive woman could be and didn't want to fall victim to Egypt's web of deception.

"Look, Fox…" Egypt started. She'd picked up a hint of southern drawl that sounded like music to Fox. "I've been asking Rone about you every since we met." She told Fox her story and unlike the first time she tried, he listened to her attentively.

Egypt's mother was strung out on crack and heroin. A cross addiction that had taken her places where Jesus himself wouldn't come get her. She was trying to sell Egypt into prostitution so Rone bought her. She teared up at the thought of being sold for a morsel of cooked baking soda and cocaine. Rone took her in and raised Egypt like his own child. He wasn't much older than her so she passed as his sister.

"Fox, the nigga treated me like I was his family. I love Rone so much I'd kill for him! Not just saying the words either. I would literally take someone's life for him." Her eyes were convincing and her words were passionate.

Fox felt them and for the first time, since they'd been reacquainted, he believed her. "Damn!" although he knew he shouldn't have, Fox had developed empathy for her."That's deep, ma." It was rare, but he was lost of words. Now he understood why she was lost and turned out.

"Fox, Rone is the nigga in the A and has been for some time now. Game ain't the word for what he has. That man has a gift to make money and I've been lucky enough to share it with him." She giggled and through her hands into the air like she was giving her testimony to the lord. "And I know… I know you think I'm a slut and all that other shit you called me earlier. We freaked it off last night two….well three coke junkies in heat, but I've dreamed about fucking you since I was fourteen. I was just as nervous as you were. I work with Lana and the rest of those hoes, but that was my first time sucking some pussy." Fox couldn't hold his laughter any longer. It just poured out.

"Bullshit!" his laughter continued. "You looked like a seasoned vet to me. I hate to say it, but you's a pussy eater. I guess you gon tell a nigga you ain't never sucked a dick before next, huh?" He stared at her in a judging manner, he was sure that she'd have a solid comeback and he was ready to hear it. *Just when I started believein this hoe!* He thought while waiting on her reply.

"Okay then." Egypt nodded and Fox smirked because he knew it was coming. "Let me ask you some," Fox nodded because he was sure that she'd ask him what

63

she had to whether he said yes or no. "Have you ever had ménage trios with two females? Have you ever had your dick sucked from the back or had your ass licked while you ate another bitch's pussy? Have you done any of that before last night?" She stared at him daring him to lie. Fox smiled at the thought of the experience he'd had with Egypt and the cocoa complexioned mami!

"Nah, but I enjoyed myself." Fox said and they both burst into laughter. Things were lightening up between them. Fox was finally beginning to understand what he'd experienced. He'd fulfilled a sexual fantasy, but she'd fulfilled a dream. Egypt's face softened because she knew she had him.

"Well if that was your first time experiencing something like that, why couldn't it have been mine too?" Fox's stoic stare spread into a smile and he nodded.

"Aw'ight, you got me." He chuckled while shaking his head. He was still wrapping his brain around what was going on. "I feel you, but this whole situation is fucking me up. I apologize for telling you about yourself earlier, but you know how it is." Egypt smiled and rubbed his chest letting him know that she accepted his apology.

"It's cool…." She giggled while rubbing his chest; I'll be your tramp. Rone said you can spend the night if you wanted to." She straddled his lap and kissed his neck. "He said that y'all were finish taking care of business so you can enjoy yourself." She unbuttoned his shirt and kissed his chest. "I can help you with that--- enjoying yourself." Fox nodded as blood rushed through his shaft.

"I'm with it, but I gotta get at brah to be sure." Fox called Rone and got the okay. Him and Egypt spent the rest of the night exploring one another's anatomy and learning more about each other on a personal level. Egypt was shocked when Fox told her that he'd dropped out of school.

Although Fox was clearly an intelligent guy it was still surprising because Rone didn't usually deal with undereducated people. He thought they were to inspire, but Fox had became an exception to the rule. Early the next morning Egypt nudged Fox while he slept.

"Fox!" she called while gently shaking him. "Fox, you have to get up. Get, up boy." She laughed. "I know this lovin is like that, but I have to take you back to the hotel." Fox chuckled while stretching out.

"Whatevah." He replied and nudged her before sitting up. "Fox, I know you're going to be busy and I'm not trying to be clingy, but I do wanna hear from you again." She said as he walked toward the bathroom. "Right. I feel you, but right now I'd rather feel you up against me in this shower." He walked into the bathroom. Egypt hastily leapt from the bed and tailed behind him.

"Ugh, you horny."

After they showered and dressed, Fox grabbed the bags that he'd accumulated during their shopping spree.

There was sporadic talking between them during their drive to the hotel, but Fox mostly stared out of the car window while thinking about the weekend that had passed. He liked Egypt's company, but he wondered what she really was about? If Rone had sicked her on him to keep him away from what was really going on. He knew how slick Rone was. They'd flown to Georgia to take care of some business, but they hadn't seen any parts of business since they'd arrived. They visited Rone's friends and partied with some broads, but they hadn't done any business. He looked over to Egypt as she drove up to the entrance of the hotel.

"I guess this is it, huh. Or are we gonna stay in touch?" he asked although he had no intention on staying in touch with her. Maybe he'd swing through and fuck her if he was in town, but anything else wasn't likely. Egypt playfully punched his arm.

"Yeah, punk! You better call me too or I'm fuckin you up!" she playfully threatened.

"Okay, I'mma hold you to that." Fox kissed her on the cheek and jumped out of the car.

Egypt watched closely as Fox disappeared into the hotel. She was upset that he had to leave so soon, furthermore, she'd heard the deceit in his voice and knew that he wasn't going to keep in touch. However, she still planned to keep her promise because she wanted him and wouldn't take no for an answer.

Fox saw the attendant when he approached the elevator. Fox nodded and gave him a pound.

"What's up, hustlah?"

"Shit, what's up with you? I appreciate y'all letting me come up and party with y'all. Rone knows how to throw a set!" Fox nodded and chuckled. His mood was nonchalant and somber.

"Yeah, brah brah knows how to throw a stone cold groove. I hope I wasn't rude, but I was occupied." He chuckled and the attendant shook his head. "Naw! It looked like you had your hands full with Egypt and her homegirl." Fox gave the attendant a quick glance.

Although Egypt wasn't his bitch and he didn't have any intention of seeing her again, he felt a pinch of jealousy.

"Oh, you know Egypt, huh?"

"Yeah! Hell yeah! She works at the gentleman's club, but I didn't know she did private parties. She's a snobbish as hoe. She be brushing guys off most of the time. I saw her flip out on one of them major rappers cats for grabbing her pussy." He and Fox laughed. "That was some funny shit." "So I guess I'm luckier than him, huh?" Fox asked glibly. "Yeah! You're luckier than anyone I know. E'ry one 'round here thinks she's a bulldagger, but I see that ain't the case. Anyway this is your floor." The elevator stopped and Fox passed the attendant a tip. Oblivious to the attendant the tip wasn't for the ride it was for the information that he'd given Fox about Egypt.

Now he felt a little better about her. He walked into the suite calling Rone. He didn't know if he was there or not. Rone came out and gave Fox dap and a manly pat on the back.

"What's up, boy?" Rone asked. He was sure that Fox had a lot of shit to tell him that he really didn't want to hear. Fox threw his bag into the corner.

"Shit, what's been up with you?"

"I'm good," Rone pointed to the bags that Fox had thrown in the corner, "I see Egypt kept you busy and took you to her favorite spot." He laughed because he knew how Egypt could get. She'd spent up plenty of his paper over the years.

"Yeah…" fox laughed, "she kept me busy, but it wasn't shopping." He smiled and Rone nodded knowing exactly what he was referring to. "So you enjoyed yourself then?" he turned to go back into the bedroom because he didn't want to hear the intimate details of Fox and Egypt's sexual adventures. Fox stopped him as he walked away.

"Rone?" He called out. "When we gon handle that business? All we been doing is partying and fuckin hoes. What's up with all the visiting, my nigga?" "Visit who?" Rone asked with a puzzled look on his face. Fox glanced over to him and noticed the look. He figured he'd either missed something or Rone was a greater actor than he was a con or drug kingpin. Either way, he was saying what he had to say.

"Cadillac, Ray, and that big knuckle dragging muthafucka Black. That's who." Although Fox feared Rone, he refused to let anyone else walk over him so he stood his ground. Rone laughed.

"Slick as you think you are, you let it slip right by you." Rone loosened his tie and sat on the edge of the sofa. He was disappointed because he thought Fox had pinned what he been part of. He rubbed his goatee.

"So you think you can just walk down on a nigga like—aye nigga, let me cop a hundred bricks of cocaine and a thousand pounds of that fruity celery green shit, huh? That's what you think, my nigga? I'm s'pose to trust a nigga not to be working with the law because we're cool? Trust him with my life like that, huh?" He laughed. It was an insidious laugh. One that made Fox feel foolish. "That's why I told you to listen because the key is in the language. Remember when we were at my house in Buckhead?"

Fox nodded. "Yeah, but I didn't know that was your spot." Rone chuckled.

"I know because I didn't tell you that, but if you paid attention some shit was implied. Anyway, that's where it happened at."

Fox grunted childishly. "Whatevah, brah. All you niggaz did was sit around talkin 'bout the weather and shit! Like we were on the Soprano's or some shit." Rone smiled. He figured at least Fox remembered something.

"Good!" Rone replied sarcastically."You remember the conversation. Well I copped a thousand pound of trees biweekly for two hundred a pop, and a thousand bricks for seven five apiece. Now, do the math." Fox took no time answering Rone.

"Bout seven mil seven hundred thousand." Fox replied confidently. He was good and Rone was shocked by Fox's swiftness with the numbers.

"Damn, my nigga! So which one came from the Cubans?" Rone was trying to give Fox a lesson that would help him alone the way. He knew the reality of the game. No matter how uncut and raw it appeared to be, there was always a snitch in the rotation. They smashed work, clacked thumpers,and bounced on the finest pussy in the hood, but at the end of the day they reported everything they'd done to the FED's. "Damn," he said while staring at Fox waiting on him to answer his question and wondering how he'd done the math so fast. He knew that Fox was intelligent, but he didn't know he was as sharp as he was.

Damn! Fox thought while trying to remember the conversation that he'd heard by the pool. It was only two days ago, but so much had happened in between those two days. He was sure that the Cubans worked in the winter so he went with that.

"The Cubans because Ray said they worked in the winter."

"Right, so how is it getting back north?"

"Cadillac said they'd get'em back home after harvest." Fox replied confidently. He knew that he'd fell asleep at the wheel because everything was right in front of him, but he'd missed it. He was usually more attentive, but the sight of Egypt's satin skin, as she came out of the swimming pool, had distracted him. Damn, he thought while shaking his head, the hoe slept a nigga.

"Right, young trap…." Rone pointed at his temple repeatedly, twenty- five percent is listening. You gotta listen in order to learning the language. When you and Egypt switched cars you were dropping off a four million dollar whip, boy!" Rone leaned back and winked at Fox letting him know that he'd been foogazied,

Fox was befuddled by what he was hearing. He considered himself to be game tight, but he'd been hoodwinked by Rone and Egypt. Luckily he was man enough to question the shit that didn't seem right to him because if not, he would have lost his position with Rone. Damn, Fox began thinking, maybe this was the test? He thought Rone had put him into this situation to see how he'd react. Rone was a major player and Fox, although he was reluctant at first, was honored to be learning from him. He popped a couple of hours of game at Fox. And Fox was surprised at how smooth the three of Rone's people were. They had their business dealings mapped out to a science. It wasn't like that in the city. Niggaz would take Fox in circles to cop an ounce of heroin. There were too many middlemen. Niggaz trying to wiggle their way in on a couple of chips, but with Rone and his team it was different. They came in, sat down, and put it

71

on the floor. Within thirty minutes everyone was leaving feeling like they'd gotten what they came for, and it was a lot more than an ounce of blow. After kicking it for a little while longer, they left out. They stopped at a steak house before going to the airport and had lunch. While eating, Rone occasionally looked over to Fox noticing a distance in him. He figured the youngster was stuck on Egypt. He wanted to put it out there, but he was sure that Fox would deny it, so he just kept his thought to himself.

They talked sporadically during their flight back home. Rone was cool with the way things had went. Although Fox had fumbled the ball, he quickly recovered it. That's what true to life hustlers did—made quick recoveries when they fell off. Every nigga crashed, but real one's didn't burn. Knowing that Fox was able to take a hit humbly was admirable to Rone because not everyone could acces a situation and put the pieces back together so swiftly. Not to mention Fox's swiftness with numbers.

CHAPTER 4

Daaamn! Sherry Thought while admiring herself in the mirror. She stretched her long slenderly toned legs out while buckling her strap on her Jimmy Choo's. It wasn't that she was conceded. That wasn't her forte, but today was a fight. A fight for position. She was getting dressed because Laticia was coming to pick her up. It had been two weeks since their last meeting and although this meeting wouldn't be the business, Sherry was sure that it would be eventful.

Sherry never considered Laticia a friend. Actually, they were silent enemies. Laticia was one of Rone's oldest friends and business partners. She meant a lot to Rone and Sherry loved her husband, so she remained civil and cordial with Laticia out of respect for him.

Rone came up hustling for Alfredo, Fox's father, in the early eighties. Alfredo was a modest hustler and Rone use to run for him before being fully exposed to the game. Alfredo wasn't much of a thinker. He was more of a brutish flatfoot hustler, so eventually Rone outgrew him and started fucking with his connect. That's just how the streets are—you look up one day and the niggaz you were putting on are pushing Bentley Coupes and Masserati's pass your S-class Mercedes. Rone was one of those aggressive types of hustlers. He stayed focused and kept a book in his face—something that he'd picked up during one of his bus rides to mule some snow back to Detroit for Alfredo. Reading was a way of life for him. It help him navigate through the mussy environment that he'd grown up in. A lot of niggaz accused him of being a social outcast because he didn't floss and club hop, but he wasn't. Rone was a thinker and those who got the chance to know him usually realized what he'd known about himself all along—he was the truth. Laticia was no exception to that. They'd met some years back when Rone was in his first year of law school.

Rone sat in a booth at Ray's bookstore in Harlem. He was reading the New York post and sipping on some coffee when he saw Ray walk in with one of the coldest bitches he'd ever seen. She stood six feet and was well built. She wasn't like most six foot woman with the athletic build. She had a woman's body---a six foot man wonderland and Rone wanted to be invited to play. Her fiery red hair was pulled into a mohawked ponytail exposing her light hue. She had minimal freckles scattered around her nose that match her hair, almost like an accessory.

"Ray? How's it going?" Rone rose and shook his hand while greeting him. He glanced over to the woman noticing the package that she drug behind her. It was as round as an onion and as plump as a pumpkin. Ray smiled loudly. He was happy to see Rone because they hadn't spoke in a while.

"I'm fine, brotha." Ray turned to the women and back to Rone, "This is LaTicia and LaTicia this is Rone." Rone and LaTicia shook hands, and Ray smiled. It was a devilish smile that spoke volume to Rone.

Rone looked over to LaTicia and back to Ray while they were sitting. This shady muthafucka, Rone thought. Ray was trying to set him up. Rone disliked surprises, but he hated set-ups. Ray chuckled after realizing that he'd been caught.

"Rone will be starting his first year in the fall and I'm sure he'll need a friend." LaTicia smiled and looked over to Rone.

"It's nice to meet you," she said softly. Rone stared into her deep oval shaped hazel brown eyes and smiled. He was sure that LaTicia was in on the set up with Rone, but he played naïve. "Likewise, ma'am." Rone threw that out there to keep the formality.

Although LaTicia was a fine broad he wasn't interested in having a tag alone. He was sure that Ray had trained her like a German shepherd watchdog. LaTicia snickered after Rone's ma'am comment.

"Please? Call me Ticia because ma'am sounds too old." She scooted closer to Rone.

This bitch is good, Rone thought after LaTicia slid closer to him. He was used to females pushing up on him once they found out he had a few dollars, but a woman like LaTicia, who clearly made and had her own money, wasn't usually one of them. Ray chuckled while pointing to the newspaper that Rone was reading when he walked in.

"I knew you'd be here reading that bullshit you love so much." Ray had a thing against the Post. Why, was something that Rone hadn't figured out and didn't have time to try. LaTicia's neck whipped to Ray and she immediately jumped to Rone's defense.

"Excuse me Ray, but I'm impressed to see a young brotha interested in what's going on in society. It's the job of the intellectual to be the eyes, ears, and voice of society," LaTicia gave Rone a flirtatious smile and winked. The wink implied that she'd saved him and he owed her one. "Are you going to inform me about the events of the day?" Rone chuckled and clapped his hands. He'd been insulted by a woman who had underestimated her competition.

"Oscar winning plagiarism." Rone said with a snide undertone. He was familiar with Ayn Rand's literature and it was comical to see LaTicia quote some of it as well.

"I've heard what you've read…" He took another shot at her, "and although I haven't had the time to read the paper, maybe we could discuss what I learned over dinner." Rone passed LaTicia his business card while standing.

"I appreciate the introduction Ray, and I hate to leave so soon, but I have some where I need to get to." Rone and Ray shook hands and he waved good bye to LaTicia. "Call me if you're interested." He was sure that LaTicia wouldn't be calling him. She'd insulted a gangster and didn't even know it. Rone had left the life jacket that she'd thrown him, in the water with her and backstroked to shore. ***This hoe fuckin with a boss!*** He thought while walking away from the bookstore.

Rone was uneasy about being setup with LaTicia from the jump. Of course, she was beautiful by any man's standards, but that didn't mean shit to him. He'd knocked dime pieces off across the country on a regular. He was just unwilling to keep them. Rone wasn't the caking type. He'd been alone so long that it seemed natural to him. Furthermore, he didn't trust woman and not many men. The streets had made him callus because there was a bowlegged bitch with a contractible pussy always looking for a come up, and a shifty eyed nigga waiting behind every bush clocker watching. That was the streets and he'd been in them since thirteen. The closest thing he'd gotten to a friend, at that point in his life, was Ray but he even misunderstood him at times. Ray mistook Rone's shrewd sense of ambition for shyness. He'd asked Rone "Why haven't you put your hooks into one of these

PYT's" but Rone wasn't on it. He had confidence and fucked well and often, but he wasn't willing to put his self out there for a hoe to trap him. He knew how hard it was for a nigga to get caked up with six baby's mommas pulling down on you at every spot you be. He had a choice to be a babysitter or a go getter and his decision was clear cut—he was a muthafuckin hustler.

Rone was a personal type of person and believed that Ray over stepped his boundaries with him at times. He met Ray through Cadillac, a mutual friend of theirs. Cadillac was Alfredo's connect before he started dealing with Rone. Cadillac was a railroad retiree. He'd jumped the tracks, and started selling heroin. After realizing blow money was larger than train smoke. Cadillac and Ray grew up in Harlem. They were both third world pool until Ray inherited an overseas connect on heroin. Ray's mother was a first generation immigrant, from Tanzania, and a mule for a Nigerian heroin cartel. He knew what his mother did for a living and wanted in. what his mother brought in wasn't enough to get them out of the ghetto, so he wanted to take a shot at it.

Ray was always an intelligent youngster. He'd watch how the Italians at the local outdoor cafes chopped it up. They were conning. Even amongst one another they were trying to get over. Of course, they were smart enough to keep family businesses in the family and that's why they didn't get pinched as often. They kept a boundary between what they did in the streets and where they ate. Once Ray became of age, he positioned himself to be noticed by the cartels that his mother was running for. Shortly after being plugged Ray became a major heroin distributor throughout the east coast.

Eventually Ray had mitts throughout the country. Midwest, west, coast, and south because his stronghold was after he graduated from college. Ray was an sociology major. He'd study people and why they did what they did, but he couldn't figure out why he loved the game so much. Although he'd stepped away from the hustle after his money had stacked up, he kept a foot in the life by association. He was the president of the fraternity, and organization that he'd formed. They were like a family who Ray had hand picked. Rone had been exceptional, from the beginning, and quickly climbed through the ranks. Ray had drove him to get his education so he could take over, but Rone was content being one of the elite members.

LaTicia stared out the window of her Park Avenue suite with the telephone to her ear.

"Hello," she greeted through the phone after hearing Rone's voice. He'd intrigued her and she wanted to see him.

"Hi, this is LaTicia Crowford," she states her full name trying not to be too informal. "May I speak to Jerone Swinney, please?" her voice was professional. Rone was surprised to hear her voice. He was sure that she wouldn't have been calling him, but she had.

"Yes, this is him. How are you? I didn't expect to hear from you so soon, but it's a pleasure." Rone was genuinely surprised so there were no sarcastic remarks coming from him, unlike earlier when he'd first met her. Now things were on his terms rather than Ray's. LaTicia smiled because she could hear his enthusiasm.

"I called to take you up on your offer, if you haven't eaten already?"she squinted her eyes hoping that he hadn't and that they'd be sharing dinner together. Rone chuckled.

"I'd like that. And you can call me Rone since we're going to be friends." He proclaimed confidently. LaTicia giggled.

"Are you checking me again, Rone?" she teased in a flirting manner. "No I don't have the privilege yet. I'm correcting you." He chuckled. Rone liked the firer that LaTicia was showing him. She was intimidated by him and that was rare. "I'll be there at seven. Cool?"

"Seven sounds fine." She gave Rone the information to where she was staying and ended their conversation. Although she was offended by Rone's sarcasm earlier, she found herself being pulled into his boisterous confidence.

LaTicia looked at the clock noticing the short time that she had before Rone got there. She rushed to her luggage and rambled through it trying to find something sexy to wear. Her eyes settle on a white Michael Kors spaghetti strap dress. She didn't have any intention on wearing the dress while she was in the big apple, but it was perfect for a dinner date. After settling on what she'd wear, she walked toward the bathroom before catching a glimpse of her in the wall mirror. She stopped and undressed while caressing herself. She loved her body.

"Ooooh." She moaned and her body shuddered from her own touch. She knew how to please herself. "Aaaaaah." She started breathing heavy while sprawled across the floor in front of the mirror. Her long slender fingers cradled her dripping wet pussy. Gushing noises sounded with every motion. Her clitoris stood erect and tender. She pinched it. "Ooooh…oh…oh!" it was coming, an orgasm that hummed like a locomotive. She used her free hand to caress her tits. Her nipples had erected into doorbells. "Ah….ah!" she felt it—the moisture ran down her thick butter pecan complexioned thigh. Uhn! I'm good, she thought while walking into the bathroom to shower. No one could control her body like her. Masturbation was something that she'd mastered as an adolescent and carried into her adulthood.

After showering and dressing, LaTicia twirled in the same mirror that she used before showering. She smiled gaily. "Bitch, you're a genuine dime!" she vainly spoke to herself and giggled before hearing the telephone ring. She rushed over to the nightstand and answered.

"Hello?" she purred into the receiver knowing it was Rone on the other end.

"Hey," Rone spoke through the telephone, "It's Rone. I'm down stairs in the lobby. May I come up?" he asked politely. LaTicia smiled. "Yes!" she said before hanging up. She sat on the bed and slipped into her strappy Chanel stilettos. She was subdued by Rone's charm. Maybe it was the home town Detroit swagger because she loved a nigga with a little thug in him. But she also saw a hint of southern gentleman in Rone. After strapping up her shoes she heard the door knock. She went to the door and peeped out. Rone was standing outside holding an arrangement of flowers. She opened and he smiled flashing his pristine dentistry, and handed her the flowers.

"These are for you beautiful." LaTicia took the flowers and stepped aside allowing him to come inside. I got the bitch with that one, Rone thought while looking around. He was sure that she wasn't expecting the flowers that he'd picked up from a street vender along the way. "I can't believe you brought me flowers!" she excitedly smelled the flowers. "They're beautiful." Rone smiled.

"I hope you'll accept them as an apology for this morning?" He chuckled. And LaTicia raised her eyelid teasingly giving him an evil eye.

"Yes, thank you." She sashayed away and purposely bent over showcasing her behemoth ass while putting the flowers in a vase. Her dress hiked up her thighs in the back showing the strain of her hamstring muscle.

Daaaamn! Rone thought while taking in an eye full of her pulchritude. He could tell that she'd spent a lot of hours keeping all of that action up. "This room is nice! I know it must have set you back a few dollars, huh?" Rone was fishing. He was sure that Ray had paid for travel and her stay, but he wanted to make sure. LaTicia chuckled while Rone looked around with fake amazement.

"Yes it is….." her giggling continued, it's real nice, but it didn't cost me anything." She lied. LaTicia knew what Rone was fishing for, but she didn't want to bring his bad side out by calling him on his probing. She'd paid for the suite herself just as she paid for every other thing in her life. This guy is off the hook, she thought. LaTicia was a bitch from the hood. She'd acquired a taste for nice shit and an impeccable mouth piece, but those were things that she'd picked up alone the way to the top. LaTicia had met Ray at school. She was one of his students. A Detroit native just like Rone. Ray had an eye for people with ambition. He knew the difference between thirst and drive. LaTicia had an ambitious drive. Like Rone, she'd started off doing odd jobs for Ray. Just pencil and paper pushing, but it was still hustling. She was still like that a--- corporate type of hood bitch. She played the catholic school girl roll swell, but every now and then her upbringing would come out.

"So you have it like that, huh?" Rone teased implying that a man had paid for the room. LaTicia looked over to him sassily.

"Yes, just like that…" she smiled and posed with her hands on her saddled hips. Rone stared knowing her ass had to be at least forty- two inches around.

"I have you taking me to dinner, don't I? And I'm sure you don't just take anyone out, do you?" she posed her question as an statement, but in actuality they were really questions—questions that she really wanted answers to. Rone laughed.

"You're right about that." Rone said convincingly. It wasn't a lie because he rarely took woman pass his hotel suite. Dinner was to intimate for him so he avoided it.

"Yeah, I usually eat dinner alone, but today is special." He chuckled after receiving an inquisitive look from LaTicia.

"Why is today so special?" she wanted to know. I know he ain't assuming he's getting layed? She thought curiously hoping that she didn't project that type of impression to him. She likes his swagger, but always took care of herself before a date. That was the first law of womanhood because men didn't usually get it done.

"Because I'm not having dinner alone…" he laughed, "you try having dinner alone for four years, and watch how special the company of a beautiful woman becomes." Rone's laughter continued and LaTicia fell in with him. "I'm honored, but we have to go. I'm starving like Marvin!" the volume of their laughter increased. Rone was damn near doubled over. He'd finally seem something real come out of LaTicia.

"So you do have some ghetto in you…." He asked while laughing, starvin like Marvin?" their cheerful laughed continued while leaving her suite. During the ride Rone apparently kept LaTicia entertained, from humming the lyrics to every song, because she giggled repeatedly. She occasionally glanced over to him and smiled letting him know that she was aware of his love for music. Rone wasn't much of a talker. He was a listener, and a doer, so the communication between them during the ride was limited. As they drove up the old colonial brick road to the restaurant LaTicia became cautious.

It seemed like a bad neck of the woods and although she'd tucked her razor under her bra, she wasn't sure that it would be enough in those parts of NY. After reaching the entrance to the restaurant her apprehension eased. There were all types of luxury vehicles in the valet line. Jaguars, Lexus, and some other nice slabs. After getting parked he led her down a few stairs into an underground restaurant. LaTicia gasped after getting inside.

The crowd was as diverse as the gumbo they served. The tables were trimmed with Mardi Gras beads and the high back chairs were creative replica's of Mardi Gras masks. LaTicia eyes roamed the room. She'd never been to a restaurant with so many ambiances. Everything was creative even the Creole drawl of the maitre D. she was seated and Rone pushed her in. she leaned close to him after he set.

"Thank you, Rone. Can I ask you something without offending you?" "Yeah, but be careful." Rone teased.

"Are you really from Detroit? You're too kind to be a city boy." LaTicia stared at him searching for a hint of dishonesty. She'd been dealing with guys from the Motor City. They were usually trying to play themselves up—like most broke niggaz did. Poor people had a habit of dressing and acting rich and that's why they stay poor. She'd been there, she'd grown up there, and she knew what the swagger there was like. Rone briefly stared at her giving her an uneasy chill.

"Maybe it's because I come from good stock? My mother is a recovering heroin addict and my father was a pimp."

That's what the stare was about, she thought. Although he sounded convincing she laughed. She figured he was trying to conjure up a joke with a good punch line. It was dark, but she was sure that it was a joke until she realized Rone hadn't joined in with her laugher. Her mouth briefly hung open before she placed her hands over it. This nigga was serious!

I am so sorry, Rone!" her apology was genuine. She thought he'd told her a joke, but this was his truth. "I didn't mean to offend you." This dude fixed to come across the table on me, she thought while discreetly scooting her chair back. She wanted to have some room to get the blade.

"I can't take offense to the truth, babygirl." Rone was unfazed by the way LaTicia laughed about his upbringing. "What it just is." LaTicia kept rambling apologies to Rone until a beautiful waitress walked up to the table. She politely smiled at LaTicia before turning to Rone.

"Hi, Mr. Swinney. How have you been?" The waitress held her smile and Rone politely smiled back.

"Hi, Patricia. This is my date LaTicia. She'll be dining with me for the evening." Patricia turned and flashed her dimly coffee stained teeth to her. LaTicia smiled back. She could tell that there was something between Rone and the waitress. *Maybe he'd laid with it and played with it, but he's with me tonight!* She thought while giving the waitress a conversation with her eyes—a silent girl talk. Although she had no right to lay claim on Rone she had.

"Oooooh! I thought you were a loner?" The waitress took a shot at LaTicia letting her know that she didn't intimidate easily. 'I'll give you all some time to decide…." She turned to LaTicia and sassily batted her eyelashes. "Enjoy yourselves." She walked away strutting her slender legs like a super model on the catwalk. LaTicia was jealous.

"I see you're popular in her, Rone…?" LaTicia smiled devilishly, "You come in her…… I mean in here often?" Rone had heard what she'd purposely let slip out and laughed.

"No and yes...." he said while thinking, *Yes I came in her well and often, but no I ain't tellin you shit.* "I haven't came in her, and yes I eat here weekly." He shook his head while still thinking about her snide remark. The communication flowed between them as the night progressed. They discussed everything from politics to their personal experience during their college years. They even shared some laughs about growing up in Detroit. LaTicia didn't expect to have as good a time as she did. She really enjoyed Rone's company and was being pulled into the magnetic charisma that he exuded. As they kicked it her attraction to him grew and she planned to address it.

Rone had LaTicia right where he wanted her. She was perishable. Just like any other sophisticated rat, he'd have sex with her a few times, but there wouldn't be a second date. She was too pretty and she knew it which wasn't a good combination. The physical changed for the worst during the natural aging process becoming useless to someone attracted to physical beauty. The brain was the only mechanism with an unlimited capacity for growth and beauty and Rone preferred woman with growth potential, rather than a well that would eventually run dry. Rone was a good judge of character. He'd had plenty of experience at it because he judged everyone. Whether it was personal, business, or just someone walking pass him he would make some type of judgment against them. He knew that people were always looking for a way to get over so he always tried to strike first, and that was exactly what he intended to do with LaTicia. After their conversation wound down LaTicia kept looking over to him and smiling. He was sure that she had something she wanted to say.

"Are you enjoying yourself?" Rone asked knowing that she was. "Yes. You're a gentleman and I love gentleman." She flirted with a smile. Rone chuckled lightly.

"How do you know that this isn't an act? I could be a fraud." He teased knowing he had her. LaTicia giggled and contorted her lips into a doubtful curl.

"I don't believe Ray would introduce me to a fraud." Or have a fake ass nigga in the fraternity! She thought while batting her long eyelashes. "Okay, I'll give you that, but I'm not as innocent as I might seem." He gave her a warning shot. "I say that because I'm authentic and it's hard to trust people."

"What's hard to trust about people?" she played naïve although she knew exactly what he was talking about. She'd been thrown under plenty of busses by people who she'd trusted. Rone sighed heavily. He was sure that she felt him and was just going through the motions. It's hard to tell if someone is sincere."

"Do you think I'm genuine?" Rone nodded. "Of course I do, but you're being on the defense since we met." Rone teased, although, he was telling the truth. She

89

had been playing a façade, that could fool most niggaz, but he could see straight through it. LaTicia smiled because Rone had called her right out.

"Yeah, but you've done enough to ease my apprehension." She took a slow sip from her wine glass. It was seductive and Rone acknowledge it's suggestion.

"Good, but don't make your final judgment because we haven't had dinner yet." He laughed, but this time LaTicia didn't join him. Instead she gave him a sly suggestive smile.

"I want to be your desert and your midnight snack. Will you spend the night with me, Rone?" She was frank. The wine and her attraction to him had pulled the freak out of her. She wasn't usually that promiscuous, but there was something in the atmosphere that pulled her into his charm. She looked up noticing Rone's reluctancy to answer" You can answer any time. Whether we spend tonight together or apart is up to you." She giggled and took another sip from her glass. "You won't offend me if it's a no."

"You surprised me and it seems suspicious." Rone stared at her with a look of curiosity, but LaTicia didn't blink.

"You can answer me any time." She politely reiterated and Rone nodded.

"Of course, but tonight is tonight only." Rone's request was candid and LaTicia nodded in agreement.

Bitch I'mma knock the bottom outta that hotpocket!
He thought while grabbing her hand and leading her out
the restaurant shortly after they'd sealed the deal.

CHAPTER 5

Sherry and LaTicia waited at the airport arrival pickup for
Fox and Rone. They shared some meaningless chitchat
while waiting. They talked about shopping amongst other
nonsense. LaTicia never trusted Sherry and was careful
not to tell her too much about herself or what she and
Rone were really into. It wasn't her business, furthermore,
LaTicia saw Sherry as an uneducated gold digger. She was
sure that a man like Rone had to be blinded by his love
for her because she wasn't intelligent enough to sustain a
relationship with him. Sherry soon became irritable with
waiting.

"I'll be glad when their flight arrives because I'm
tired of waiting." Sherry complained with a loud sigh.
"Shit, we've been waiting at least an hour pass schedule."
LaTicia looked at her watch noticing that they'd only

been at the airport for thirty minutes. Although their wait wasn't as long as Sherry had complained, LaTicia agreed with her nonetheless—that it had been too long of a wait.

"I know that's right." LaTicia agreed with a giggle and slipped the heel of her foot out of one of her shoes. "These shoes are dear to me, but they're hell on my feet!" she laughed and Sherry chimed in with her. LaTicia's joke was funny, but Sherry laughed for another reason.

Sherry laughed a laugh of ridicule. She looked over to LaTicia's four inch stiletto heels and knew that she'd worn them to impress Rone. She was sure that they'd shared something outside of business, but she couldn't prove it and she'd never ask Rone something so trivial. LaTicia always threw Sherry an indicator that something was going on between her and sherry's husband, but Sherry refused to give her the pleasure of acknowledging it. She wasn't gone to let LaTicia or any other woman fuck up her fairy tale marriage. Eventually Sherry's laughter tapered off. "Girl...." Sherry began, "You are too funny!" she laughed. "We have to get together more often. I'm always available since I finished with remolding the house, so whenever you have some free time.... Let's do it." She bragged inconspicuously, but LaTicia picked right up on it.

This bitch is an amateur who's fucking with a pro! LaTicia thought while snickering. She'd picked up on Sherry's attempt at boasting, so she decided to do a little trumpeting of her own.

"Yeah, I'm with that," LaTicia giggled. It was a haughty giggle that said that she had something sucked into her holster. She was confident that Sherry wasn't ready for the bomb. "I'm so busy though. Between getting the law firm off the ground and taking care of things for Rone I'm usually exhausted." She claimed victory with vindictive smile and snicker, and Sherry went quiet.

"I need to get out though…" LaTicia continued before going silent. Rone crept up on Sherry from behind and sensually caressed her shoulders. LaTicia's body shifted into a jealous edge and Sherry was startled by the sudden touch of someone until she recognized the five carat wedding band that she'd custom made for her husband.

Sherry relaxed and let Rone massage her neck, shoulders, and back while she teasingly made eye contact with LaTicia. I know you're watching, beeeotch! Sherry thought while smiling in a way that signaled she'd had the last laugh because ultimately she had the man. LaTicia batted her eyes and looked up to Rone.

"Hey, Rone!" she squealed. It was Sandra off 227 type of shriek that mimicked a screech followed by a lewd fuck face.

"Where's my brother?" Sherry quickly asked Rone before he could say hello to LaTicia. She'd been battling for position with females her whole life, especially redbone bitches like LaTicia, so it came swift and natural to her. "Here he comes." Rone said while pointing into his direction. "He had to use the restroom." And damn he couldn't have came sooner. He thought. He'd noticed the rift that he'd been trapped between immediately. This was something that had been going on between Sherry and LaTicia for a while, and Rone was always caught in between them. Rone let out a light sigh as Fox walked up. Fox leaned in and kissed Sherry cheeks.

"Hey, sis…" Fox stated before looking over to LaTicia. Damn this hoe cold! He thought before looking back to his sister. "Who's your friend?" he tried to sound mature while giving LaTicia's mountainous backside a quick glance. Sherry laughed at her brother's lustful stare.

"Fox, this LaTicia. A friend of ours and she is too old for you….too old." She took another shot at LaTicia just in case she didn't hear the first one.

LaTicia's eyes rolled sassily. This dirty bitch! She thought while thinking of something to counter Sherry's last attack. This bitch goon make me fuck her little brother out of spite! She laughed at the thought of actually doing something that low.

"Pssh!" LaTicia blew air from her mouth while waving Sherry off. Aint shit old about LaTicia, but her last name and her money, so you need to stop!" she rolled her eyes at Sherry before turning back to Fox. "I've heard a lot about you." She told him. "How was your trip? Did you enjoy yourself?" LaTicia asked question after question trying to pull him into her direction. Sherry had already clamped down on Rone so LaTicia went at the next best thing, to annoy her, her brother. Fox walked over to LaTicia and sat next to her.

"Yes I did." Fox answered with a smile. After all that he'd experienced in Atlanta, he was sure that he was ready for a more mature type of woman. How could he go back to knocking off hood rats when he'd just fucked a brothel.

"Am I making you uncomfortable?" Fox asked noticing there wasn't a lot of room between them on the small airport bench. Rone looked over to Fox and smiled.

Look at my lil nigga work! Rone thought while admiring Fox's forwardness. He was sure that LaTicia wouldn't fall into his game, but he still made a mental note to warn Fox about her, just in case. Rone knew that pursing her was a slippery slope and he didn't want his protégé to get caught in the cold trying to climb out.

"No!" LaTicia waved. Actually she was flattered that a young cat, liked Fox, was attracted to her. Not to mention, she could feel the heat coming off Sherry's forehead from seeing them blatantly flirt with one another. "Fox, your manners and presentation is impeccable." LaTicia said and touched his thigh as a warning shot to Sherry to stop the dagger throwing. I'll fuck him so don't test me, is what the touch said to Sherry.

95

"You remind me of how someone we know used to be." LaTicia shot an eye over to Rone after she finished her statement.

"I see you over there." Rone said to LaTicia. He'd immediately picked up on who and what she was referring too. Shit! Just when I thought I was in the clear. He thought before walking over and giving LaTicia a hug. "I just missed my wife, but I always got a little love for you too." He teased trying to appease both women without insulting either. Sherry was pissed. Fox was flirting with LaTicia and LaTicia was flirting with Rone. It was hard for Sherry to keep her composure, but she did out of respect for her husband. While walking through the airport Sherry threw her arm around Fox and they started talking.

Fox told Sherry about his trip omitting the parts about what they'd done in the suite and at Rone's house. He was sure that neither event was supposed to be repeated. Fox wasn't even sure that Sherry knew about the house in Georgia because she'd never mentioned it to him and that was rare. While walking he couldn't keep his eyes off LaTicia and she noticed his attraction, although, he was trying his best to be discreet.

LaTicia turned it up twisting her hips seductively causing her ass to jiggle. She was making sure Fox got and eye full, only the show wasn't meant to please him, instead it was meant to piss his sister off, because LaTicia was sure that Sherry was watching too. This ignorant ass little girl can't fuck with me!" she thought while boldly making her ass pop. Even Rone had noticed LaTicia's erratic behavior and shook his head.

Rone loved LaTicia to death, but he hated to be within the same vicinity as her and Sherry let alone in their presence together. It was always an uncomfortable situation. Of course, he loved his wife too, but him and LaTicia had history that couldn't be sold out by marriage. He needed her and she needed him, so Rone knew that he'd eventually have to put a stop to her and Sherry bickering over his affection because there was no way that he was being without either one of them. Rone pulled Fox to the side after they reached the parking structure.

"You have to ride with Ticia," Rone explained, "Once you get to where she takes you, you have to stay until I get there. I have to take care of some business with your sister so I'll be a while, but I'll be there before night falls. I got something for you." He patted Fox's back and Fox smiled. "Ah'ight! I got you, but don't be all day. I'm tryna go holla at my mom before she goes to sleep." Rone nodded and walked off toward sherry while Fox walked into LaTicia's direction. Rone grabbed his wife's hand and walked off, but her neck swiftly turned into Fox's and LaTicia's direction.

Where this bitch goin with my brother? Sherry wondered while nearly dragged, by Rone, into the opposite direction as Fox and LaTicia. She could tell that Rone noticed her uneasiness with Fox going with LaTicia, but she didn't care. That was her brother and she deserved to know where he was going with a hoe that she couldn't stand.

"Where is she going with my brother, Rone?" Sherry asked abruptly as they walked up to her car. She was still looking into the direction that Fox had went with LaTicia.

"I'll explain everything to you once we get to the house. "I'm tired as hell." Rone yawned before playfully slapping Sherry across the butt. "We still on for tonight?" they were supposed to be going to a concert later on that evening. Sherry's face remained solid.

"Yeah, were still going, but I wanna know where that bitch is going with my brother?" she insisted upon getting an answer. Although Rone was becoming irritated with Sherry's tone, he kept calm.

"Trust and believe that nigga is gon be alright. He good wherever or whoever he's with." Rone chuckled after remembering how quickly Fox came up with those numbers at the hotel. He'd done it effortlessly and Rone was impressed.

"I think the lil nigga might be one of them geniuses or something." He nodded. "Yeah, he's cool but I'm gonna watch'em for a little while longer before I let'em loose on the world." He opened Sherry's door and walked around the passenger's side. Sherry folded her arms across her chest and grunted. It was a defiant grunt that assured Rone that she hadn't gotten an answer to what she'd asked and she wanted one.

"Yeah…" Sherry replied nastily, "I know my brother and I'm thinking of his best interest. And I don't think it's with that scandalous bitch LaTicia." She stared at Rone watching his anger swell. He'd went from zero to sixty in less than a millisecond. Rone looked around like he was searching for some one.

Who is this bitch talkin to? He wondered while looking around because he was sure that she wasn't quizzing him about what he was doing. He slammed the passenger's door shut and rushed back around the car to her.

"I…." Sherry tried to say something but was briskly cut off.

"Shut the fuck up!" Rone shouted angrily. He wasn't his normal cool natured self. He stood inches from her face because he wanted her to understand him clearly. "I make the muthafuckin decisions around here! Your only job is to agree with them!" He shook his head disappointedly before turning to walk away. He stopped and looked back over to her.

"Whatever your problem is with Ticia…. Leave it alone, babygirl. Leave it alone because it ain't gon do shit, but cause problems that neither one of us need." They both got into the car and Sherry drove off without so much as breathing another word.

Fox and LaTicia walked up to Rone's Mercedes. It had accumulated a lot of dust from the parking garage during the three days that they'd been away in Atlanta.

99

LaTicia laughed as they approached the car. She wanted to break the silence between them so she wiped her finger across the dust and looked at it before showing Fox.

"That's when you know someone has money." She laughed sillily "Having a nice car like this one and don't take time to keep it up." Although Fox didn't think the joke was as funny as LaTicia let on, he chuckled alone with her.

"Yeah, I feel you." After getting into the car, LaTicia looked over to Fox and struck up a conversation. She wanted to see where his head was at. I know it's going to take you some time to really warm up to a sistah, but you can trust me. Rone and I are best friends and I'm sure you and I will become good friends too." She smiled innocently and Fox glanced over to her with a smile. We gon be better than friends, ma! He smiled while thinking about what he'd like to do with LaTicia. Every since he'd started being around Rone pussy was just falling out from everywhere.

"I'm a little stand offish, but I try to respect my elders." He threw that out there to test the waters depth. He was ready to push some game on LaTicia, but he wanted to know where her boundaries were. "You know, I don't wanna say nothin outta the way." Tha statement about her being his elder sent LaTicia into a frenzy. She hated being considered old, especially by someone who wasn't too far behind her.

"Boy! You better stop listening to everything your sister says! First of all I ain't your elder. And second, well there isn't a second, but I ain't your elder." Both of them laughed. This time Fox laugh was genuine. She'd fell right into what he'd planned.

"Well, I'mma come straight out with it since you put it like that…" he glanced over to her while pulling out of the parking structure noticing that she was finer than he originally thought. He was used to popping pimping at females his age and on his level, but this was a new arena for him so he was caution about what he was going to say.

"You're the finest sister that I've seen walk this earth! I was gon compliment you earlier, but my sister interfered. I haven't ate yet, so let's stop and get something to eat and get to know each other?" he wanted to see her reaction to his boldness, and she smiled. It was a smile that she tried to control, but couldn't. I got the bitch! He reassured himself after seeing her reaction.

"Boy, you are too much." She laughed while maintaining her joyous smile. "Jump on the lodge. We're going downtown. Maybe we'll stop and get something to eat once we're there. "She giggled again and glanced over to Fox. "You are too much." LaTicia was flattered by Fox's staring, but she had no ideal why he was looking at her so strange. She offended him, but he wasn't ready to give up.

"Oh, so now I'm a boy, huh?" he chuckled although her comment wasn't funny. You ain't gon be sayin that once I put this sledgehammer up in you. He smiled and nodded. "I see what it is. So since we gon be rolling together, we have to make a compromise." LaTicia's smile finally broke into a straight face.

"What?" she asked. "Fox, you must be on something." She was cautious not to call him a boy again, but she was waiting for him to answer because she was interested in what he meant by compromise?

"I'm sayin!" he chuckled, I'm young, no doubt, but I know when I'm attracted to someone. I definitely know I'm attracted to you. So when we're hanging out, taking care of business, or whatever. You should cancel the stilettos, cover the cleavage, and please no thong underwear." Both of them burst into laughed and Fox knew that he had her. Her laughter drowned his. She could barely breathe because she was laughing so hard. Although she'd never admit it to anyone, she really enjoyed the youngster and was impressed with his charisma.

LaTicia was having a good time. The conversation flowed between them thought-out their drive. They'd even spoke briefly about Fox's decision not to return to school in the fall. She tried to convince him otherwise, although, she had to admit he had a legitimate reason not to. LaTicia knew the necessity of education because she had one, so she still felt like his reasons were questionable, so she changed the topic before she bruised his juvenile ego.

"So, do you have a girlfriend?" she asked out of the blue. Fox looked over to her and smiled.

This hoe curious! He thought before answering her. "Nah, but I'm taking applications. You interested?"

"No," LaTicia laughed, "and you just blew it! We can't stop to get food now, playboy," she laughed as they were coming up off the expressway. "Ah'ight, ma! You got me." Fox conceded, although, he wasn't really giving up so easily. He'd seen her wink, so just like rolling a six on an eight point; if she wink she'll definitely fuck!

"Just drive down Jefferson." She demanded with a chuckle while pointing. This young nigga is relentless, she thought after glancing over seeing the thirst still in his eyes. "Do you know where the Jeffersonian is?" Fox nodded and looked over to her like he was insulted.

"No doubt!" he replied confidently. "I'mma D-Boy through and through. My aunt used to work across the street from there at this spot for retarded people."

"You mean mentally challenged people?" LaTicia made and attempt to correct him, but Fox made it evident that he wasn't trying to be politically correct. He shook his head defiantly.

"No," he continued shaking his head, "I mean retarded. I saw one of the muhfuckaz eat their own shit." they both giggled, although, LaTicia was trying to hold hers in. "To top it off! The nigga got pissed when the counselor tried to pull him away from it." They both continued laughing. "Ugh, you are nasty as hell!" LaTicia laughed while trying to catch her breath. "That really canceled lunch. I can't eat with that thought in my head. Ugh!" she rolled down the window to get some air because she was disgusted. They were still laughing, at what Fox said about the mentally challenged guy, when they drove into the parking lot of the Jeffersonian. He'd entertained her throughout their entire ride to the apartment. She could tell that he was charming and humorous youngster, but what she didn't know was that his comedic ways were a ploy to get between her legs. Once they'd made it up to the apartment, LaTicia turned to Fox and invited him inside.

Fox walked in noticing that the apartment was kind of empty. It wasn't his place to judge, but an attorney who was doing business with a grand hustle nigga like Rone should have been able to afford better. There was a forty- two inches television and a leather sofa set in the front room, but that was extent of it. He glanced over to LaTicia and noticed her smiling ear to ear as if she'd showed him some trump real estate. He smiled to accommodate her, although, he really wasn't impressed.

"This is nice." He lied while nodding and looking around like there was something impressive to see. She waved for him to follow her around. "Come on, Fox." She requested and he walked behind her.

Daaamn! I know this hoe doin this shit on purpose! He thought while holding his swelling penis. LaTicia's ass was bouncing with every step that she took. It looked like a take from a ying yang video! LaTicia smiled while walking down the hall. She was sure that Fox was enjoying the show that she was putting on for him. If this nigga was a little bit older I'd let him get some of this wet-wet! She giggled and turned around catching Fox cradling his manhood.

"This is the master bedroom." Fox walked in behind her looking over the balcony noticing the Detroit River and the Canadian skyline. Although the room wasn't furnished it was still a nice view. After showing Fox the rest of the apartment, she turned to him and pass him the keys.

"These are yours." She smiled. Fox looked from her to the keys and back to her.

Damn! That was swift. I done got the keys already! He thought presumptuously.

"Damn, baby! We ain't even had foreplay and I get the keys." He said with a chuckle. "You move fast." LaTicia laughed alone with him. She was sure that he was joking with her. She'd flirted and gave him a show to jackoff to later, but there was no way that she'd actually mess with him. "Negro please, negro freeze! This is your apartment. You can finish furnishing it whenever you'd

105

like to. You have a store credit at Art Van's for six thousand. There are towels, blankets, and plenty of hygiene. The refrigerator is full and the rent is paid up for a year." LaTicia gave him a stern look that let him know that the game of flirting were over. She was serious now and expected him to be as well.

"Fox, this is your starter kit. You ain't getting shit else for free, except advice. That's something you can get from me or Rone at any time." Fox's stone face cracked into a laugh.

"Ah'ight! You got me. I know I've been talkin boo'koo shit, but you bust my head with this one." He tried to hand her the keys back, but she didn't accept them. Neither did her poker face change. She was serious. They'd given him apartment to go alone with the truck."I'm not playing with you. This is yours. The utilities will be paid for a year also. Rone wants you to stay here until he gets here. I'm leaving, but you and I will be getting together tomorrow so we can talk more." She turned to walk out of the apartment before stopping and turning back toward Fox. She was really trying to see if he was still watching her lady lumps.

"I forgot...." She chuckled, Rone said he needs your things out of his car before he gets here and your telephone number is on the refrigerator." She waved before walking out.

Fox pounced onto the sofa, looking around in amazement. Now, the apartment that seemed so mediocre for LaTicia, was suddenly a place because it was his. Fox was an optimist who believed in good fortune, but what had happened for him throughout this weekend wasn't usually the scenario in his life. His father had died leaving him in a world of chaos and corruption, that he'd been trapped in for the past three years, but after giving his new residence a once over, a calm had suddenly came over him. He'd know that there would eventually be a light at the end of the dark tunnel he'd been traveling down, since his father was murdered, and now it was here. After looking through the kitchen cabinets, Fox found himself in the master bedroom. He walked through the sliding glass doors that led to his balcony and smiled. This was his first piece of American dream. He looked over the mayor's mansion into the Canadian skyline and sighed still in disbelief.

"Sheeit! Fuck the west side! This here is what's up!" he shouted into the tint of the night fall that was coming across the Detroit River.

****

Sherry had a chance to think about some of the things that was haunting her conscience. She understood the life style that Rone lived because her father lived one similar to it, and she'd grown up watching what it was like for her mother. She was willing to accept some things, but it was time to address other things that she felt crossed boundaries.

She was fed up with LaTicia's blatant disrespect of her and Rone's relationship. She wanted her husband to know that she knew about LaTicia's relationship. She wanted her husband to know that she knew what LaTicia's sexual acts, while around Rone, implied. She was sure that Rone knew what LaTicia was trying to do and she wanted him to put her back in her place--- second place.

LaTicia did a lot of work for Rone's companies, but Sherry felt like she could do better. She didn't have the education that LaTicia had, but her street smarts were supreme to LaTicia's. Not to mention, she was cheaper and more trustworthy than LaTicia. She knew that because she was a good judge of character, during their weekly meetings. And she'd learned a lot about LaTicia's character during their weekly meetings.

They'd meet weekly so LaTicia could explicate the direction of Rone's business to Sherry. Afterwards Sherry would sign the checks for the expenses. They'd usually have their meetings over lunch depending on their schedule compatibility. The tell came when Sherry realized she was battling LaTicia for position with Rone. Each time they met it was a fashion show. They'd dress up as if they were going out on a date with someone who they'd just met. The flamboyant meet and greet type of deal, but it was all a personal competition for Rone's attention, just like at the airport. Sherry was tired of the back and forth drama and wanted Rone to end it before she ended it herself.

Sherry looked over to Rone as she pulled into their driveway. He was asleep. What they'd had words over, had bothered her all the way home, but at that moment she realized how trivial their spat was. LaTicia had almost won by making Sherry feed into her own insecurities. Rone loved her, supported her, and most of all he inspired her, therefore, her jealousy was inappropriate and after looking at him sleep, after a long business trip; she realized how wrong she was. She shook him.

"Rone, wake up, stinky butt!" sherry teased and Rone stretched groggily and smiled.

"Ah'ight, Cheeks." Cheeks was a pet name that Rone had given her a few years before they got married. He'd always kiss the deep dimple on her left cheek which was where the name came from. "I was tired. I probably had jet lag or maybe it was the corn beef sandwich I ate on the plane...." He chuckled lightly, "You know how black people do it." Sherry laughed alone with him.

"I know you were letting some gangster shit fly outta your ass all the way down the expressway!" she playfully punched his arm while they both laughed. The mood that had overtaken them at the airport had been put aside. Sherry loved her husband and didn't want to let anyone, especially LaTicia cause her to question whether he loved her or not.

Rone turned the lights out immediately after they walked into the house. That was one of his strange habits. Although Sherry loved him, she'd always kept a close eye on him because she'd heard some gruesome stories about some of the things Rone was rumored of doing in the streets. There weren't any stories about him beating or killing any woman, but she was still apprehensive because murderous tendencies didn't stop at the respect of woman. A killer was a killer, and Sherry was aware of that.

Sherry drank and cleaned up around the house while Rone slept. She hated to start the party without her husband, but she'd been the one dealing with LaTicia's shit all day, therefore, she deserved a drink. She needed to loosen up a little. While cleaning the linen closet she heard Rone calling her from the den. She walked toward the den to see what he needed and was met by him walking down the hallway.

"What time is the concert?" Rone asked. "Because I still have to take care of some business with Fox." He walked into the bedroom followed by his wife.

"Boy, that concert doesn't start for three more hours." She answered drunkenly and smiled as Rone got undressed to get into the shower. She'd finished a half bottle of champagne and was ready to put in work. After all, she'd been alone and horny throughout the entire weekend while Rone was away, with Fox, taking care of business. She smiled while following behind him as he walked toward the master bathroom.

"That means we have enough time to do whatever you want to until then." She said while undressing. By the time Rone made it into the bathroom Sherry was naked and in tow of him.

****

Antoine rushed to the telephone. He was sure that it was Fox calling. He'd been waiting to hear from his guy all weekend.

"Hello?" Antoine spoke into the receiver, and smiled at the sound of his friend's voice.

"Tee? What's up wit it, hustlah?" Fox was just as excited to holler at Antoine as he was to talk to Fox.

"Shit! What it do, my nigga?" Antoine chuckled. "I been waitin on yo call all day. I thought you was s'pose to be back yesterday. "Yeah, I did too. But we stayed a extra day....man fuck all that though! Whatchu got up later on?"

"Shit, what's up? You tryna go to the after hour or somethin?" Antoine was anxious to do something because he'd been stomped while his mans was gone. They hung out daily, so seeing Fox leave all of a sudden was hard on Antoine, especially since Fox was his only friend. Antoine had developed a brutish type of personality over the years that they'd been hustling, so the other youngsters in the hood who were getting money shied away from him. Bullying on the block always started with a couple of jokes and knockouts or two, but once a block bully found out what he could get off, it was on. He'd started going in the other trapper's pockets and all kinds of shit, and that was what the other youngsters trying to come up in the hood avoided by not dealing with Antoine.

"Yeah," Fox replied, "we can do that. I'll be to scoop you up after I finish taking care of this business with Rone."

"It's on, my nigga."

"Aye," Fox caught him before he hung up the telephone. "Take all that shit you got left and hit the plate easy….real easy. Rubber band two packs to each pusher and throw the rest of whateveh in the trash outside somewhere," Fox was sure Antoine knew what he meant by hit the plate easy. That was a code that they had. It meant, put it out there straight top side.

Antoine looked at the phone suspiciously. He wondered why Fox wanted to put what they had out like that. They usually stretched everything to the edge so he wondered what was up. It didn't matter too much though because Fox was his guy and that's how they got down. They both called shots and neither of them usually went against the grain. It was an unspoken rule between them not to disrupt the cipher. "Aw'ight, I'm all over that right now, my nigga….." Antoine hesitated briefly. He wanted to question Fox about what was up, but he didn't want to offend him. They were partners and there had never been any shady deals between them, so he had no reason to doubt Fox's judgment. He was just curious about what he changed without him knowing it had.

"Is…you know? Antoine procrastinated with the ideal of coming right out with what he wanted to ask Fox. "You know is ev'rythang aw'ight?" he was worried about Fox's sudden generosity.

"Oh definitely", Fox chuckled, "shit's better than it's ever been in my life or yours." He assured Antoine. Fox would always make away for Antoine. No matter what him and Rone did together, he'd always see to it that Antoine ate too. "Feel me, hustlah?"

"No doubt, I just had to ask, but I'mma have that poppin." Antoine said a few more words before hanging up. After getting off the telephone, Antoine locked his bedroom door and got the rest of the heroin, that he hadn't sold while Fox was gone, from the razor slice in his twin size mattress. He rubber band two needles to each pack or blow and took the paraphernalia outside and tossed it into his neighbors trash can.

After returning to his bedroom, he sat on the floor trying to figure Fox's new found generosity out. Somethin gotta be wrong 'cause that nigga tighter than fish pussy. Antoine thought while sitting on the floor near the foot of his bed. He shook his head. It was right in front of him, this nigga fixed to leave me hangin! His face contorted into an abhorrent snarl.

Although him and Fox had been like brothers since grade school, Antoine knew that Fox would eventually outgrow him. Fox had carried him since they'd met. He would always make sure Antoine had whatever he himself had. Money, females, or whatever. He was the reason why Antoine and Keisha were together now, but knew that all good things came to an end. He stoop from the floor and walked to the window.

"Fuck it!" he whispered to himself. "If he trya do his thang, I gotta do mine. I'mma get at this paper my muhfuckin self!"

Fox walked to the door after hearing someone knocking. He was sure it was Rone on the other side of the door, but he peeped through the peephole just to be sure. Things were quickly changing in his life and he knew that he'd have to be more cautious, because grimey ass stick-up cats in the hood were always looking for their next come up. It was Rone so he opened the door. "What's the pass work nigga?" Fox playfully barked at Rone while using his young muscular body to block the entrance. Rone chuckled slightly lifted his shirt exposing the butts of two blue steel 9mm berretta semi- automatics. He held his shirt up long enough for Fox to get the hint. "These the passwords, nigga." Rone replied jokingly before brushing pass Fox while entering the apartment. Fox chuckled and closed the door behind Rone.

"Good password," him and Rone burst out laughing while Rone eyes canvassed the front room of the apartment.

"What's up? You gon show me around this muthafucka or what?" "Sheeit! I thought you already saw it. You paid for it." Fox laughed and waved for Rone to follow him around.

"I ain't pay for shit! This business, baby!" Rone laughed in a haughty manner while following Fox into the hallway leading to the master bedroom. "These the perks of fuckin with Rone! All courtesy of the M.O.B." His obnoxious laughter tapered off as they walked onto the patio. Rone didn't like attention so he watched how he projected himself to people who did know him. Fox sniffed the air around Rone as they walked back into the apartment. He knew that there was something off about the way his brother-in-law was acting. He was drunk and Fox could smell it on him. He wasn't used to seeing Rone so relaxed and he wondered what had changed him so much—other than the alcohol.

"Nigga… you been drinking?" Fox asked while staring at Rone. It shocked Fox to see Rone intoxicated. Damn! Fox thought while staring at him. I didn't even know the nigga drinks! Rone smiled loud and drunkenly.

"Yeah," he slurred his reply and nodded. "Big brah done had a taste or two. Me and your sister are on our way to a Frankie Beverly concert. That's her man so…..ya know." He wildly threw his hands into the air admitting that his wife had pulled rank on him. "Oh, sis down stairs? Why didn't she come up?"

"Me," Rone pointed to himself, "I'm feelin good, but her ass is drunk. Come on, I wanna show you something." He waved for Fox to follow him as he turned to walk out of the apartment.

As soon as they walked out of the building Sherry leaped out of Fox's truck. Fox smiled because his sister was looking good. She wore a soft powder blue short cut Louis Vuitton dress with a L'Impetuex Suhali handbag that matched her dress. Her satin tie Salvatore Ferragamo platform sandals loosely swung from her hands as she walked towards them barefooted. Fox laughed because he could see her drunkenness as they met up.

"What's up, big sis?" Fox smiled as she staggered closer to him with a drunken smile.

"Hey, Fox!" Sherry slurred and wrapped her arms around him hugging him.

"Sis liquored up, lil brah." She whispered loudly. Rone laughed and playfully slapped her across the butt while telling her to get into the Mercedes. "I told you she was plastered." Rone said while pointing to her as she walked to his car. "Look at her." They both laughed at her lush swagger while walking over to Fox's truck.

Rone got into the driver's seat and Fox jumped into the passenger's side. Once they were inside, Rone pulled the two berrettas from his waist and passed them to Fox. He reached over into the glove compartment and passed a concealed button, that had been mechanically place inside, then he turned to Fox.

116

"Look, young trap." Rone said and pressed the break holding it while he hit another button by the fuse box. The back of the glove compartment fell forward exposing a stash spot. "Tuck them burners in there." Rone told Fox and he did as Rone had requested. "Whenever you leave this truck take one of them yahmeans with you. I'ont give a fuck if you're running in and out—take it. When you get back in the truck put it back in the box. Don't drive around with'em out, Fox." He emphasized that with a coldblooded stare. He meant what he'd told him and he expects Fox to accept game.

"Most of all, don't hesitate to use 'em because we can beat a murder case, but it ain't a piece of currency they done made that can buy your life back. You feel me?" Fox nodded assuring Rone he felt him.

"Hell yeah I feel you." He gave Rone a pound as a reassurance. Fox knew what time it was. He watched the news nightly and saw countless headlines about carjacking murders, and he wasn't trying to be the next one. So he definitely felt where Rone was coming from because he'd kill in cold blood before he allowed his to flow in the streets.

"Good." Rone said with a nod. "As long as you feel me....we good." He gave Fox another pound and jumped out of the truck. After Rone and Sherry drove off, Fox sat in the truck for a while. He knew that he was all in and there was no turning back. He had to eat and would make sure that everyone around him was full also.

117

Antoine thoughts were everywhere while waiting on Fox to come pick him up. His hustling would have to be done solo something that he'd never experienced. Fox had done a lot of hustling by himself, but Antoine had always been a teammate of a sort. He was sure that Rone had given Fox an opportunity to touch a dream, and that was what was pulling Fox away from him and their petty hustling. While contemplating his next move, Antoine heard loud music thumping outside of his bedroom window. He peeked out and saw a candy painted Expedition sitting on dubs out front. I know this ain't my mans! He thought while rushing through the house and outside. Damn! Antoine grabbed his nuts while checking out the ink on the truck.

Fox leaped from the driver's seat and folded his arms into a D-Boy stance. He knew that Antoine was fixed to hit the moon. They were always happy for one another because what one of them had the other was welcome to enjoy. "Nigga!" Antoine shouted hysterically. "This ain't you is it?" he knew the answer when he saw the smile sweep across Fox's face.

"No doubt, hustlah!" Fox broke into laughter and Antoine rushed to look inside.

"The monogram seats! What the fuck! You fixed to hit the bitch lottery with this muhfucka!" Antoine happily embraced his guy. He'd read about cats getting blessed like that in a few books, but it was reality in Fox's life. Fox laughed, but it wasn't in a boastful way.

"I told you, my nigga." Fox explained with a nod. Big Rone blessed me. Leather goods and the whole nine. I got something I want to show you, but we gotta wrap this little shit up first." He leaned hard while cruising down Antoine's street. All of the young bitches on the block who they'd fucked stared at the chrome spinning pass them, but neither Fox or Antoine stopped to acknowledge them.

"We fixed to take this shit to another level, my nigga." Fox encouraged Antoine about their new hustle.

"What's up, my nigga? Talk to me." Antoine was driven after hearing Fox say we. He'd sworn that his boy was going to push him out the whip after getting plugged in with Rone.

"Did you bring that work?" Fox asked and Antoine nodded.

"Yeah." Antoine replied and reached into his crotch pulling out a few bundles. "Here it go right here. I did it just like you asked me to."

"Good, so how did shit go while I was gone?" Fox was curious because Antoine could be a slacker at times.

"It went. That's all I can say, my nigga." Antoine answer was nonchalant because he knew Fox was checking up on him.

"Cool." "So what's up?" Antoine pressed for conversation. "What the fuck popped off down there?"

119

"Rone threw a little party." A smile swept across Fox's face after thinking about what he'd done with Egypt and the Cocoa complexioned mami that night. Although he wanted to tell Antoine about his trip, he didn't because he didn't want to seem like a braggart. Neither did he want to slip up and tell Antoine about what type of paper Rone was really dealing with. Rone was his connect now and he wasn't going to fuck the trust up by telling Antoine their business.

"It was cool though. We kicked it."I feel you." Antoine replied, although, he really wasn't feeling Fox's standoffish attitude. He and Fox had shared every detail of their lives, even the beatings that he was getting, but something had changed now. He didn't like Fox's new secretive behavior. He felt like the trip to Georgia with Rone had changed his Fox swag.

During the ride to the after hour spot the two of them kicked it some. It wasn't like their usual flow, but it was a steady exchange between them. Antoine didn't know what to think. He didn't know whether to be happy for his boy's good fortune, or to hate on him because it was evident that Fox was putting himself in another league and leaving Antoine behind. Fox turned to Antoine and sighed as they parked.

"Tee, I hear that shit in yo voice, my nigga." Fox complained. He'd heard all the skepticism within Antoine's tone. They were best friends so he knew when something was off about his peoples. He shook his head in disappointment because he was sure that Antoine was doubting him.

"Stop doubt yo mans, Tee. I ain't never shitted on you before and I ain't gon start." Fox said while trying to convince Antoine to relax, but he wasn't buying into it.

"It ain't nothing." Antoine's reply was somber. "I know you an opportunist, my nigga. Do you?" he knew that there was no way Fox would turn down the type of work Rone could supply him with so they could stay in the bars doing hand to hands.

"Fox shook his head. Nigga, just roll with yo mans, hustlah! I'mma hit the hoe you just hold the leg."

Antoine glanced over to Fox. He was tired of holding the leg. He wanted to fuck, and he would –with or without his comrade. They both jumped out the truck and went inside.

Fox was greeted like ghetto royalty as they walked inside while Antoine received his regular cautious stares from everyone. The older bitches rushed up to Fox in flocks. They'd been trying to fuck him for years, but he wasn't with it. He'd heard about the tragedies that came alone with running up in dope fiend broads. Cats would either be turned out to their own sack by the same hoe, or they'd leave with three letter death sentence. Either way, Fox wasn't interested, so he stayed clear.

Antoine walked through the spot straight over to the bar. Although he didn't drink, he liked to post up at the bar and catch females as they passed. Unlike Fox, Antoine would get head and plug a basehead every now and then. He felt someone's stare so he turned and caught Trey-pack, a young nigga out of their hood. Trey-pack peddled three dollars rocks the size of boulders. Antoine and Fox didn't sell crack, but whoever pushing that package on their set had heavy competition because Trey's stones were massive. I wonder why this muhfucka always staring? Antoine asked himself while giving Trey a cold looking mean mug. This was the wrong timing for anyone to be getting out of line, especially a nigga with a hustle because Antoine was looking to replace somebody. While checking Trey, Antoine noticed Fox strolling around the bar passing out the packages that he'd bundled up. What's wrong with this nigga? Antoine watchful eyes noticed Fox wasn't getting paid for them. Fox was friendly people type of person, but he didn't socialize with the fiends the way he was right then. Antoine wanted to know what was up so he walked over to Fox. Fox turned as Antoine approached him.

"What's up Tee money? It ain't shit, but dope fiend bitches in here tonight." Antoine said as a hint that he was ready to leave and Fox caught on."Ah'ight, let me holler at Trey for a second and we out." he walked over and gave Trey-pack some hood love.

Antoine was steaming after seeing Fox embracing Trey-pack. This nigga was just grillin me, and now, my mans tossin game wit'em!" Antoine blood broiled at what he was seeing. Fox was consorting with a potential enemy. He walked out and waited by the truck for Fox to come out.

Shorty after he got outside, Fox came walking out. Fox walked over and they both got into the truck. He could see that something was still eating at Antoine, but he didn't know what. He'd assured his boy that they both were going to eat so it couldn't be that. Envy had never been an issue between him and Antoine and Fox hoped that it wasn't going to be one. Damn! Fox thought suddenly. Maybe this nigga's moms is trippin again.

"I got something to show you." Fox nodded after his statement. He knew that Antoine mood would pick up after he heard what Fox was working on. "Show me the money, my nigga." Antoine resorted with a fake laugh. He wanted to know where the money for those blows that Fox had given out was at. "How much we make?"

"Nothin!" Fox answer was frank. "Those were gifts to the muthafucka's, who 'bout to make us rich."

"What! Nigga, you just gon give some shit away? What the fuck is wrong with you? That heat must've fried yo muhfuckin brain while you was down south!"

"Nigga, fuck that short shit. You've been acting like a suckah all day! What the fuck wrong with you?" Fox's temperature rose. He was becoming heated with the way Antoine was acting.

"Ain't shit wrong wit me! Somethin wrong with you, nigga. Just givin shit away like you got a opium field in yo muhfuckin backyard." Antoine slouched into his seat and Fox looked over to him with anger in his eyes. He wanted to steal on Antoine, but he didn't. They hadn't had a fist fight since grade school, but Antoine was calling for it.

"I ain't 'bout to argue with you, nigga. We gon end this shit before it gets ugly between us."

There was little talking between the two of them during their drive to Fox's apartment. Both, Fox and Antoine, knew that something had caused a change between them, but neither of them knew exactly what it was. Antoine was having remembrances of some things that had taken place during their childhood. He realized that throughout their lives he'd been Fox's right hand man, but never the man himself. He'd been a latchkey, but he refused to continue being a flunky. Be figured Fox was ready to eat alone and he'd have to make his own way from here out.

Fox watched Antoine through his peripheral while coming off the freeway. He tried to read his facial expressions. Something had changed between them, but Fox didn't know what or understood why. He was sure that Antoine wasn't envious of the attention that he's received from fiends. Hell nah! He brushed that thought off. It couldn't be that. Everyone preferred doing business with him because they thought he was a pushover compared to Antoine. Nah, maybe it's Kiesha?

He knew that Antoine and Kiesha stayed into it. Whether it was Kiesha frequent disappearing acts of her gold digging ways, they feuded relentlessly. Fox shook his head while pulling into the parking lot of the building.

"Who lives here?" Antoine asked.

"This one of Rone's chill pads. He said I can use it because he don't use it anymore."

"Yeah, that's some real shit." they both got out of the truck and walked toward the building. Fox stopped in mid stride.

"Hold up, my nigga." Fox ran back to the truck. He remembered what Rone said about the pistols so he popped the hatch and tucked one into his waistline.

During the elevator ride to Fox's floor he saw it. The hate illuminating off Antoine's skin. This hoe ass nigga jealous! Fox thought while getting off the elevator. This shifty muthafucka! He couldn't believe Antoine was envious of his come up. He'd always made it happen for the both of them, and now he was being confronted with baller bigotry. Throughout their friendship Fox had always kept Antoine's best interest, and he had assumed Antoine kept his too, but after what he was seeing, he wasn't as sure as he once was. "Make yo'self at home, my nigga." He metioned, while walking over to the telephone. Antoine walked over to the sofa.

"Can I sit on the couch?" Antoine asked glibly, although, he'd just heard Fox tell him to make himself feel at home. It was a snide remark made solely to get beneath Fox's shin. He was deliberately trying to upset him, but Fox didn't bite. Instead he laughed at Antoine.

"Nigga if you don't sit yo silly ass down, we gon have some problems." Fox wasn't falling into Antoine's childish antics.

His reply to Fox's idle threat was cold. He grabbed the remote to the television and began scanning through the channels. Fox laughed at him while shaking his head.

"Yeah, I know it ain't. You graduate next may and I'll be eighteen in September. It's been a long time, dawg. Sheeit, 'bout eleven years to be real." Fox tried to break the tension by reminding Antoine how long they'd been friends and how close they'd been over the years.

"Yeah, 'bout that long."

"Tee, I made a nice piece of change fuckin with Rone this weekend." Fox reached beneath the sofa seat and pulled out a shoe box. He opened it and pulled out the roll of cash that Egypt had given him. He hadn't spent a dime of it and it was still rolled into a knot thick enough to choke a boa constrictor.

Antoine's complexion tinted into a hateful bronze. *This nigga tryna show off!* He thought while trying to keep his comments inside the sanctity of his own mind. He and Fox had been friends for years and now their friendship was being tested. Antoine felt like his best friend was trying to stunt on him. How this nigga gon play me! The muscles in his neck stiffened and his eyes became dark.

"What? You tryna boss up on a nigga, Fox? Ain't no surprise, nigga! I knew you was gon pull out once you started fuckin wit Rone! Drop me the fuck off and do you, nigga!" Antoine aggressively stood from the couch while Fox stared at him in disbelief.

Now he knew why Antoine was flipping out. "Nigga, sit down and give your ears the same chance you gave your mouth." Fox demanded while Antoine stood over him with menacing glare. He pointed to the bankroll that he held. "This paper be us, my nigga. We…" he emphasized, "'bout to turn this hustle up. I already hollered at Wheat and he said he'd push us a hundred grams for eight stacks. Us, not me. Us, my nigga." He tried to easy his guy's worries.

Antoine slowly fell back into his seat. What was once envy had quickly been replaced with humility?

"I feel shitty as fuck." Antoine explained. "I thought you was tryna abandon a nigga out here in these treacherous ass streets."

"What?" Fox's question was more of a statement. "You on some bullshit. Nigga, we fam'ily…." Fox paused while shaking his head. Antoine's admission bothered him. This was the first time Fox had really questioned their friendship, and although Fox was young, he game tight enough to know that, once a relationship is questioned it could never go back the same."I'mma drop

127

you off because you goin through some emotional bitch ass shit that I ain't tryna fuck with. I'll scoop you up in the morning, but right now you gotta bounce, my nigga,"

Antoine nodded. "You right, my nigga. I gotta get my head right. Shit just been crazy while you was gone." They rose from the couch and walked out of the apartment. Antoine continued apologizing throughout the entire drive to his house, but it was too late because the damage was to their friendship had already been done.

****

After dropping Antoine off at home, Fox decided to stop by an old friend's house before going home. He waved through the bumper to bumper traffic amazed by the hustles blatant disregard of the cops. Barely clothes bitches paraded up and down seven mile pushing baby strollers and soliciting hustlers. They didn't care what type of hustlers he was, whether it was raping or robbing, as long as his whip was something that stretched out long enough for them to get pounded out in the back seat, and there were plenty of them. Young cats leaning hard in Benzes, Jaguars, Range Rovers, and other expensive whips that unemployment niggaz shouldn't be pushing. Everyone was partying wildly and the scene intimidated Fox. As he pulled to a stop, behind a car full of honeys, a tinted out Lexus truck pulled beside him. It was close enough to dent his door if they jumped out. Bitch! Fox thought, while trying to reach for one of the burners. Nigga's tryna jack me! The stash opened and he reached in for his cannon.

"What's up, young Fox?" Quake yelled while rolling down the tinted glass. Fox's heart rate settled and he shut the hatch.

"What up?" Fox replied. Although he didn't like Quake, this was a time that he was happy to see him. He wondered what he'd done with the white Lexus LX470 truck. The one that he'd just drove up in was wet as hot pussy and the chrome that it set on threw off a three dimension gleam.

"I see you looking good, lil brah." Quake gave Fox's truck a quick unimpressed once over. "And skatin clean." He nodded at the spokes and Yokohamas that the Expedition sitting high.

"Yeah, we move up, but you keepin it movin. Huh, nigga?" Fox was talking about the rotation of Quake car game.

"Yeah, I got some pant on this muhfucka, but it's really time to upgrade." The light turned green and traffic started moving in the middle of their conversation. "Get at me fo that twork, baby!" Quake nodded and sped off with his spinners rotating in two different directions.

Fox laughed. It didn't surprise him to see Quake chasing bitches up and sown the mile. It was customary for cats like him to placate to a broad with an ass like Buffy. Erk was different than Quake. Fox actually felt him. He didn't fuck with him, because the two of them came as a package deal, but he liked his swag. And young chocolate tender that he kept in his passenger seat was royalty. She'd always give Fox a smile that said she wanted to fuck, but he never crossed that line with Erk. It was respect for the streets. He refused to let a hoe drag him into a war over some pussy. "No sir," he whispered to himself while jumping out of the truck.

He walked up the driveway of Jackson's home. What the fuck is that? He wondered while hearing a loud shriek coming from the backyard. Jackson's parent's car wasn't there. Fox knew that they worked midnights so he was sure that it wasn't them, but someone was fucking.

"Oooooh.....oh!" a familiar voice came from Jackson's bedroom window. Fox stood below listening and trying to figure out who the voice belong to. There were more moans and words of passion being whispered.

"Fuh…fuh..fuck me…me..me!" the sound of slapping skin got louder and louder. "Oh!" the woman's voice panted an earthly groans.

"Captain Jack!" Fox yelled up to his window while chuckling. He was voyeur and Jackson had given him an audio show. Suddenly Jackson leaned out of the window sweaty and breathing heavily.

"Who dat?" Jackson asked while scanning the backyard never seeing Fox standing right beneath his bedroom window.

"It's Fox! Country ass nigga!" Fox laughed and stepped backward so Jackson could see him.

"Wuzzup, bwoy? When you get back dis way? I'm on my way down." Jackson ducked his head back into the window and quickly appeared at the back door. "Come on in, pimp!" Jackson was excited to see his guy. He'd heard that he went to Georgia, his home town, but he didn't know that he was back.

"What's up, my nigga?" Fox gave Jackson dap as he walked into his home and headed toward the basement. That was something that had become routine throughout the years. They could always kick it at Jackson's crib, but the kicking it had to be done in the basement.

"Did you go to Turner field while you was down south, homie?" Fox chuckled. "Nah, but I sucked on some pussy, my nigga!" they both fell out laughing after what Fox had said. Unlike Jackson, Fox wasn't into giving oral sex, he only liked to receive.

"Squa business, bwoy? You ate some pussy? As much shit as you be talkin 'bout me?" his laughter continued. He couldn't believe Fox had fell victim to the Georgia peach.

"Whatevah, nigga. You eat pussy for sport! Nasty as nigga." They laughed. "My situation is different. I had two cold as bitches on me, brah! So I had to perform, feel me?" Fox nodded in a gaily manner and Jackson fell right in laughing and wanted to hear more about Fox's trip. Sometimes Jackson seemed like more of a best friend than Antoine, but Fox had grown so close to Antoine because he had to carry him where Jackson could roam around himself. The two of them sat around kicking it for a while before Fox came out with the real reason for his sudden visit.

Fox knew that Jackson wanted to open up a towing company after he graduated, but he didn't have the money. He wanted to pull Jackson in now while he needed the cash because there was no one else who he could trust, especially with his and Antoine's friendship looking shaky. He needed someone else to watch his back and Jackson needed the paper, so he was sure that things would work out between them.

During their talk, Jackson assured Fox that he was all in. he also made it clear that he wasn't taking any disrespect from Antoine. Fox was sure that it would come, but Jackson was man enough to handle up with Antoine, so he didn't see the harm in his request. After they came to an agreement on a few things, Fox left so Jackson could get back to his session with the mystery broad. He walked out of Jackson's house feeling more confident than he'd ever felt in his life. He was ready to make moves, and just as his foresight predicted, him and his crew went full time in the game. It was hustling season, and they weren't missing a crumb!

CHAPTER 6

Fox and Antoine walked out of the Broadway. They'd just done some shopping. The money had been floating through in stacks they were too large to fold for Fox, and Antoine's bankroll had stacked up as well. Antoine looked over to Fox and chuckled.

"My nigga?" Antoine said and held up the leather jacket that he'd just copped. "You think I'll look stupid if I throw this bitch on right now?" Fox laughed.

"Hell yeah, nigga! Not only will you look like a ignorant ass nigga, but you'd look like a hot ignorant as nigga." Fox said and shook his head. He couldn't believe Antoine was still so showy. They'd been getting money for a few years now and he still had something to prove. This nigga needs to prove he can pay Wheat that eight stacks! Fox thought while walking up to Antoine's Tahoe. Wheat had put some bad words on the streets about Antoine, and Fox was starting to catch a reputation behind it because everyone knew that him and Antoine were teams. He couldn't even take Antoine to buy work because of the debt. Fox had become embarrassed of Antoine, especially in the game where reputation meant so much.

"Nigga," Antoine resorted and laughed as if Fox had told a joke. "You crazy. It's fall, baby! Leaves is fallin and shit. I'm puttin this muhfucka on right now." He stripped the jacket out of its plastic and put it on. Fox stared at Antoine as Antoine primped in the window of his truck. He was making a mockery of himself and Fox knew. This wasn't the first time either, and Fox was getting tired of Antoine's bullshit.

"Yo silly ass act like you just start getin money or something." Fox spat at Antoine and he laughed. Everything had became a joke to Antoine. Fox just stared at him. His disappointment had descended into a subtle

134

contempt. "I did!" Antoine laughed you the one had a good moms and pops, and a brother-in-law who holdin the earth." His voice had a hint of jealousy in it and Fox picked up on it. Although it hadn't surfaced in a while, Fox had known it was there. Jealousy was like that, it would bevel when someone is doing good themselves, but once they recognize someone else is doing better it would resurface.

"Fuck you, nigga. Maybe if you stop spending your money on stupid shit, you could hold the earth." Fox's contempt was beginning to show, so Antoine quickly tried to avoid any further altercation.

"Whatevah, nigga. Is we scoopin captain Jack up or what?" "Nah he already at the apartment. I gotta shoot through Rone's and take care of some business, so y'all on y'all own today." Antoine chuckled after Fox was finished talking.

"Yeah, I forgot." He replied with sarcasm. "Rone's business is more important than ours!"

I'mma end up whippin this nigga! Fox thought while rushing around the truck and over to Antoine. "Stop hatin on my peoples, nigga! You letting these couple of dollars change you, brah! If it want fo Rone you wouldn't be pushin this truck or wearing that hot ass leather, son!" They stared at one another for a brief moment. Fox wanted Antoine to see the anger building within him. They'd been best friends since grade school, but money had a way of ending good friendship, especially when someone feels cheated.

Antoine assumed Fox was paying less than what he led them to believe. He'd came to that conclusion because Fox wouldn't allow him to tag along when he copped their work. That's why Antoine was holding out on the money that he owed Wheat. It wasn't that he didn't have it because he did. He just wanted to let the situation play out before he sprung it on Fox that he'd known what was going on. And Fox's nonchalant attitude about everything was bothering Antoine too. He figured if Fox didn't seem to be bothered by the dept than why should he.

Fox was still apprehensive about the direction of their friendship. He couldn't trust Antoine after seeing the envy in him when Fox hooked up with Rone. It was strong and hateful type of jealousy that Fox was sure could turn deadly if it progressed. He couldn't understand why Antoine was so blind with it. Fox was getting long money with Rone and had no reason to be dealing with Antoine other than to help him, but the green envy eyes kept him from realizing that.

"There Jackson go over there," Fox said while pointing to Jackson. Jackson was casually leaning against his GTO. "I can see him," Antoine replied with a laugh. "A nigga can't miss them big ass sideburns."

They both laughed at Antoine's joke because Jackson had some sideburns that looked seventies. They jumped out of the car and gave Jackson dap. Fox smiled while checking out Jackson's whip.

"I see you done finally put paint on this muthafucka! Hw wet now, brah!" he was excited to see what Jackson was doing with the old school Pontiac. Fox had a thing for older cars, especially Chevy's. He'd spent tens of thousands customizing his own two door Caprice Classic.

"Fo'sho!" Jackson smiled proudly while giving Fox a thankful pound for his compliment.

"You need to upgrade." Antoine commented, and smiled insidiously while patting the hood of his truck. This was something that Jackson had become accustomed to. Everyone knew that Antoine was a hater, but no one spoke on it.

"Nigga, I got betta shit to do wit my bread!" Jackson laughed at Antoine to his face because he knew about the debt. He was even considering covering it to spare Antoine the humiliation, and their crew the beef. Trey-Pack had already pulled away from them because of Antoine's reputation in the streets, and from what Jackson was feeling Fox was gradually packing his bags too. "Plus, we ride old school in the south!" Jackson continued to defend his classic and Antoine eased up.

Whatevah, nigga! Let's bounce 'cause Fox got more important shit to do." Antoine glanced over to Fox with an instigating smirk. "It's just me and you, Captain." He gave Fox a pound and jumped into the truck.

137

"Aw'ight, bwoy." Jackson gave Fox a manly embrace before getting into the truck with Antoine.

Fox's eyes followed the truck as Antoine drove out of the parking lot. He watched as the Tahoe disappeared into the busy midday traffic. Although Fox never wanted the day to come, he was sure that his and Antoine's friendship was screeching to an end, because the guy who just pulled away from his apartment building wasn't the friend he used to be. Antoine had let the hustle take over his life.

Antoine swerved and swayed through the bust rush hour Detroit traffic. Him and Jackson didn't usually talk much, but today was different. They were popping game back and forth since they'd left the building. They talked about everything, including the game.

Antoine was the typical hood nigga. He thought that the end all be all was the hustle. That the dope game would rescue him from the perils of the ghetto, but Jackson had another perspective.

Jackson's dope boy dream didn't stretch that far. He was sure that he'd have to do a lot more than push heroin to make it out the hood. He'd seen plenty of drug dealers get major paper only to be victimized by it. If a nigga in the ghetto has money he becomes prey for a community of niggaz looking for a come up, and unlike Antoine, Jackson wasn't interested in becoming no one's prey. Jackson had saved the bulk of his money since he'd been hustling with Antoine and Fox. He was planning to

6 MILE CHRONICLES   The Birth of A Hustler   Mi'kiel Los

start a towing and wrecking company in the spring. Consequently, that would be the end of the game for him. It was a wrap; Antoine changed the subject after hearing Jackson's plans.

Antoine had heard it all before. Hustlers talking about getting out of the game, but for him it was different. He couldn't concede because getting at the bread wasn't a game for him, it had become a life style. A way of life that he planned to live until the day he died.

"So you gon put some feet on that muhfucka or what?" Antoine asked as they drove up to the front of the 70 West apartment. He really cared less, if Jackson was going to put rims on his car or not, he just wanted to stop him from rambling. Jackson opened the door while chuckling.

"Naw, brah. I'm staying original wit it pimp." He leaped out of the truck and rushed into the building.

Jackson knocked on Que's apartment door after getting inside the building and making it up to his floor. Que was one of the soldiers that Fox had recruited to hold down the Cass Corridors. The corridor was one of the roughest parts of the city for a nigga trying to stack his chips like Pringles. You had to be a goon around those parts of the city and Que was a goon. Que opened the door shortly after Jackson's first knock. He was sure that Que had seen him while he was outside because he kept a squad of lookouts posted around.

"Wuzzup, Que baby?" Jackson gave Que pound and looked around to the room they'd just seen a hamburger after a month long fasting. I'll take the top off ya head bwoy. He thought while looking at a grimy looking cat who sat in the corner eyeballing him. That one was a new face so Jackson held his felonious stare just to set precedence.

"What up doe, Captain Jack?" Que asked before closing the door and locking it.

Jackson looked back. Although he'd been through this a few times before, it hadn't gotten any easier to come to terms with. He felt trapped because he was in a room full of cats that were eager for a lick, not to mention, he really didn't know Que that well. Que was Fox's peoples. Him and Fox had went to school together on the eastside after Fox's mother moved them.

"What's up, gangstah's?" Jackson finally greeted the other men while making his way through them. Niggaz were sprawled across the floor, slumped into the raggedly couches, and standing near the ancient steam radiator near the window. They all gave Jackson silent hood head nods and the one that he'd made eye contact with simply sucked his teeth.

Jackson watched puzzled while Que unlocked multiple pad locks that he'd recently attached to the bedroom door. What da fuck is dis nigga on? Jackson thought while watching him. He was sure that the locks weren't there the last time he had did the pickup from his trap. After Que had unlocked the door, they went inside leaving the rest of Que's goons on the other side of the door. After getting inside Que slapped a few chain locks that he'd put on the inside of the door on.

"Damn, nigga!" Jackson chuckled. There was just as many locks on the inside as there was on the outside. "You got dis muhfucka like the Arab store, bwoy!"

Que looked up to him without smiling. "Sheeit! A nigga gotta be safe out here in these muthafuckin streets." He pulled a safe and a Ak47 from beneath the bed. He looked over to Jackson without any emotion in his face. "I'm just being safe, Jack." Que said and threw the safe on the bed. He used his back to shield the safe from Jackson while he unlocked it. After he unlocked the safe he pushed it over to Jackson without opening it and posted up at the door with the chopper.

Jackson wanted to burst out laughing at Que's theatrics. This nigga can't be for real! He thought, while opening the safe. Jackson looked from the money that was inside the safe to Que then back to the money. Finally a smile crept across Jackson's face. He couldn't help, but smirk to keep him from laughing.

After getting to the elevator, Jackson burst into laughter. I gotta holla at Fox 'bout this nigga! He thought while laughing there was no way that he'd be returning to that spot because he felt uncomfortable around Que's clique. Jackson became startled as he walked out the building. The police had blocked Antoine's truck off. He walked pass the squad car and Antoine's truck without making eye contact with either of them. He walked across the Woodard and posted up at a city bus stop while watching what was going on. One officer drew pistol and ordered Antoine out of the truck. When he got out the other one drew his revolver and forcefully pushed Antoine to the ground while holding the gun on him. He cuffed his hands behind his back and searched him pulling a huge roll of cash from his pocket. Meanwhile the other cop searched his truck. The search didn't last too long so it was evident what they were looking for—drugs and money.

Jackson was pissed about how the law was treating his mans. "These muhfucka's some bitches!" he said to himself while watching the cop tuck Antoine's bankroll into his pocket. He was sure that this was a shakedown because the officers had taken the cuffs off Antoine. Damn, he thought suddenly. He'd been feeling bad for Antoine and was willing to pay his dept when Antoine had been carrying enough bread around to square half of it himself. At least they didn't find the thumpers. He thought while watching Antoine walk back to his truck at gun point.

The officers held there pistols on Antoine until he got into his truck. "What the fuck?" he said to himself out loud while staring at the two pistols that lay in the passenger's seat. He sighed. "Damn!" he figured the three grand, which they'd just peeled him for, was worth his freedom because he would have been spending that on bond anyway. He fixed his seat before driving across the

142

street to where Jackson had been watching from. He rolled down the window.

"Get yo coward ass in, nigga!" Antoine demanded jokingly because he would have done the same thing if their places were reversed. Jackson jumped into the truck giggling.

"Damn, bwoy! I thought they was gon put the Rodney King on yo ass!" they both laughed hysterically as Antoine drove off into traffic.

"Yeah, my nigga! They put the pillage game down on me, but they left me my burners and my freedom, so a gangstah can't complain." He chuckled. "In my eyes it was a good deal."

Jackson was surprised to see Antoine taking what had happened so well. He expected him to hit the moon with rage, but he reacted completely different. "Right, I feel you." Jackson replied assuring Antoine that he understood. "Wuzzup wit dat nigga Que though?" he laughed and shook his head about what had went down at the apartment. Antoine chuckled as if he'd already known what was up.

"Yeah," Antoine nodded, "Dude bugged the fuck out ain't he? He's a muthafucka, but he's trustworthy."

I'm sayin pimp! He be goin through all that bullshit like he really holdin. Pullin out safes and choppahs. I'm thankin it's some real paper in dat muhfucka and he come out wit a few hun'ned!" both of them laughed after

Jackson told Antoine about what had taken place in the apartment.

Although Antoine was laughing and playing nonchalant about what he had just happened to him, he'd really been shaken up by the police robbing him. This was his first real brush with the crooked side of the law, but he was sure that it wouldn't be his last. In the game you had to take a couple of losses to get a few gain, so Antoine took his in stride. They went on to finish the rest of their pickups without any other altercation, other sporadic arguing between themselves, but that was normal. That's just how their friendship worked, but in truth they really did have love for one another.

After seeing Antoine and Jackson off, Fox went up to his apartment to shower. After dressing, he called Egypt. They spoke on the telephone often, but Fox hadn't been back to Atlanta since they'd spent that weekend together. He felt Egypt, but there was nothing exclusive between them. They were just friends who enjoyed each other's company.

"What's up, babygirl?" Fox asked after hearing Egypt's voice on the other end of the phone.

"Hi, boo!" Egypt's voice was filled with excitement. She was always happy to hear from him Fox. "How you doing?"

Fox smiled. I'm good. I was thinking about you, so I called. Did you get my gift?"

"Yep…ummhmm." She teased flirtatiously. "I appreciate it too." "Yeah?" Fox chuckled lightly. "You can show me this weekend because I'll be down there."

"Good because we miss you."

"You and who? I know you ain't talkin 'bout Lana?" Fox teased, although, he knew what Egypt was talking about.

"That shit with Lana was a onetime thing." She childishly smacked her lips and giggled. "I'm talking about me and Ms. Pretty." Ms. Pretty was what she called her lovehole.

"Is she a freak?" Fox asked sillily and laughed. "Nah, "I'm just fuckin with you. Look, ma. I just called to let you know I was coming, but I gotta shoot a move. I'll see you later."

"Okay, booboo. See you when you get here."

"Ah'ight." Fox hung up the telephone and left the apartment smiling. He didn't understand what had happened between him and Egypt, but he was developing feeling for her. As he walked down the hallway towards the elevator, he saw a familiar face approaching him. He chuckled while giving LaTicia a once over.

"What's up, cutey? You lookin good." He hugged her snugly holding his embrace. Fox knew that LaTicia was feeling him, but she had a hang up with his age.

LaTicia smiled nearly melting in his arms. "Thank you, Fox. You're leaving?" she asked disappointed because she wanted to spend some time with him. Fox had a way of making LaTicia feel better about herself, and she enjoyed that quality in him.

"Yeah, I was on my way to see Rone." "Oh, I'm sorry. I've been so busy trying to get my practice off the ground that I haven't spoken to him in a while. Sherry's been managing his companies for the last few months."

"Yeah, I'm hip." Fox replied with a smile. He was proud of his sister because she had been doing her thing expanding Rone's businesses like elastic. "I'm in a rush, what's up?"

"I just came by to check up on you... see how you were doing. I was going to take you to lunch, but I guess we'll have to do it some other time." She stepped aside so he could walk pass her. "Go ahead. I don't want to be your excuse."

Fox chuckled while shaking his head. "You somethin else, Ticia." They walked to the elevator together. I should grab all that ass. Fox thought while they were in the elevator. He wanted to put it on the floor because it was evident that she felt him, but he kept his distance. He respected her inhibitions about young men, although, her beliefs didn't apply to him. He was also afraid of what Sherry would say because Sherry couldn't stand LaTicia.

146

Rone sat in his living room quietly reading while waiting for Fox to arrive. He'd been hearing some bad things about Fox and his crew. Things about them owing depts. To Wheat, a cat from the east side who Rome despised, and Rone couldn't understand why Fox would be owing anyone. Fox was compromising Rone's operation by trying to establish his own. He was impressed with the youngster's ambition, but there was a thin line between ambition and stupidity, and Rone was afraid that Fox was coming too close to crossing that line.

Rone was expecting this to happen. He knew that him and Fox would eventually have to have this talk because Fox was a leader, and would eventually want to branch off. He was hoping that he could pull Fox back closer to what they were doing because there was too much conflict in stretching his arm both ways and it could get ugly. The telephone rang disrupting Rone's thoughts.

"Hello?" why didn't you tell me you and Fox were coming down here this weekend?" Egypt asked inquisitively because Rone usually gave her heads up before he came to Georgia.

"Because I'm not. Who told you I was coming that way?'

"Fox called me earlier. He told me that you and him were coming down here this weekend." She misquoted because Fox had only mention himself. "Oh,

he did? Sheeit, he lied than. He's coming, but I'm not."
Rone was frank.

"Okay, do you want me to do anything for him?"
"Yeah, get him a rental and a room. His business is short
so y'all can toss it up how ever y'all choose to."

"Why is he coming then?" Egypt asked nosily.

Rone chuckled. "I'ont even explain to my wife! I
just need him out of my way for a few days. I figured
you'd keep him company since you were out of school for
a few more weeks. I know your hot ass want to see him
anyway. I want you to fly back with him too since you
haven't been home in a while." "I do want to see him."
Egypt snickered. "Okay, I'll have everything ready by the
time he gets here."

"Good. Be safe too because you ain't ready for no
babies, E. I hope you hear me." His voice was cold and
demanding and Egypt giggled. "Yeah, I hear you, dang!"

"Ah'ight then." Rone placed the telephone back on
its base. He briefly thought about Fox's and Egypt's
relationship and the direction it was going into, before his
thoughts fell back into Fox's clique and what they'd been
involved in. he didn't want to offend Fox because he
knew how Fox felt about his niggaz. So he settled on a
humble approach because he didn't want their talk to
become aggressive.

"That must be Fox," he whispered to himself after
hearing someone knocking on the door. He hoped Fox

was ready to hear what he had to say. Even if Fox didn't trust his judgment and go with it, he at least wanted Fox to hear him out. He opened the door letting Fox come inside.

"What up, big brah?" they walked over to the couch and sat across from one another.

"Trap, you getting to relaxed." Rone came right out with it. He wasn't the type to beat around the bush. He would get straight to the point because he hated when people toyed with him.

"Y'all young niggaz owing muthafuckaz and shit!" Rone had intended on being subtle with him approach, but he was pissed. He couldn't believe Fox was out there fucking up like that, especially with what he stood to lose. "What?" Fox asked. Damn! Who the fuck put me out there like that? Fox wondered because he didn't owe no one shit. The streets owed him and he wanted to keep it that way.

"Brah, if I know your business you can believe the police knows too. Niggaz talk too much out there in them streets, Fox. Muthafuckaz will bark your muhfuckin name until someone hears it! That's what envious ass niggaz do!

Fox was getting confused. He was sure that Rone was talking about the debt to Wheat. He knew that the word was roaming the hood, but he didn't know it would travel all the way back to Rone. Fuck it! He thought. He'd go pay the dept himself. Eight racks wasn't shit to him, although, he was tired of cuddling Antoine.

149

"I'm saying Tee ain't built for this shit, Fox! I know that's your mans, but he ain't gonna be if y'all keep doing business together." Rone stared at Fox. "Stop fucking with him like that."

Fox was silent after hearing Rone's request. Although he'd planned to break ties with him after Antoine got his cake right, his ego couldn't allow Rone to think he was making that decision for him. Fox shook his head defiantly.

"Me, and the nigga Tee, twelve years in the making, brah. I respect yo judgment; I ain't dropping my peoples off like that." He saw the seriousness within Rone's eyes, but he could give in, although, he knew that he should. "Rone, you a cold hearted muthafucka, baby."

Rone stood up. He was upset and it showed. He threw the paper that was laying across his lap to the sofa. He didn't understand why Fox couldn't see what he saw. Antoine was making a mockery out of himself and Fox by proxy. "My nigga! Look around you." Rone looked around his home theatrically. "It's just me and you baby! Before you came in it was just me." He chuckled evilly. "It gets lonely at the top, but it's safer that way." He walked over to the door and opened it. It was a signal for Fox to leave.

Fox stared at his brother-in-law as he motioned for him to leave. Rone was putting him out of his house. Damn! He thought while walking to the door. I done fucked up the plug!

"Ah'ight then, brah." Fox said in a hushed tone while walking out onto the porch. Rone closed the door behind Fox without saying another word. He walked back to the sofa and continued reading. Just like he'd told Fox, it was him alone and at the top.

Fox drove down Livernois on his way to their safe house. He could barely stay focused on the road because he was so discombobulated. He was curious about what Rone had seen in Antoine. Maybe it was the same envy that Fox had already known about or maybe it was the shit that he'd picked up alone the way and it was unwarranted, because Antoine hadn't served any real drama. A fist fight or a head busting, but no real bloodshed. I wonder why this nigga on me so tough? Fox was puzzled about Rone's relentless pressure for him to drop his guy.

Although Fox and Antoine were on ends lately, Fox didn't want to bail on him because they were friends. Besides, arguing was the nature of their friendship. Especially after Fox decided to bring Jackson into their hustle. Whenever the three of them were together Antoine always acted shady. Fox didn't understand why because they'd all known one another primarily the same length of time. Jackson and Antoine argued the most, but Fox was sure that they did have love for each other because they kicked it without him from time to time.

After getting to the safe house, Fox walked to the door and it was opened by Ms. Webb, and older woman who owned the house, before he could knock. Fox smiled and tightly hugged her after entering the house.

"Hey, Ms. Webb. How've you been?" Fox smiled and closed the door behind himself.

Ms. Webb giggled. "Everything was fine until your loud ass friends showed up with all that arguing and shit!"

"I'll talk to them. Are they still in the basement?'

"Yeah.." she giggled, "That's where animals are supposed to be." She laughed at her own joke while walking away.

Although Fox didn't show it in front of Ms. Webb, he was steaming. He couldn't believe the blatant disrespect that Antoine and Jackson showed Ms. Webb; especially after all she'd done for them. He was sure that it would only be a matter of time before they jacked the spot off, and made her stop letting them use her basement as a safety net for their hustle. He heard ranting as he walked down the stairs. Damn, he thought, these niggaz is still at it! Antoine turned and was the first to notice Fox as he walked into to basement.

"What up doe?" Antoine asked seeing the anger in Fox's eyes. He'd been around Fox long enough to spot when he was upset, but he played naïve although he wanted to know why.

6 MILE CHRONICLES   The Birth of A Hustler   Mi'kiel Los

"Ain't shit up!" Fox resorted with a wrathful snarl. "Why you niggaz down here actin like y'all ain't got no respect?"

Jackson chuckled. "Nigga, you ain't got no kids yet, pimp." His look implied that Fox's tone was disrespectful, and Antoine chimed right in.

"Yeah, nigga! Fuck's wrong with you? We pay the bills 'round this muthafucka!" he pounded his chest while making his final statement. Fox pounced onto a beanbag that sat in the corner near and old floor model television. He looked from Antoine to Jackson and back over to Antoine. He was disappointed in both of them. They were reckless and at that moment Fox understood why Rone was insistent about him dropping them from his team. He shook his head, these niggaz just don't get it. He thought while realizing what had to be done.

"Y'all niggaz ain't got respect for shit!" Fox spat out at no one in particular, and Antoine laughed as if what he'd said was a joke. "Fuck you, nigga," Antoine chuckled and slouched deeper into the seat of the old sofa he sat on. "This blow money is fo'sho money though, baby!" he tossed the duffle bag that sat behind him, onto the floor near Fox's feet, and smiled. That sight of the bag changed Fox's sour mood.

"What we do?" Fox asked with a hopeful smile whisked across his face. Things had started off slow for them, but had gradually picked up over the weeks since they put it down. The buzz about that Sis'ahola, the name

153

that they'd coined their blow with, had taken off so it was only a matter of time before they became walking dollars sighs.

"We did good, bwoy!" Jackson laughed after thinking about how their day had been. "E'erybody was slumin 'cept fo Que! He still slow." He glanced over to Antoine and they both burst into laughter. "His hustle might be slow, but he a animated muhfucka though!" They all laughed after what Jackson said. Even Fox knew about Que's theatric.

"He must've pulled the Fort Knox move on you niggaz?" Fox chuckled. "It's cool though.." he nodded, "that spot gon blow eventually. I'm tellin you niggaz. I used to run for a cat who had a spot in the Corridor, and that bitch used to bang like the Crips and Bloods."

"Yeah, he cool. Plus, he only been opened for three weeks. Give it some time." Antoine assured them of what Fox had already known.

They counted the money together. This was a precaution that they took so no one felt cheated, but somehow Antoine always felt that way. He still believed Fox was pulling some underhanded moves on them, although, he couldn't prove it. As they counted the money, Jackson reenacted the robbery that the Detroit narcotics police pulled off on Antoine. Although the incident wasn't funny while it was happening, Jackson's reenactment had them all belting with laughter. He'd made it sound like a comedy movie.

"Ah'ight…" Fox managed to say while catching his breath. 'Nigga, quit trippin! That shit was that funny." He tried to slow Jackson's teasing up after noticing Antoine's uneasiness. He held a stack of money up and smiled.

"Sheeit! We did good, my niggaz! Ten thousand in two days." Fox nodded while looking over to each of them.

"Damn, pimp!" Jackson was excited. He'd planned to get out the game, but if cash kept coming in like that, he would stay in it to win it! While Jackson and Fox slapped fives and gave each other pounds about their come up, Antoine slouched into the sofa vehemently watching their camaraderie. He was upset because Jackson was Fox's yes man. These niggaz do this shit every session! He thought while jealously watching them revel in their success.

"What's up, Tee baby?" Fox asked after looking over to Antoine noticing his absence from their celebration.

"Yeah, bwoy!" Jackson added cheerfully. "You always hype until the paper come out, pimp." He'd noticed how Antoine mood shifted when the money was sorted. I bet dis nigga tryna plot on takin it all? He thought while analyzing the look in Antoine's eyes. Dis nigga grimy!

Antoine tried to soften his look after seeing their reaction. He was certain that his spiteful thoughts were

155

coming across in his facial expressions, so he tried to throw them off.

"Sheeit, everything cool." Antoine replied with a nod, and without making eye contact with either of them. "I was just thinkin 'bout Kiesha." He lied unconvincingly and Jackson burst into a mocking laughter. "Problem is…" Jackson paused and sucked air through his teeth, "Kiesha ain't thinkin 'bout you." He said provokingly because he knew Antoine was lying about thinking of her. Dis nigga was thinkin 'bout lickin us! Grimy ass nigga. He thought while him and Antoine mean mugged each other.

"What, nigga?" Antoine aggressively rose after questioning what Jackson had just said. I know this hoe ass nigga ain't testin me! He thought while giving Jackson a hateful stare. Fox jumped in trying to defuse the altercation. He knew how Antoine felt about Kiesha, therefore, he had no doubt that the simple rift could escalate to another level of drama.

"Come on with that bullshit!" Fox swiftly intervened. "Y'all niggaz trippin!"

Antoine wasn't stopping. He was ready to set it off on Jackson's ass. He had his thumper tucked deep into his jeans and would let it rang if it got too ugly. Yeah, Jackson was his guy, but testing his gangster was crossing the line. This nigga questioning what my bitch feelin! Hell nah! He thought while approaching Jackson.

"Nah, nigga!" Antoine asked Jackson aggressively. I'll kill this nigga! He thought angrily. "I guess she thinkin

156

'bout another nigga, huh? Hoe ass nigga, get some pussy than rap with me!" Antoine stopped and backed away from Jackson. He was sure that he'd go too far if he moved any closer, and although he was upset, at that moment, he wasn't ready to end their friendship. He gave Fox a pound.

"Fox, put mines with yours, my nigga." Antoine turned and stared back to Jackson. "I'mma bounce before I put hands on this nigga. I'll hollah at y'all tomorrow." He walked toward the stairs and Jackson called behind him. "Aye Tee?" Jackson yelled, but Fox stopped him.

"Let'em go, dawg! He'll be alright." Fox assured him, although, he was really uncertain about Antoine himself. They divided the money into piles before leaving. There wasn't much talking during their drive back to Fox's apartment. Fox was thinking about his upcoming trip to Atlanta, to see Egypt. Meanwhile, Jackson secretly reveled in the satisfaction he got from harassing Antoine.

****

Egypt rushed Fox as he walked through the airport security check. She drove into his arms smiling from ear to ear.

"Hey, baby!" she squealed before passionately kissing him.

"Damn, ma. That was a helluvah grettin." Fox smiled while holding Egypt's round hips and giving her a once over. Daaamn! He thought while shaking his head. She was finer than he'd remembered and he couldn't wait to tap that. Egypt's smile was suggestive and she rubbed his back.

"Good thing were in public because I missed you." She teased and giggled girlishly. Fox looked down to her pelvic area and ran his tongue across his lips.

"Yeah, I miss you too."

"Mmmhmm." She mumbled with a suggestive nod. "You ready?" she grabbed one of his rolling suitcases and walked off leading the way through the airport, to her car. Egypt had been thinking about the nature of their relationship a lot lately. She knew that a long distance relationship was trying, but it would be worth it to her if she could have Fox. She wanted him desperately and was willing to do whatever it took to keep him in her life. Egypt's circumstance had been everything, but fairy tale so a challenge wasn't shit to her.

Once they got to her car, she opened the trunk and Fox threw his luggage in. during the drive they talked nonstop about what had been taking place within their lives since they'd seen each other.

Fox was surprised about how intimate their dialogue had became, and he wondered about their relationship. I'ont even know what it is 'bout this bitch, but she got a nigga. He admitted to himself while listening to Egypt's detailed rant about her life. Although he felt this way, he'd never tell Egypt because he didn't want to seem too clingy and push her away. Fox's face cringed into an angry stare as they drove up to the hotel. He looked from Egypt to the hotel and back to Egypt.

"What the fuck you bring me here for?" he asked angrily. This bitch trippin! He thought while seething. "I came all the way to Georgia, to see you, and I gotta stay at a room?" this hoe got a nigga fucked up! He stared at her in disbelief.

"Boy.." she giggled and waved his ranting off, "We ain't dropping shit off, but your bags. You and that big ass dick, is coming with me." She assured him by rubbing her hands across the bulge between his legs, and Fox quickly calmed down.

"Oh…'cause sheeit! I was 'bout to be mad as a muhfucka." He grabbed his bags from the trunk and went inside to check in. after getting up to his room, he immediately called Rone to let him know that he'd made it there. He was still uneasy about Egypt wanting him to have a room, but that was something that he'd check into after he finished taking care of his business.

Sherry removed her reading glasses from her face and put them onto the table. She ran her fingers through

159

the silky strands of her hair and sighed. She was stressed out from the work that she'd been doing for Rone. The telephone suddenly rang while she took a break from rambling through paperwork. "Hello?" Sherry answered, and it was Fox.

"Hey, big sis. Is Rone around?" Fox asked through the telephone and Sherry rolled her eyes jealously

She wasn't used to sharing her brother with anyone. It was just them for a long time, so it was hard knowing that Rone was stealing some of him from her. He rarely acknowledged her since he'd started hustling with her husband. She walked through the patio and handed Rone the telephone, without saying a word, before stomping off. Rone watched as she walked away before putting the phone to his ear.

"Hello, Jerone speaking." His voice was formal and professional because he didn't know who was on the other end of the telephone.

"What's up, brah?" Fox asked with a laugh.

"What's up, young trap? I didn't know who the fuck this was on the phone." He chuckled.

"Yeah, I feel you. I just wanted to let you know I made it down here." "Was Egypt on time to come get you from the airport?" Rone asked, although, he was confident that she'd been late. "Yeah, why? What's up?"

"What?" Rone asked with a chuckle. "She was on time…… yeah, she must be feeling you, brah." His chuckling continued, but Fox didn't join in. "Yeah, she was on time , but she ain't feelin a nigga. She put me up in a muhfuckin room. Paid for the shit and everything." He was still curious about why she'd done that, although she had her own apartment. Rone chuckled. "Dig, lil brah. This a late birthday present from me. Everything is paid for and Egypt got five stacks for you to blow."

"Thanks, but no thanks." Fox chuckled. "I got my own paper now. I'm through with the handouts, brah brah." He couldn't accept any more money from Rone, especially knowing that he didn't need it.

"Nigga," Rone responded. He was offended because Fox hadn't accepted his gift. "You couldn't have possibly heard me say that the shit was a gift. It's disrespectful to turn down a gift." He was adamant about Fox taking the money.

"You know how it is." Fox felt guilty about not taking the money, but he would feel guiltier if he took it and didn't need it. "You done so much for a nigga already. I ain't tryna drain you, but thanks. I appreciate the gift." His thank you was sincere, although, he was still uncomfortable taking the money.

"Enjoy it then, my nigga. Before you start kicking it, stop by Ray's house. He needs to talk to you."

"Ah'ight! I'm on it, brah."

"Make sure you don't get on the plane with that bread either. If you need some help spending it, Egypt will help you." Rone teased.

"Ah'ight then. I'll hollah." Fox tried to rush Rone off the phone.

"Yeah, do that." Rone hung up and walked into the house to find Sherry. He walked into the kitchen and saw Sherry leaning against the counter top sipping a strawberry daiquiri and reading over some paperwork concerning the expansion of their expediting service. Rone was impressed with the way his wife had taken over the business. Both of their companies had grown excessively since she'd been handling the day to day operations. She was very intelligent and self motivated, and had brought in contracts with larger more established companies, which was something that LaTicia could never do. Although Rone was big on education, he was certain that his wife possessed something that couldn't be taught—a natural charisma that was unmatched. "Hey, Cheeks?" Rone approached his wife interrupting her concentration.

"Hey, baby." She replied with a soft whisper.

"Is everything alright? It seems like something is bothering you." Sherry put the paper that she was reading, onto the counter top and turned to talk to her husband.

"I'm just tired." She smiled weakly trying not to complain too much. "I've been working so hard trying to

162

being in new clients and shit. Maybe I need a break?" she was hoping that Rone agreed with her, but he laughed. "Yeah, I know how shit can be, but we gotta eat so we gotta work." He was blunt. You the one asked for the shit when you ran Ticia away. He thought while chuckling and Sherry smiled at him.

"I know, but damn!" she laughed knowing Rone was mocking her. "Come here, ma." Rone pulled her closer to him and kissed her. He looked into her beautiful brown almond shaped eyes and kissed her while caressing her shapely ass and Sherry breathed heavily.

"Baby you just don't know how much I need that. Kiss me right here." She pointed to her clavicle line.

Rone's kisses became raunchy as he undid her blouse letting it fall back exposing her bare chest. Her dark tits hung high with erect raisin shaped nipples. She moaned a prurient moan as Rone lifted her onto the counter top and removed her skirt and panties.

Sherry's breathing deepened as her husband lips traveled down her naked body kissing, sucking, and nibbling.

"Oooooh…!" she moaned libidinous sounds after feeling Rone's stiff tongue enter her. Her body stiffened and her pussy was dripping wet. His tongue moved across her clitoris.

Rone pulled the foreskin around the entrance of her love hole exposing the clitoris further. It was erect

163

and he tickled it with his tongue causing her body to quiver.

"Oh.......ahhhh!" she shrieked loudly. Billows of thunderous moans followed as selflessly pleasured his wife into climax. He knew that she deserved adulation and he met her needs as he always did.

Fox lay across Egypt's water bed thinking about what she'd done to him earlier. She'd freaked him hard and heavy and now she walked into the room wearing sheer lavender Roberto Cavalli negligee. It fell just above her thick dark brown thighs. She was carrying a tray full of food. Damn! This type of shit will make a nigga move to the south! He thought as she placed the tray beside him on the bed.

Thanks, ma." Fox said and smacked her across her ass causing it to jiggle before she sat. "You showed a nigga a good time, baby." Egypt giggled and smiled while watching him eat. He'd opened up her flood gates after they got to her apartment. *Damn I'm felling him!* She thought. She'd fallen for him, although, she knew gangster love stories didn't end good.

"You worked up an appetite." She laughed and lewdly rolled her hips mimicking Fox's stroke. "The least I can do was feed you." They both laughed and she slid closer to him. Fox knew Egypt had developed feelings for him, and she wasn't alone, because he was feeling her to. He still remained cautious though. He believed Rone was the mastermind behind his and Egypt's setup. He was sure the Egypt was Rone's watchdog, but he still enjoyed her company nonetheless. As he ate, Egypt shyly looked over to him.

"Fox, can I ask you a question?" her tone was meek. Fox nodded. Here comes the hoe shit! He thought. The bitch gon pull the pregnant role on a pimp. He knew that something was coming because usually when a woman asked you to ask a question it was life changing. "Yeah," he answered, "you can ask me whatever you want. The way you put that pussy on me…ask away." He laughed.

"Where are we going with this because I like you…a lot? I thought about you every day after you left." Her tone was convincing, and Fox felt her. He put his fork onto the tray that she'd brought the food in on. Damn, he thought because he was sure that things were going to get deeper than he'd planned it too.

"Straight face. I aint even thought about it." He lied without hesitation knowing that he thought about her and where he wanted their relationship to go. There was no doubt if he felt her because he did, but he wasn't willing to commit to something he wasn't sure about. He didn't know if she wanted to be his woman more than she wanted to be Rone's watchdog, and that posed a problem with him. Rone was his mans and he respected the way he put his play down, but he wasn't comfortable with having a broad keeping tabs on him, especially a female that claimed to be his.

"So you don't feel anything between us?" Egypt tried to make eye contact with Fox because she noticed he was trying to avoid it. "What, you don't think I could make you happy?" She grabbed the fork from the tray and started feeding him.

"No question!" Fox laughed while chewing the food that she'd fed him. "I know you can make me happy. I'm eighteen. Proper head and a hot fudge sundae would make me happy." He tried to ease the tension that her question had brought between them, but it didn't work. She dropped the fork and playfully threw a pillow at him.

"Stop doing that! Nigga, you know you're gamed beyond your years so stop throwing your age around like it put restriction on your mental. Ooh, you make me sick when you act like that." She stood and tried to walk away. Fox swiftly grabbed her pulling her back onto the bed. He pulled her closer into his embrace after seeing tears fall from her eyes. He didn't mean to hurt her feelings, but he couldn't just lay down for her either. "E, aint even like that. I was just bullshittin." Fox kissed her tear drenched cheek. "I was just trying to make you laugh." He wiped tears away from her eyes and Egypt chuckled. Damn, she even cold when she cryin. He thought when she snickered.

"Nigga, she sniffled, "You be talking all that Bengal tiger shit knowing youa soup hound. Wiping tears from a bitch eyes and shit." she shoved him in his chest affectionately.

166

"I was tryna be romantic and shit, but now I gotta get domestic," he pulled her into his lap and tickled her. His action kept Egypt optimistic. She knew that he was still apprehensive about her sincerity because of the night they shared during his first trip to Atlanta, but she didn't have any regrets. Egypt believed in seizing opportunities, and in her world, having an ménage trios with Fox was the opportunity of a lifetime. "Egypt I gotta hollah at Ray, so I'mma jump in the shower so you can take me to his house." You aint getting in the shower without me." Egypt quickly leapt from the bed and dropped her negligee before hustling up behind him as he walked into the bathroom

**********.

Antoine sat outside of the 70 West apartments while waiting on Jackson to Antoine didn't like working with Jackson because Jackson wasn't an authentic hood nigga. He was a wannabe dope boy that wasn't built for what him and Fox were creating. *I hate dealing wit this country ass nigga*. Antoine thought while keeping a watchful eye on the niggaz who were hanging around the building. There were always a few hustlers trying to pick up their scraps, but today there was something off about the scene. This what I'm sayin, if my nigga was here I wouldn't even be worried. Leavin me wit this nigga. Antoine was tired of Fox leaving town every other week leaving him to take care of everything with Jackson. He'd

167

brought Jackson into their fold so it should be him who had to roll with him

Antoine was also still upset about the stunt that Jackson had pulled a few weeks back. He wasn't sure, but he thought Jackson may have feelings for Kiesha himself. What other reason would he say some shit like that? He'd heard Jackson making snide remarks about his and Kiesha's relationship before, but never so direct. He knew Jackson was a snake from way back, but Fox insisted on bringing him in.

Fox believed they needed another player in order to blow, which turned out to be right, but Antoine didn't like the way Jackson flaunted his and Fox's new found closeness in front of him. He was certain that Jackson was trying to put a wedge between his and Fox relationship. This nigga gotta lot of nerves tryna come 'tween me and my nigga. Hoe ass nigga think he slick. He saw Jackson walking out of the building.

"Fuck wrong wit this nigga?" Antoine whispered to himself while clutching his tool. He reached beneath his seat and grabbed his throw away .380 and pulled the Berretta from his waist before wildly leaping from the truck.

"Shit ain't sweet, nigga!" Antoine yelled and swung the berretta firing two shots.

"Blocca…. Blocca."

The bullets whistled pass Jackson's head hitting a young nigga that was behind him in chest and throat.

"Blocca…blocca, blocca!"

Gunshots rung from everywhere and both of Antoine's pistols were spitting fire as Jackson ducked and dodged bullets. Jackson scrambled to Antoine's truck and reached beneath the driver's seat hoping to get Antoine's loose strap, but it wasn't there. He looked up just in time to see the fire spit from the barrel while Antoine let it rang out.

"Blocca…blocca."

Rone frantically rushed into the house calling for his wife. "Cheeks?" he called out. He'd just got some news about a shooting in the Cass corridors involving someone from Fox clique. He knew that thing would end badly with the company that Fox was keeping. Sherry sprinted into the living room after hearing Rone calling for her. She was used to hearing that type of urgency in her husband's voice so it startled her. "Why are you yelling like that?" she noticed Rone's dark expression and feared the worst. "One of them silly ass young niggaz done got blasted!" "What young niggaz?" Sherry asked. She was puzzled because the only young guy who Rone dealt with was Fox and he was in Atlanta. Rone knew that what he was about to tell his wife would disturb her.

"I think it was Tee, but I'm not sure. What's his mother's number?" Rone wanted to call his mother to get the confirmation before he reacted. Sherry was shook.

169

"Hold on, let me get the phone book." She rushed off toward the bathroom. I hope nothing happened to my brother. She thought while flipping through the pages of her telephone book. Please GOD let everything be okay! She rushed back into the living room with the number. Rone grabbed the number already knowing what the outcome would be once he got Antoine's mother on the line. He dialed the number and waited. After getting her on the line, Rone listened as she told him a story that, hoped was embellished. He shook his head, how could this nigga be so loose? He wondered while listening to the details of the shooting. He hung up the telephone and hugged his wife.

"I've got some bad news, baby." He said and tears rose and fell from Sherry's eyes. "What Rone? Please don't tell me he's dead. I can't take that blow right now, baby please." She whined while sinking deeper into his embrace. "Nah, get yourself together while I make a few phone calls." Rone walked off toward the den.

Sherry went into the bathroom thinking about the secrets that loomed over her family. Although she was relieved that Antoine hadn't been a victim of homicide, she was still concerned about him. She knew that there were secrets within their family that would wound Antoine and Fox deeper than any weapon. Secrets that she had to let them, know before it was too late. I can't live with this shit! She thought while washing her face. I love my husband, but I love my family more! She pulled her hair into a ponytail and put gloss on her lips before walking out the bathroom. As she approached the den,

170

she overheard Rone talking to someone on the phone. She inched toward the door and eavesdropped. Rone looked upset as he spoke. "I'll meet you at the court house in the, in the morning, but for now claim that truck as on the job accident liability." He closed the conversation out and hung up the phone, he grabbed his car keys and his cell phone from his desk and walked toward the door catching Sherry ear hustling. "I'm ready, baby." He's at receiving hospital, but they have him under arrest too. I told his mother not to come to the hospital because she sounded like she'd been drinking." Rone shook his head, it's a shame what happen to that bitch. He thought as him and Sherry left their home.

****

Egypt and Fox was exhausted as they walked into Egypt's apartment. They'd kicked it all day after Fox visited Ray. They'd went to a few black universities. It was Egypt's attempt to inspire Fox. She wanted for her friends what she desired for herself, and she wanted an education. After settling in, Fox lounged on the sofa thinking about their day. He chuckled, E think she's slick. He thought. He was on to what she was tried to do by taking him to the colleges. He appreciated it, and he enjoyed himself, but an education was the furthest thing from his mind. Fox was set on going heavy at his paper, especially after talking to Ray. Fox looked over to Egypt noticing the distress in her as she checked her voice mail massages. She was upbeat and joyous when they arrived, but his look was distant now. Her nigga must've called? Fox shook his head. He wasn't surprised because a female as fine as she was had to have a man, he just wished she could have been real with him. Egypt listened to Rone's voice massage. "This Rone!" I need you and Fox on a plane tonight! One of Fox's niggaz got slugged!" she turned to Fox. She felt bad for him. She didn't know his friends personally, but she lost plenty of people in her life, so she knew what death by murder felt like to the ones who survived them.

Fox walked over to Egypt. I'mma salt the bitch's game. He was sure that she'd heard something that she didn't want him to hear. He wanted to know what had suddenly changed her mood.

"What's wrong, E?" He lowered his head to make eye contact with her. "I don't know what's wrong, but Rone said he needed us on a plane to Detroit." She looked nervous and Fox immediately picked up on it. The nigga must be coming over, so the hoe tryna get ghost. He thought. He wondered how could he have been so gullible. The tramp damn near caught a pimp off guard. What she was trying to pull confirmed what Fox had known all along—she was all game. "Let me hear the message." Fox demanded not believing one actually existed. He was sure that Egypt was busted because she had a concerned look about herself. Fox pressed the repeat button and his eyes grew larger as he heard the massage. Not my nigga! He was sure that Wheat had tried to hit Antoine over the debt that he owed. Egypt tapped his shoulder. "Fox, there another message before that

172

one." She said and started the messages from the beginning. Fox listened as a familiar voice frantically spoke into his ear. "Fox, dis ya bwoy!" it was Jackson which let Fox know it was Antoine who had caught hot ones. He'd given Antoine and Jackson Egypt's telephone number for emergencies only, and a shooting of one of his niggaz constituted urgency. The massage from Jackson continued. "We need you home baby!" it's getting ugly out here." He hung up the telephone. Images of Antoine's blood stained body sprawled across the cool fall pavement passed through his mind. He wondered if his mans was maimed, paralyzed, or dead? Egypt could see the rage within Fox's eyes. She wanted to help him, but she didn't She thought knowing how rage could be misplaced when it was fresh. She played it smart and used some game that Rone had given her years ago. Egypt left the room to stash Fox's money into the safe. She knew the hustlers protocol because she'd been raised by one. She grabbed her credit card and went back into the front room with Fox.

"Come on, baby." Egypt said and grabbed his arm. She wanted to let him know that she was there for him and he could trust her. "I put the money in the safe and grabbed my charge cards." She tugged his arm pulling him towards the door. Fox was still in an enraged trance. After getting outside, Egypt stopped and made eye contact with him. "Fox, I'm here for you. I know you're shaky about me, but I wanna be with you." She hugged him and got into the car.

Fox leaned against a handicapped parking sign collecting his thoughts. Damn! He thought knowing that his life was changing. Antoine could be dead, and Egypt had made him feel something for a female that he didn't believe in. he knew that there was feeling between them, but this was the first time that he'd considered having a relationship with her.

After getting into the car with Egypt, Fox started telling her about his friendships with Antoine and Jackson. Intimate shit that he'd never told another woman. Egypt had always wanted a friendship like theirs, but bitches were usually too jealous of her to keep it solid. He was giving her his truth and it bounded them in different way. She knew that she loved him. That was Egypt's truth and she told him.

After getting their flight, Fox settled in Fox tried to figure out what had   happened. Antoine always carried his strap which made Fox wonder what had went wrong. I should be springing bail money instead of visiting a 'spital or a morgue! He thought, hoping Antoine didn't freeze up on the draw. He'd witnessed cats talk boogie down Bronx gangster shit, scaring everyone on the block, only to let a humble nigga pump their asses full of led. Nah, not my nigga! Fox sunk deeper into his seat preparing himself to hear the worst.

****

Rone and sherry waited for LaTicia to show up. They'd been told that they couldn't see Antoine because he was under arrest. The police didn't want anyone speaking to him until they had a chance to question him. Sherry was pissed. She'd watched Antoine grow up with Fox. They were family and she couldn't see him. She paced the floor of the lobby anxiously awaiting LaTicia, and when LaTicia came strutting through the sliding entrance doors a feeling of relief overcame Sherry. This was the first time that she was actually happy to see her. LaTicia walked over to them and they all walked over to the receptionist' desk together. LaTicia smiled affectedly. "Hi, I'm LaTicia Crawford and I'm here on behalf of Antoine Jones. May I see him?" she held her polite smile because she could tell that the receptionist was a bitch. The receptionist gave a nasty stare before grabbing the telephone. Rone had already assured her that Antoine's attorney would be coming shortly, so she guessed LaTicia was the lawyer. Look at this high trotting bitch. She smirked while holding the telephone beside her ear. "No, but I'll call the attending doctor. You can speak to him." She pursed her lips. "I'll also call the police who are handling his investigation so you can speak to them too." LaTicia reluctantly thanked the receptionist and pulled Rone to the aside to talk. She was missing something. "Where is the other guy?" LaTicia asked Rone thinking Jackson had been shot too. She scanned the lobby hoping to see someone show up. Rone shrugged his shoulders.

"I have the slightest idea. They said two people got smoked. One of them could be him." Rone was the least bit concerned about the health of either of Fox's boys. He'd told them to stay in their lanes, but they'd cross

175

them anyway, so whatever they got served was what they'd ordered.

"Shit, Rone!" LaTicia said angrily. She was furious because she'd warned him about dealing with the young niggaz. In the first place. "What the fuck happened anyway, and why are you dealing with those young motherfuckers?" I hope this bitch ain't trying to check me! He thought while giving LaTicia a warning look. There was no way she could believe he'd be dealing with them. Rone despised Antoine and he barely knew Jackson. What they did on the streets was Fox's issue, not his.

"I ain't doing shit with them niggaz!" Rone's voice rose into a soft rumble. He wanted LaTicia to feel him. "Those Fox's mellows. I'm just here for support!" "You're getting sloppy, Rone!" LaTicia walked away, and Rone waved her off.

Nah, baby girl. I'm getting tired of this shit! Rone thought while walking out to the sitting area and sitting next to Sherry. He was ready to throw in the towel. Hustling had become old to him. His run had come to an end. He was a veteran, no doubt, but he had heavier obligation to his wife than he did to the game. After he clear the path for Fox he was retiring. Rone rubbed his wife's back and shoulders while wondering how many families he'd caused to feel like his wife was feeling about Antoine's situation. He himself had risk the same fate daily before he came up. He'd done hand to hands and sold petty weight, but he'd never been on the end of someone's burner. He was always the shooter, but now he wondered if, at the end of his hustle, would he face the same fate of the two men that Antoine had sent back to their essence or the countless others that he himself had taken away from the living. Yeah, this is it for the god. Rone thought while leaning back into his seat. Sherry nudged him.

"Baby," Sherry pointed to LaTicia as LaTicia walked through the surgical doors. She's going back there to see Tee." "Alright….." Rone nodded and rubbed her shoulders. "I'm going to sit here with you until she come out." he returned to his thoughts.

Sherry could see the distance in Rone's stare as they sat in the waiting area. She was curious to know what was bothering him. She knew that he didn't care for Antoine. Rone had stressed that to her and Fox, on several different occasion, so it was unlikely that he was taking the shooting hard. Why is he even here? She wondered while glancing over to him. She was certain that he was ready to leave, but stayed to support her, so she tried to give him an escape.

"Baby." She said softly. "I'm ready to leave." She played impatient. "Yeah," Rone nodded, "Me too, but we're not going anywhere until we find out the status of Tee's injuries and arrest." His reply was blunt. "You don't even like Tee. Why in the fuck do you want to stay so bad?" Sherry was ready for a confrontation. She was already upset and now Rone had given her a reason. Rone recognized his wife's anger, but it was useless to argue. She was right, he didn't like Antoine and he'd never tried to hide it and wouldn't try to now. He chuckled and rubbed his goatee. "You're right!" Rone said boldly. "I don't like the little dumb muthafucka, but I love you and Fox so I'm staying on y'all behalf." Sherry's, neck whipped into his direction. She couldn't believe he'd tried to run game on her. She knew him and what he was all about—that dollar. Support didn't have anything to do with why he was staying at the hospital. "Nigga, please!" Sherry grunted in disgust. "You're here because that truck was in the company's name. Ain't nobody stupid! I know about that shit. Have you forgotten? I do the books."

"This ain't the time." Rone said calmly, although, a rage was swelling within him. He wanted to smack the top of Sherry's head off for disrespecting him the way she was, but he understood her, and knew that her frustration about Antoine's situation was affecting her judgment.

"Here comes LaTicia." Rone said changing the direction of their conversation. He stood to go over to LaTicia, but Sherry quickly grabbed his hand pulling him back into his seat. "Let her come to us." Sherry demanded firmly. She was tired of seeing her husband running to LaTicia. She'd known that Rone was calling her earlier, before they left for the hospital, and that set off a flame inside of her.

"Get the fuck up!" Rone yanked her arm nearly pulling it from its socket. "Bitch you better quit playing with me!" he had reached his boiling point with Sherry's jealousy. I'm going to end up busting this bitch head! He thought while walking toward LaTicia dragging Sherry along. Sherry let go of Rone's hand once they reached LaTicia. She was sure that she wanted to talk to Rone because that's usually how it went. LaTicia would purposely pull Rone away from Sherry letting Sherry know that, although, she was Rone's wife, she was still an outsider. Sherry stood a short distance away from them trying to read their lips and body language. Her fury roared inside after seeing LaTicia flirtatiously touching Rone's chest. She knew that LaTicia was taunting her. This trick think she's fucking with a light weight! Sherry though while ready to strut over to her and send a right hand down her pipe. LaTicia hugged Rone while looking over his shoulders and into Sherry's eyes.

"Nah, bitch!" Sherry whispered to herself while walking over to them. This is the last straw! I gotta go up side this heffer's head now! They'd been there for an emergency and LaTicia was still at it. She wouldn't let up on their little rivalry, so Sherry was ready to end it herself. As she reached Rone and LaTicia, LaTicia broke her embrace and waved to Sherry. "Bye, Sherry." LaTicia smiled and walked away swaying her hips and ass sensually. Sherry turned vehemently watched LaTicia disappear as she walked through the hospital exit.

Fox unlocked his apartment door letting Egypt go in first. He closed the door and rushed straight to his telephone. He tucked his cell phone into his back pocket and began punching number from his land line. He looked over to Egypt and held the phone up.

"I'm in the other room making a few calls. Make yourself at home." "It's alright, baby. I understand." Egypt sat on the couch and looked around. She didn't know Antoine, but she still had empathy for him because of her feeling for Fox. Fox dialed number after number, but he kept coming up empty. No one who he'd talked to knew what happened and Rone wasn't answering his cell phone. He began to think the worst case scenario had taken place. My nigga probably dead. He thought while holding the phone. He dialed Antoine's mother's number, but was interrupted by Egypt knocking on his bedroom door. 'What's up, E. "I'm tryna handle something right now." His voice sounded agitated.

"Someone is at the door." Egypt responded shyly. She'd heard the frustration in Fox's voice and didn't want to upset him any further, but she was sure that he'd want to know who was at the door. It's probably one of your hoes. She thought as Fox brushed pass her rushing to the door. She walked back to the front room and sat on the sofa eyeballing him. Fox pulled a Desert Eagle from his recliner and walked to the door. Although no one outside of his crew knew where he laid his head, he was still being cautious. He didn't know if Wheat had sent his goons on a mission to finish what they'd started with Antoine. I'll let this muthafucka hollah threw the door first! He thought while walking over to the door. He stood beside the door.

"Who is it?" he asked hoping it was Rone.

"It's yo bwoy!" Jackson's voice came through the door, and Fox quickly opened it letting his guy in.

"What the fuck happened?" Fox asked. He was irate and wanted to know how Antoine had gotten himself shot.

"Shit crazy, brah!" Jackson paused and looked over to Egypt. Damn this bitch fine! He thought. "Who dat if?" he rudely pointed over to Egypt. "That's Egypt. What the fuck happened, nigga?" Fox wasn't trying to get off track. He wanted to know why his mans was laid up in the hospital somewhere. He'd only been gone for two days and they'd let shit fall apart. "Let me hollah at you in the other room, brah." Jackson was skeptical about talking around Egypt. It wasn't that he didn't trust her; it was that he didn't know her and he knew how deceitful females could be. One day they could be in court listening to everything they'd said be repeated by Fox's bitch. Fox tilted his head. He wondered why Jackson was being evasive. Maybe this nigga tryna snake me? Fox thought while discreetly stepping back. He wanted to have some room in case he needed to up his strap and put something hot in Jackson's body. They'd been friends since grade school, but Fox knew how money separated friendships, and if Jackson was trying to get over on him their friendship would be no different.

"Nah, nigga." Fox casually shook his head while stepping closer to where Egypt was sitting. "That's my girl and we 'ont keep secrets, dawg." Is this nigga tryna make a move? He wondered while closely watching

181

Jackson's hands. He was ready to make something thunderous sound if his guy tried to crook him. "What the fuck is going on, dawg?" Fox was ready to up his strap. "I feel you, Fox but I ain't comfortable sayin what I gotta say 'round yo peoples." Jackson's tone was subordinate. He didn't want to disrespect Egypt, but he wasn't going to violate the code of the streets to please Fox's Georgia peach.

Fox finally calmed realizing Jackson was right. Although he trusted Egypt, he had no right to making Jackson fall into his view. He gave Egypt a head gesture to go into the bed room.

"Your right, my nigga. I was trippin." Fox said while watching Egypt disappear into the bedroom as he told her to. He'd seen a smile whisk across her face, as she closed the door, and he knew it was because he'd acknowledge her as his girl.

"Damn, pimp!" Jackson smiled respecting his boy's game. "You got shawty trained, brah!" Fox shook his head. "Nah, homie. It ain't even like that. Anyway, what happened?" he continued to urge a response to his question.

"I was comin outta the 70West buildin. Once I hit the pavement, I seen two niggaz comin outta the alley uppin they pipes." "Then what?" Fox wanted the meat of the story. He had made some assumption of his own about what had taken place and he wanted to see if they matched up with the truth.

"Sheeit! Tee must've peeped the play 'cause he jumped outta his truck yellin and shit. I looked behind and seen another nigga creepin on me." Fox was puzzled. He wondered where Que was. He'd listened to Que talk about how he had West on lock and how wouldn't a nigga in their right mind try him, but Antoine was in the hospital with peepholes through his body. "Where was Que? I know he let off a few rounds outta the window from that block rocker?"

Jackson shook his head. "All that shit fo show 'cause homie ain't even throw a rock at them niggaz, brah. On some real shit, a nigga didn't even need'em. The nigga Tee dropped the first cat with two shots then spent on the other nigga." Jackson spun showing Fox his rendition of what he'd seen Antoine doing, during the shoot out. "Then he put 'bout eight or nine off in the other nigga." he nodded assuring Fox that he wasn't bullshitting, and Fox laughed at Jackson's antics.

"Hold up!" Fox had missed something. "If he was the shooter how did he end up at the 'spital full of holes"? Jackson shook his head and sighed.

"Sheeit, them narco's! The one's who robbed'em that day. They were the first ones on the scene. The nigga Tee dropped his heaters, but they still let off on'em. His hands was at five after eleven and e'erything." Jackson threw his hands into the air, like he was being held up, to show Antoine's stance while being shot by the cops. "You talked to his mom?" Fox asked hoping Jackson hadn't told anyone, other than Rone and Sherry, about what had happened.

"Naw! Hell naw. I been layin low. I wanted to hollah at you first." Jackson was visibly shaken by what he'd seen. And he didn't want to be implicated as an accomplice to the killings either.

A lot of thought went through Fox's head. He ain't told nobody? He wondered how Rone found out." Fox asked curiously, and Jackson shrugged his shoulders.

"Sheeit! Hell if I know because I ain't said shit!" he wanted to make it plain that his lips were closed.

Fox stood in the living room confused. He knew that something was flaky about what happened, but there was too much missing to put the puzzle together. He wondered why Que hadn't helped Antoine lay the Jack boys down and how Rone had found out so quickly, if Jackson hadn't told anyone what had happened. The telephone rang and Fox rushed to the room to answer it. "Hello?" he answered after snatching the telephone from beside Egypt. "What up, young trap?" Rone asked in a causal tone. "Don't panic. Tee is cool physically, but he's being detained on gun charges for now." "I need to hollah at you. Can I come through?" Fox was anxious to find out how Rone knew about what taken place so quickly. "No Rone said bluntly, "Me and Sherry just got in. we've been at the hospital all night. I have some business to take care of in the morning, but I'll shoot by your spot in the evening." "Bet." Fox nodded. "That's cool. So when does Tee go to court?" "Aye, nigga. Let me and Ticia handle this. You don't need to be nowhere near this bullshit." Rone demanded sternly. "Ah'ight. I'll hollar tomorrow then. Fox hung up the phone and threw it back onto the bed beside Egypt. He'd seen her watching him while he was talking to Rone, but he didn't mention it.

Egypt followed behind Fox after he hung up the phone. She'd been eavesdropping the whole time that him and Jackson were talking. Although she didn't do dirt, she'd been around enough of it to know when someone was a snake and that's the impression that she was getting from Jackson. She sat on the couch pretending to watch television, although, she was really keeping a watchful eye on Jackson. She just didn't trust him.

Fox looked over to Egypt as she inconspicuously watched him. He figured she want to spend some time with him so rushed Jackson off. "Ah'ight, my nigga." Fox gave Jackson a pound and Fox closed it behind him.

"Fox, "Egypt called while he was standing near the door after locking it. Fox turned and looked at Egypt. "What's up, E?" Fox was sure she was ready to pry. Nosey ass hoe. He thought while walking toward her.

"I know I don't know that guy, but something isn't right about him, baby." She nodded. She'd seen nervousness in him that shouldn't have been in a street nigga. Laying cats down and talking penitentiary chances was an everyday thing in the dope game. A hustler should be willing to kill and die at any time, but didn't see that sanguinary nature in Jackson. Homeboy's a hoe! Egypt thought.

"You're right. You don't know'em so don't speak on my nigga. Especially insinuating some devious shit." Fox grunted, who the fuck this hoe tryna corrupt! He thought shaking his head. He too thought something was off about Jackson's demeanor, but he wasn't going to let Egypt think she'd convinced him of it. His ego alone wasn't having that. A hoe would never strip him of his integrity like that. The nigga was to relaxed though! Jackson was nonchalant about Antoine being locked down with slugs in his body after saving him from a robbery murder. I hope this nigga ain't tryna slick me? Fox sat next to Egypt on the sofa without saying another word. He'd said what he meant and he expected his bitch to abide by his lead.

Egypt was sure that Fox had seen the same thing that she did. He's to hood not to have peeped his man's game! She thought while nestling up against Fox. It was her way of letting him know that she was aligned with him. She just hoped Fox's love for his friends wouldn't blind his judgment of reality because something wasn't right about Jackson.

Fox pulled into the supermarket parking lot. It had been a few days since Antoine's shooting and he'd thought a lot of things out. Jackson had put something together that he hadn't mentioned the night of the shootings. Fox had rolled down on him while he was sitting out front of one of their trap houses.

"Wuzzup, Fox?" Jackson leaped off the hood of his car and walked toward Fox's Chevy. He'd cleaned it up putting candy paint and chrome everywhere, including his twenty inch blades. When the sunlight hit the gloss on the candy apple red paint, it looked like it was sizzling. "Let me hollah at you, hustlah." Fox chuckled while snugly clutching the trigger of his .40 caliber. He'd been restless for two days, thinking about Antoine ordeal, and it wouldn't go away. At least, not until he got to the bottom of it, and Jackson was where he would start. Jackson's wary eyes scanned the block as he approached Fox's whip. Something was telling him to be cautious. Not from Fox because Fox was his mans, but the streets were talking like there was a war going on and their clique was the target. He walked up to the driver's window. "Wuz…" Jackson stated before Fox reached out pulling him into the barrel of his burner. "What da fuck's up?" he spoke through clinched teeth because Fox had his pistol pressed stiffly against his chin. "That's what I wanna know, nigga." Fox responded in a low mumble. The trust was gone at that point, so Fox was all in and wouldn't hesitate to send something hot through of his cranium. "What you mean?" Jackson nervously asked. This nigga fixed to kill me! He thought while trying to keep still, because he was sure that the hairpin trigger of the .40 caliber would sound if he so much as flinched the wrong way. He'd been around fox long enough to know that he'd kill to avenge Antoine.

187

"Nigga, I'mma ask you once, muthfucka." Fox pushed the throttle deeper into his throat signaling his seriousness. "What the fuck happened at the 70West apartments?" his stare told Jackson that his death would proceed a lie, so he finally came clean.

"It was one of Que niggaz!" Jackson blurted. He'd known every since the shooting had happened, but he was to coward to say anything. It was the grimy looking cat that had sucked his teeth at Jackson. The nigga had been eyeballing the last few times that he'd stopped by, but Jackson never mentioned it so he felt partially to blame.

"Yeah, brah!" Jackson swore. "I would never cross you! It was Que's nigga that Tee bodied!" Jackson was relieved when Fox released his grasp of his shirt. He was sure that his life was going to end, but Fox had spared him.

After hearing Jackson out, Fox understood why something didn't sit right with him. Jackson had known who the shiest was all alone, but withheld it from him. Fox's first mind was to get in touch with Rone, but he quickly thought against that. This was something that he had to handle on his own. Rone had carried him to the threshold and it was up to him to cross the line between being a hustler and being in the game.

Fox pulled the twin .40 calibers from his stash spot and got out of the car. He casually walked through the supermarket parking lot. It's on now, baby! He thought while walking crossing Woodward near the 70West building. There was no turning back. Que had crossed a line that could only be solved with murder. It would take his life to atone for his betrayal.

He saw Rone's face and heard his coldhearted voice, in his mind, while crossing the street. "Most of all, don't hesitate to use'em because we can buy a murder case, but it ain't a piece of currency they done made that can but your life back." What Rone had told him was the hood gospel and he knew that. Whether he laid in his bed or a cot in Jackson penitentiary, after this, was up in the air, but he was going to get at Que regardless of the consequence.

Fox leaned against the building watching the fiends going in and out. He didn't smoke cigarettes, but this was a time that he needed a drag, something to ease his nerves, because he didn't want anyone to see him going into the building. Fuck it! He thought after lifting off the wall and discreetly walking into the building. I'm in here! He took the elevator up to Que's floor. Fox wanted to take him by surprise because it was him against Que and an apartment full of his goons. Fox knocked on the door. "Who is it?" someone from inside the apartment asked. Fox wanted to send a few shots through the door, but he just remained silent instead waiting beside the door with his pistol up. The door opened and Fox swung from beside it letting his burners guide him.

"Bocca…! Fox shot the cat that had opened the door in his stomach and grabbed him around the throat

189

using his as a human shield. Fox knew the he was limited on time.

"Bocca.. bocca.. bocca!"

He laid two of Que's goons down and walked down on Que. Que was scared out of his mind. He threw his hands into the air. "I'm sorry, my nigga!" Que pleaded frantically. "I didn't know! I sorry dawg!" "Blocca..! The shot that Fox fired into Que's forehead left a tunnel the size of a fifty cent piece. He pushed the goon, that he'd been using as a shield, on top of Que. Bocca!" he let one fly through the back of his neck killing him instantly before scrambling out of the apartment.

CHAPTER 7

Antoine nervously stood next to LaTicia as the judge spoke. The judge stared at Antoine with disgust. He wanted to throw the book and the bench at him, but he didn't.

"Mr. Jones, as sickened as I am to do this. The law is the law, and the law is on your side today." The judge grimaced. "All charges are dismissed." He banged the gavel and LaTicia turned to Antoine.

Aw shit! I just won my first murder case! She thought while smiling and extending her hand to Antoine for congratulatory shake, but Antoine dismissed her hand and pulled her into a strong embrace. He smiled uncontrollably.

"Thank you Ticia!" he couldn't believe he was free to go. After all of the shit he'd been through, something good happened to him. "You're welcome!" LaTicia replied with a smile. She was happy to see Antoine free, but the comfort of knowing her practice was going to explode after this win was more exciting. She winked at Antoine.

"I'm taking it that you won't be going through this again, right?" LaTicia asked presumptuously and Antoine nodded. She walked toward Rone and Sherry and chuckled. I see the hate in your eyes beeutch! She was sure that Sherry was happy to see Antoine free and certain that she wished it wasn't because of her skills.

191

LaTicia slipped her sunglasses onto her face. To keep the hate out hoe! She stopped in front of Sherry.

"I appreciate what you did for Tee, LaTicia." Sherry thanked LaTicia and smiled affectedly. She hated to do it, but after what LaTicia had done, she felt obligated to.

Rone chuckled after hearing Sherry's insincere thank you. He'd recognized her counterfeit gratitude immediately, and was sure that LaTicia had pinned it as well.

These hoes crazy as hell, he thought before hugging LaTicia. "Me too," Rone reiterated with an authentic sincerity. "Yeah, appreciate what you did for the young nigga."

LaTicia melted into Rone's arms smiling loudly. She peeked over his shoulders seeing the hate fill in Sherry and amplified her flirting. Her and Rone's friendship for entertainment purposes. "I appreciate all the support too." Antoine commented after seeing the cold stare that Sherry had given LaTicia while she hugged Rone. He was sure that Sherry wanted to whip LaTicia ass, so he tried to change the tone of the group. Sherry smiled.

"It's cool, Tee." Sherry hugged Antoine. "I'm just glad it's over. We got cha back though." She giggled, and Rone fell in with a chuckle also. "Yeah, Tee baby." Rone quickly glanced around the courtroom. "You pulled through this one, but they don't always come this easy.

192

Feel me?" he was referring to Antoine's victory in court because there was a lot of niggaz, some who he knew himself, that had left the judges realm with nature life bids for less than what Antoine had done.

"Yeah," Antoine agreed solemnly after hearing the ridicule within Rone's tone. "It was easy this time, but it wasn't cheep because that hot lead that went through my body wasn't a small price to pay." He curtly smiled at Rone before mocking him. "You feel me?" Antoine was challenging Rone. Letting him know that, unlike Fox, he didn't fear him. "Hell muthafuckin nah I don't feel you!" Rone's voice rose. He was offended and he caught on to Antoine's mocking. I ain't gon let nobody shoot me! I don't give a fuck! Police, bitch, nigga, or baby! If a muthfucka up pipe on me, he gon lay where he stoop!" his month snarled showing his viciousness while boldly sending Antoine a subliminal message of his own, before Sherry intervened.

Outside and everything, and y'all niggaz wanna start this dumb shit." she grabbed Rone's arm. Come on let's go" "I know that's right!" LaTicia second what Sherry had said. Uhnuhn! They ain't fucking up my celebration! She thought while walking out the courthouse.

Damn, they gangin up on a nigga. He thought in amazement after Sherry and LaTicia had agreed on something. This was the first time that they'd agreed on anything other than the fact that they didn't like one another. "Fishbones, my treat." Antoine offered after stepping onto the courthouse stairs. He wanted to break the tension that his and Rone's brief dispute has caused.

"Bet it up my nigga." Rone agreed, although, he really wanted to bust Antoine's head for disrespecting him in front of his wife. "I'll call Fox so he can meet us there." Rone said while reaching for his cell phone.

"Let's go, LaTicia demanded. "I'm starving." She swayed off the porch, and Antoine lustfully watched as her hips bounced from side to side. Daaaamn! He thought while intently watching her ass twirl around in her tweet skirt. It was tailored to cuff beneath her cheeks giving them a mountainous rise. And her blazer bushed her breast up accentuating her cleavage. This bitch is a dimepiece, baby! LaTicia was the only woman, other than Sherry, that he'd had contact with during his stint and an attraction had built, especially after the way she'd taken care of his case. Twelve hours after he was shot, LaTicia filed law suits against the Detroit police department, the city, and the two officers involved in his shooting. Although Antoine had killed two men prior to the police arriving, he immediately yielded to their authority dropping his pistols and raising his arms into the air. But eager policeman still shot him, although, he'd surrendered immediately. He was shot in the chest and beneath his armpit proving that his arms were raised. LaTicia pressed the law suits to get Antoine some leverage against the gun charges, but the city officials were only infuriated. They charged him with the murders and remanded him without bail. Antoine spent six months inside of the Wayne County Jail before coming to an agreement with the

194

prosecutor. He had to drop the law suits for impunity of the murder charges.

Antoine gaily inhaled while walking off the courthouse porch. He'd waited six months to do that; although, he thought it would be a life time. Rone looked over to him and shook his head. Stupid ass nigga lucky he breathing this filthy ass air! Rone thought as they walked to his car.

Fox was hype after getting the call that everything had worked out and Antoine was free. He immediately called Jackson. Although he'd upped pipe on Jackson, they'd buried the hatched because Jackson knew why Fox had done it. But line had been drawn so Fox was still watching him. "Captain Jack?" Fox spoke into the telephone after hearing Jackson's voice. He thought he'd heard someone else that he knew too. "Wuzzup, bwoy? They must've let Tee out or you done hit the lotto?"Jackson laughed. Although he'd forgiven Fox for what he'd done, he hadn't forgotten. That was something that he'd carry around for the rest of his life, especially after Fox threatened him not to tell Antoine. "Yeah, they let up on'em....." Fox paused before asking, "Who was that in the background? She sounds she familiar?" he questioned him suspiciously. "Nah, pimp. You don't know shawty." Jackson chuckled. "You can't get all the pussy, dawg. Let another nigga fuck sometimes."

Fox laughed although he knew Jackson was running some bullshit up under him. I though this nigga learned that this shit was real! He thought realizing that he'd be lied to. Jackson had an easy tell in his voice that any street cat could pick up on.

"Whatevah, nigga." Fox replied without signaling Jackson that he'd pinned his lying ways. "I'm 'bout to bounce, but we gon get together later on tonight. Ah'ight, brah?" "It's on. Just hit me up."

Fox left the room puzzles by the voice he'd heard. It was the same voice that he'd heard panting from Jackson's bedroom window a few months back. He was usually putting things together, but he couldn't seem to put a name or face with the mysterious voice. Maybe it was because he'd been so busy lately.

He'd made contacts all over the mid-west networking with major players in states surrounding Michigan. He'd been blessed with a serious plug and he planned to keep it. All of his time had been invested in the game. He'd also set shit up for Antoine while he was away. It was clear that him and Antoine had two different mentalities and Fox didn't want to hustle with his boy any longer. Their hustling season had ran its course, so Fox made a way for Antoine. He'd stumbled up a heroin connect through Raymond while he was in Atlanta on business. Sixty-five a kilo, but he would have to move whatever they sent him. Fox had no use for the connect, but he didn't want to turn it down so he proposed Antoine as an alternative. They accepted, but didn't want to meet Antoine until they felt comfortable enough to do business with him. Fox was sure that Rone had something to do with that, but he didn't mention it. Fox assumed responsibility until the time came to introduce them. Rone had spoiled Fox. Although he made his own decision, he respected Rone's insight. He'd been in the game for decades hassle free, so everything he said was worth listening to. Fox was certain that him and Antoine couldn't keep their friendship solid and hustle together. They were both to strong willed and would eventually collide.

Rone, Sherry, LaTicia, and Antoine waited at the restaurant for Fox to arrive. Antoine was anxious to see his guy because they hadn't spoken since before the shooting had taken place.

Antoine wasn't upset that Fox didn't come to visit him because Rone kept his books fat and Sherry came to see him twice a month during his entire stay. That was more than his mother did, and she was family, so he couldn't complain about Fox's lack of support without considering from his own family. He did wonder why Rone had went through all of the hassle of paying his attorney fees and stacking his commissary account up considering Rone didn't like him. It was evident because he'd came up with confusion. Rone wasn't use to anyone standing up to him and Antoine didn't fear him. "What's up, Tee?" Rone asked noticing his distance. He wasn't sure what Antoine was thinking about, although he would have liked to know. "You want a bottle of champagne for a victory drink, brah?" he tried to pull Antoine out of his trance like state and back into the chemistry of the group. "Nah, big Rone." Antoine replied distantly. "I don't drink, but I appreciate the offer."

LaTicia heard the coldness in Antoine tone. Damn! She thought, this nigga might be colder than Rone! She wondered what the beef between them was about, and she would surely be asking Rone, but right then she intervened before the tension became any thicker.

"Boy," she said to Rone, "you know he's too young to be drinking." She chuckled trying to bring some humor to their table, and Antoine chuckled. "Nah, LaTicia. It's cool. Besides it ain't 'bout my age. My mom has a drinking problem, so I just say no." his tone had fell into a detached pitch and everyone fell silent as an result of his honesty. They all had known about his mother problem, but it was still shocking to hear an admission of something so personal from someone so young.

"Aye, my nigga," Rone began and grabbed Antoine's shoulder showing him that there was no more aggression. "I'm apologizing for that. I knew about your mother's situation, so should've used better judgment." Rone's apology was sincere and it lightened the mood. Antoine smiled and chuckled lightly.

"I'mma be real with you, Rone. All the shit that you've done for me........." He chuckled again before continuing. "It's gon be hard for you to offend me." He reached accross the table and gave Rone a pound assuring him that there were no hard feelings and that he was ready to bury the hatched. LaTicia suddenly interrupted their moment.

"Here comes Fox." LaTicia said and pointed to him as he walked through the entrance. Shit! He's fine! She thought while eyeballing him. Antoine jumped and embraced his nigga! "What's up, brah? You lookin real playah like." He complemented Fox after giving him a look over. Fox was fresh to death in denim Girbraud jeans, and Gucci blazer and loafers to match. Antoine was shocked at the transition his guy had made over a six month span. He looked like money now. Damn, this nigga clean! He though while smiling, proud of his best friend.

Fox chuckled. "I wish I could say the same. You clean and all, but a shave would be more just the release you just got." Fox teased and everyone laughed. He walked over and gave Sherry a kiss on the cheek and Rone a hood head nod. Damn them titties lookin perky! He thought while standing over LaTicia looking down her cleavage.

Sherry watched as LaTicia smile spread widely across her face. If this hoe is fucking my brother too! She thought while Fox sat next to her. She'd already put up with LaTicia and Rone's boisterous affair, but her and Fox was a no no. this hoe's a real dopeboy groupie!

"Hey, Fox!" LaTicia squealed his name like a school girl with a crush. "What's up ma?" Fox slid his arm around LaTicia's waist pulling her into his chest hugging her. It looked playful, but he purposely rubbed the bottom of her breast.

Antoine stared at Fox's move. He'd seen him rub his hand across her chest and wondered how soft her breasts were. Damn my nigga is cold wit it! He admired Fox's game.

"So what up, my nigga? What did you get into for yo birthday?" Antoine asked meaninglessly because he didn't know what else to say. "Shit really!" Fox answered coolly. "Me and Egypt kicked it because she was leaving the next day." He didn't want to give too much detail because he knew how envious Antoine could get at times. "Nigga stop lyin. I know you tossed it up, plus Egypt ain't reality." He'd been teasing Fox that Egypt didn't exist. Of course, he'd seen Fox with some fine bitches, but nothing as cold as he'd described Egypt to be. Fox laughed.

"You ready, boy?" Fox asked warning him that he had jokes too. "You fresh outta the county, brah! And you want to do this with grease still on your palms?" he teased sending the table into a thunderous laugher. Everyone sat around the table eating and enjoying one another's company for a while. Antoine entertained them with unbelievable stories about his short stint in the county jail. Fox was proud of Antoine's new found humility.

Damn! Fox thought while watching Antoine working the table. It's crazy how a nigga do some time and comes out a new man. Antoine was never known for his networking ability or people skills, but at that moment he was showing that he actually possessed them. He'd set the tone of the table even causing Rone to take another look at him.

Rone could see a change in Antoine, but that didn't change what Rone had originally questioned about him. Rone was still skeptical about Antoine's loyalty to Fox. He'd seen niggaz like Antoine along the way and all of them crashed out at some point, he just hoped it wasn't too late when Fox recognized him for what he was. Fox had became restless sitting around having meaningless chitchat, and he wanted to talk to Antoine about what he'd been working on. "What's up, Tee? You ready to bounce?" Fox asked abruptly. "Yeah, let's pull." Antoine said while standing and reaching into his pocket to pay the check. Rone grabbed his forearm as be reached into his pocket. "Young Tee, you know I can't let you pay for this. Maybe next time." Rone said knowing that next time depended on if Sherry was present, because Rone was from the old school and wouldn't think of letting another man pay for his woman's meal.

"Ah'ight then." Antoine nodded. I feel you." He gave Rone a pound, kissed Sherry on the cheek, and waved goodbye to LaTicia before him and Fox left.

Jackson's cell phone rung and he leaned onto his elbow. That's probably Fox and Tee? He thought while nudging the board who Fox had heard through the phone earlier.

"Aye, shawty. Hand me that phone." He demanded and Kiesha rolled over and snatched his cell phone from the night stand beside her. "Here, baby." Kiesha said and handed him the phone. Jackson looked at the caller ID and shushed her.

"Be quiet. This Fox. I'm 'bout to answer and he already heard you earlier." He answered the phone. "Hello?" "What up?" Fox's voice came through the telephone. "I got Tee with me right here. We "bout to scoop you up." "Aw'ight. Give me 'bout an hour, so I can get my shit together." Jackson said knowing he needed some time to get rid of Kiesha before they showed up at his house.

"Bet it!" Fox replied and hung up. Kiesha leaped from the bed and sassily put hands on her hips while staring at Jackson. "Are you gonna to tell him because I'm not telling him shit!" Kiesha was irate. She was sure that Antoine would kill both of them once he found out that she was pregnant with Jackson's baby. Jackson laughed. "We ain't tellin'em shit! you getting an abortion anyway, so why Antoine do to those two niggaz at the 70West there was no way that he would tell him he'd been pounding his woman out. "Nigga! I'm six month pregnant! How in the hell am I gonna get an abortion?" Kiesha shouted. This nigga is scared of Tee! He's a bitch! She thought as tears swelled in her eyes. She was sure that he'd find out and that terrified her. I don't even know why I was fuckin with this lame! Jackson shrugged his shoulders. "He thank it's his baby anyway. Fuck it! Leave it that way shawty!"

"This shit ain't cool Jackson! You know this is your baby." She pointed to her swollen stomach. "What goes around comes around motherfucker and I hope this come back t bite you in the ass!" Jackson shook his head and chuckled. This raggedly ass hoe outta her muhfuckin mind! He thought while examining what she'd said to him. He wanted to smack her upside her head, but he was sure that whipping her would only cause more problems for him.

"Wrong? Wrong?" Jackson was furious. "Bitch! We been fuckin since the seventh grade and I'm wrong?" he couldn't hold it back. Whack!" he slapped the shit out of her sending her flying onto the bed. Kiesha lay across the bed holding her face in disbelief. She'd been stupid for messing around with him, and now he was throwing her beneath a bus because he was too afraid to man up against Antoine. "You're right!" she screamed vehemently while grabbing her clothes. "Sorry motherfucker! You ain't wrong! I'm just stupid for fucking with your coward country ass. No good bitch!" "Yeah, yeah, bitch." Jackson said calmly not caring about her tantrum. "Just shut the fuck up and shut up with the shuttin up, bitch." he lay across the bed watching as she ran through his house and out the door with her clothes loosely hanging from her arms. He just laughed heartlessly. Stupid ass hoe thank she 'bout to put the baby on me she crazy. Guttah ass bitch. He thought while walking to the shower after she left.

Antoine slouched into Fox's couch. It was the first piece of real furniture that he'd sat on in months and he reveled in while looking around at all the upgrades Fox had made to the apartment. "I see you finally finished furnishing this muthafucka." "Yeah." Fox nodded. "Egypt helped me put it together before she left last time."

"She sounds like good peoples." The mention of Egypt made Antoine think about Kiesha. "You know Kiesha is six month pregnant." Yeah, Sherry told me about that pops." Fox teased. "Have you talked to her yet?" he asked curiously. "Nah, my nigga. I wanted to pop up on her. You know. Surprise and shit." he chuckled, and Fox shook his head. "Or get surprised." Fox joked, although, he was as serious as colon cancer. "A nigga could be in that pussy as we speak muhfucka." Fuck you, nigga!" Antoine laughed, although, he'd considered that possibility himself and that was what had changed his mind about surprising her.

"Freaky as you say Egypt is. She the one probably up in her long as a back wood Mississippi python." They both fell out in laughter. They watched television for a while, while catching up on lost times.

Fox was trying to see where Antoine's head was because he was cloudy before the shooting. And Antoine was trying to figure out a way to ask Fox about the distance that he'd created between them, while he was locked up, without offending him. That was a time where he really needed Fox, but he wasn't there.

"Aye, Tee?" Fox said interrupting the silence. "You know shit got real sweet while you were away." Fox tried to set the tone and direction of their conversation.

"Yeah." Antoine nodded. "I heard you was out here shakin yo ass." They both chuckled. "They say you done got major out here in these muhfuckin streets." He was proud of Fox. "No doubt, but you ain't get left out nigga. You left me in the county stankin." He teased, although, there was some truth to what he'd said and Fox had sensed it.

"Nigga, you must be delusional. Hold up." Fox said before disappearing into the bedroom and coming out with a duffle bag. He tossed the bag to Antoine's feet and gestured for him to open it. Antoine was certain that Fox would have a little something for him, once he was released, but that still wouldn't excuse his lack of support while he was doing time. He opened the bag. God damn! He thought while taking a double take at the stacks of dough that was inside. It had to be at least twenty thousand inside.

"Damn, brah!" Antoine blurted. "You done came the fuck up." He fingered a few of the stacks and Fox shook his head. "Nah, my nigga." Fox said and leaned back into his Minotti Capri chair smiling. "We done came up. It's a hundred stacks in there too."

"Quit bullshittin, nigga." Antoine took a closer look at the stacks of money noticing that they were all hundred dollar bills. "That's you, dawg!" Fox smiled knowing that Antoine would be impressed. "But that ain't it. It's that time, brah." His facial expression fell into a somber stare. "What time?" Antoine asked after seeing Fox's mood change. He hoped Fox wasn't talking about getting out of the game because he would be on his own with that call. Antoine was lifetime participant of the game. "I got everything jumping for you while you were gone. You got spots, workers, and plugs. The only thing that was missing was you." "Whatchu talkin 'bout?" Antoine was still confused and didn't understand that Fox was parting ways with him. "I'm not fucking with the heroin no more. I'mma do my thing with this coke, baby. I set everything up, but from here on out you on your own." Fox threw his hands into the air and dusted them off. "It's been real, but our business is over." Antoine shook his head. "They say a nigga gotta watch what he ask fo or he just might get it. Fox, man.... I been in yo shadow for years, brah." He leaned in and gave Fox a manly hug. "It's a perfect ending to a new beginning, my nigga."

Fox stared at Antoine after their hug. He'd expected him to throw a tantrum like he had always done, but he responded like a man. Fox wondered what happened to him while he was in the county. He'd heard stories about prison time changing niggaz, but this was his first time witnessing it firsthand.

"Nigga," Fox chuckled before continuing. "You must've been in there readin them Muslim books and shit, because that was deep." Antoine laughed. "Nah, I just got my GED and did some soul searching, dawg. I had some serious shit in my head." "Yeah! I know, muhfucka. You was really buggin if you thought I could've said fuck you." Nigga I bodied four muthafuckaz about what happened to you! He thought, but would never tell Antoine or anyone else about what he'd done. There was certain things that shouldn't be spoken aloud and four murders was one of them because that was information that you shouldn't trust no one with. "On some real shit, brah!" Antoine said and laughed. He wanted to soften what he was about to say. "I ain't like how close you and Jackson had got, my nigga. That shit was hauntin me."

"Why? You my nigga, and he's my nigga, there shouldn't be a problem 'bout that." "You're right, but I had some personal issues that made the envy come out." "Right," Fox said with a nod. He was glad to hear Antoine finally admit to his jealously.

"Nigga, I was sitting in the truck steamin about that shit. I seen Jackson silly ass come outta the building, and nigga was creepin up behind him. He ain't even know, but I peeped it."

Straight up?" Fox asked showing his interest because he wanted to hear Antoine's version of the story. "Straight the fuck up! The nigga Jackson thought I was upping my strap on him until I dropped the first nigga. His eyes got wide as hell!" Antoine laughed. "Nigga quit bullshitting."

"Nah, dawg! I bullshit you not. The nigga gave me a look like he'd done something to me that I didn't know about." Antoine sat back and nodded assuring Fox that he was telling the truth. "Shit from what he told me you putting it down, my nigga!" Fox said changing the subject before he had to tell Antoine the reason why Jackson thought his life was on the line. It had finally came to Fox. The voice that he'd been hearing was Kiesha's, Antoine's girl.

"The shit happened so quick! One minute I'm in the truck waitin on Jackson to come outta the building, and the next I'm in the ambulance chained down with two bullets in my ass and two bodies on my jacket." They both laughed. "Sheeit, while you was playin convict I was down south making movies, brah. Everything is gon move through me until my connect wanna meet you." "I thought the boy was coming outta the east coast?" Antoine asked curiously.

"Don't worry about where it's coming from. Just know you're gettin whole one's foe sixty-five." "Those some good numbers, baby." Antoine smiled knowing Fox had put some tax on him.

"Hell yeah, they some good numbers, especially when the first one is free. Mr. Webb is waiting on us and we gotta go scoop Jackson up." "Ah'ight, lets bounce. I'mma leave my package here, but I'll be to get it tomorrow." Antoine pushed the duffle bag beneath the sofa and followed Fox out of the apartment.

The remaining months of 1997 were a ha Antoine bubbled up becoming a premier hustler in the heroin community. He flaunted his new wealth without shame buying houses, cars, and flamboyant jewelry. He was the man—his own ma, with his own hustle. The streets talked and when they spoke his name it was with respect and fear. Laying two niggaz across the pavement in cold blood and walking away from prosecution would get you that type of respect and fear. His and Kiesha's child was born, it was a boy. They named him Jah'lil and their relationship got stronger as a result of their son's birth. Antoine's life changed, he'd even sent his mother to rehabilitation center.

Antoine had stepped out of Fox's shadow and into his own stride revealing what he could do in the game. The next two years was a season of growth, but like Nas said "A thug changes, and love changes, and best friends become strangers.

CHAPTER 8

Antoine's watchful eyes scanned the club while sipping on patron on ice. He still wasn't much of a drinker, but he'd push back a few occasionally. After his release from jail him and Fox went on a two year uninterrupted grind. The money was flowing like liquid, the hustle was consistent, and the city was theirs. Everything was lovely and they were at the pinnacle of their hustles. Antoine smiled at the thought of where him and Fox had come from. Starting off, moving syringes in the hood into gaming their way up the food chain. He put his arm around Fox's shoulder and chuckled. "It's hoes everywhere!"

"Yeah," Fox nodded. It was a nonchalant nod. "Everywhere and nowhere at the same time." He chuckled because he wasn't impressed by none of the bottom feeding bitches who were in the club.

"No doubt. You're right, but I'm still tryna fuck something tonight, brah!" they both laughed and touched glasses.

Damn! Fox thought while canvassing the club. He'd seem this years before it had happened. It was a vision that only a true hustler could have because him and his guy were in a league of their own. The major league moving slopes of snow and blow from Peru to Kalamazoo.

"We living the good life, my nigga." Fox laughed and nodded his head. "I would have never thought we'd

210

be here. I always knew we was gonna blow, but damn, my nigga."

"Yeah, I knew it though. There wasn't a doubt for me, baby!" Fox laughed. "Even when you threw that hot ass Pelle on in 70degree weather, I knew."

"Fuck you, muthafucka." They both laughed. Two fine young broads pulled up to them while they were talking. This was something that Fox and Antoine had became accustomed to. Groupie love was one of the perks of being a birdman. Woman would come from far a wide to set it out and tonight would be no different. One of the females was fine ass red bone with some huge tits. She was wearing a dress that fell just above her thighs and right below her pussy. Her ass was round, but it was as fluffy as niggaz in the hood like them. She walked over to Antoine pushing her voluptuous cantaloupe like breast forward, and started a conversation. She had a straight up type of approach that impressed Antoine.

Meanwhile the other female extended her hand to Fox. She wanted to portray herself like a lady, but Fox saw right through her two dollar ass façade. He'd been around enough boppers to pinpoint one when she showed up—and she was definitely a bopper. She was wearing a pure white Chanel pants suit with a soft peach scarf belt that wrapped around her thin waist. Her ass was donkey with a butt cuff that any nigga would want to mount. She stood sideways showcasing her saddle hips.

211

"Hi, I'm Kizzie." She said with a polite smile that offered more than her name. Damn, she thought while shaking his hand, this nigga is fine! Fox flashed his smile and shook Kizzie's hand. Although he wasn't interested, he wasn't a fool. This bitch got a Tennessee tottie body! He thought while twirling her around. He wanted to take her on a trip to the local motel and blow her back out, but Fox knew woman like Kizzie came alone with problems, especially once they found out who he was.

"I'm Fox, but I'm engaged, babygirl." He wanted to slip away from her before he ended up in some troubled rafting. She giggled as if what he'd said didn't bother her. How long have you had that problem?" Kizzie smiled like she'd ran major game down Fox's throat, but what she was spitting he'd put down years before. Fox laughed in her face. He was sure that she'd borrowed that line from a nigga who's pushed it off on her. This bitch don't know who she playin with! He thought while slowing his laugh into a soft chuckle. Although what she'd said could have been misinterpreted as disrespect, Fox knew exactly what she was trying to do and had failed at.

"What? You're tripping, babygirl. Being disrespectful ain't the way to a man's heart or pockets." Fox tapped his pocket letting her know that he was aware of what she'd came for. She was a hood bitch who was trying to find her way out and he couldn't be her cabbie.

Kizzie moved closer to him causing her peach alligator stilettos to scrape the floor. She wasn't giving up

212

because she was use to getting what she wanted. Her soft feature was usually a trap for ballers. And this nigga is a baller! She thought while taking a sip from her drink. Her mouth was so close to Fox's he could smell the margarita on her breath. "I'm sorry," she apologized with a timid smile. I'm just nosey like that. So can I buy you a drink?" she wanted to buy his forgiveness, and Fox was tempted because she was fine. Damn! He thought while giving her a once over. Her body was banging. I gotta get away from this hoe 'fo she get a nigga! He laughed. "No thanks, babygirl." Damn, I hate turning all that good pussy down. Fox thought while shaking his head. He was already in a situation that he had to walk away.

Kizzie's look of confidence that she'd originally came over with was fading. Fox had shitted on her and she couldn't understand why. Something was off about him. What's this niggaz register? She wondered while curiously staring at him. Her eyebrows went up and she sassily put her hands onto her thin waist just above her hips. "You must be conceited or gay, but you're definitely one or the other!" Kizzie chuckled as if she was teasing him, but that's what she thought and the latter was closer to what she really believed.

I should slap this bitch up off her muthafuckin feet! He thought while giving her an abhorrent stare. He was sure that she just upset about him pulling back and didn't really believe what she'd implied because he'd take her out the parking lot and disprove that theory immediately.

"Nah, babygirl." Fox shook his head denying what she said. I'm just committed." He lied.

Committed to what?" Kizzie looked confused while playing the naïve role. She was sure that she would eventually break him. You ain't the first nigga that played hard to get son! She thought and smiled while waiting for his comeback. Fox had tried being respectful to Kizzie. He prided himself I being a lady's man, n gorilla shit.

"Committed to getting money, fuckin my girl, and stayin away from sack chasin bitches like you." Fox turned and walked away. Stupid ass tramp! He thought as he strutted off like a boss that he was. Once he was the bar, he straddled the stool and enjoyed the scenery. It was Friday which usually brought out the working to upper class people. Factory workers, city employees, and the entrepreneurs. In the Motor City, most of the upper echelon drug dealers referred to themselves as entrepreneurs. They did that as a attempt to cover up their true occupation. Fox was one of them, but his cover up had become his truth over. Earlier in the fall, Fox had bought three eighty unit apartment buildings with the help of Rone, Egypt, and LaTicia. So in truth he had became a genuine businessman. While sitting at the bar his cell phone started vibrating. "Hello," Fox answered. This is Ticia, Fox." LaTicia voice came through the phone and Fox's face cringed.

"Yeah, what's up?" he asked although he knew she was calling with some bullshit. "I was just calling to let you know that I understood where you were coming from

214

earlier." Her voice was humble, unlike what she was like earlier when they'd talked.

"I'm glad because you on some hoe shit earlier." Fox let her know that he appreciate how she'd reacted earlier. I know…. it's just that we've been having sex for two years, Fox. I always knew how you felt about Egypt, but I want to keep my baby." Fox's face tightened. It was the same thing that they'd talked about talked about earlier the day and his conclusion was the same now. This bitch gon make a nigga stomp the baby outta her dizzy ass! Fox thought while trying to keep his composure. He'd known alone that LaTicia was trying to fuck up his and Egypt's relationship, by trapping him with a baby. Although she was an attorney she still had hood in her and Fox was aware of that. The baby might not even be mines. He lied to himself knowing that he was the father. "Look, Ticia! I'm tryna enjoy myself, but I'll stop by before I go home." He hung up the phone without saying goodbye. His first thought was to go snatch Kizzie up and pound her out while he was upset, but she wasn't worth the hassles that came with her. Instead, Fox walked over to Antoine, who was entertaining a group of dimes including the one with the huge tits. He threw his arm around Antoine's shoulder and smiled at the woman. Fuck it! He thought while looking them all over. I might as well bang one of these hoes tonight! Antoine pushed Fox forward into the den of groupies.

"Ladies?" Antoine started. "This is my nigga, Fox and he wanna know how it feels to fuck five bitches at

215

one time." he chuckled while patting Fox on the back of his shoulder.

Fox's face was flushed. Damn! He thought, Tee gettin gritty with these hoes! He looked around noticing that the broads were actually interested in getting down. This might cost a nigga, but I'ont give a fuck! He already turned down one piece of pussy and there was no one that he'd be doing it again tonight. Suddenly Kizzie walked up from out of nowhere and rolled her eyes at Fox.

"He don't want any of y'all." Kizzie shook her head assuring the woman that she was telling the truth. "He wants a man! He has to like dick if he if he doesn't like this!" she bounced her thick hip to the side and twirled in an attempt to flaunt her body.

Fox's face darkened with anger. I'mma kill this bitch! He thought while walking up on her.

"Bitch! You think you that cold? A nigga just fuck with a raggedy ass tramp bitch like you?" he laughed sinisterly and swiftly wrapped his hands around her throat lifting her off her feet.

"Hoe! You, your game, and that knock-off ass Channel you wearin is lame!" he squeezed tighter choking the hell out of her before Antoine stepped in grabbing him. Fox let her go after realizing what he was doing.

"You a arrogant ass bitch!" Fox yelled into her face while Antoine stood between them.

Antoine didn't want his mans to catch a murder case over a hoe, so he stood in airplane position trying to keep him from snatching her up again. He looked over to Kizzie wondering why she was still standing around. Bitch, you better run! He thought while trying to hold Fox off her.

"Hold up, brah!" Antoine didn't want him to fall victim to a broad as vindictive as Kizzie seemed to be. "Not over a bitch, my nigga." He nodded to Fox as a gesture to pull back, and Fox facial expression softened. He was like that , there wasn't an in between Fox was either calm or raging.

"Yeah, you right, Tee baby. I'm up." Fox said and gave dap before turning back to the women. " I Apologize ladies, but y'all need to drop the dead weight." He nodded to Kizzie letting them know that she was the dead weight that he was talking about.

"I'll get with you tomorrow." Antoine said and patted Fox on the back. "Ah'ight then." Fox replied and dug into his pocket. He pulled out a thick roll of money and passed it to Antoine.

"Make sure these ladies don't have to spend any money tonight." He made a head gesture to Kizzie. "Even this bitch." He walked off with Kizzie eyes following him. She was lust filled and stupefied after the sordid display of words that Fox h d laid on her before walking off.

217

Mary J. Blige's voice blared through the speakers in LaTicia's living room while she sat around moping. She'd passed herself off to others as the epitome of a strong, independent black woman, but she herself knew her shortcomings.

I can't believe I'm laying around here upset, barefoot, and pregnant by a twenty-one year old! She thought while sniffling back tears. "I need my ass whipped." She whispered to herself and rubbed her barely swallow stomach. All because of his bitch. She was sure that Fox wasn't willing to step up because of his relationship with Egypt. "Fuck it"! She was ready to face her pregnancy alone, but what she wasn't willing to do was have an abortion. Knock…knock….knock!" Someone banged on her door causing her a thunderous crashing sound. She was sure it was Fox, but she played naïve. "Who is it?" LaTicia asked while standing beside the door. It's me!" Fox answered knowing she'd recognized his knock and was playing games.   LaTicia signed before opening the door.   She knew that an argument was prevalent, and she wasn't ready for it again. They'd already had words earlier and she was still exhausted from that.   She rolled her eyes as Fox walked straight pass her without saying anything.   Everything within their relationship had changed after she told him about her pregnancy, especially the affection they usually shared.

"I can't get a hug, a kiss, or a tap on the ass today, huh Fox?" LaTicia asked sarcastically and pursed her lips. She slammed the door. "Nah!" Fox Replied bluntly and fell into the sofa. "Fox, why are you acting like this? It's your baby too?"

"Yeah, you're right. So I should have some influence on the decision." LaTicia's neck whipped toward Fox. *I know he don't think he has a say so over my body?* She wondered hoping that she didn't hear him right. *You can knock the bottom out of this pussy, but you still don't own it!*

"It's my body, Fox. I'm thirty-three years old. I can't be running around having abortions. What if I can't get pregnant again?" Fox shrugged his shoulders. "I'mma tell you like this. We both made a mistake. The problem is, I know it's a mistake and you think it's a gift from GOD or some shit like that!" As soon as Fox completed his sentence tears started pouring out of LaTicia's eyes. *Here this hoe goes with this cryin and shit.* He thought.

"I'm in love with you, Fox! I want you and our baby!"

"I ain't no muthafuckin possession! You can't have me!" He shook his head defiantly. He wanted her to feel him. "Know that, LaTicia. You can't have me." He repeated stiffly and it upset LaTicia.

"Fuck it, Fox!" She sniffled back tears. "You're right! I can't have you, but I'm having my baby!"

"A nigga can't win with you!" He leaped from the couch and stormed out of her house leaving the door

219

opened. LaTicia bolted behind him and kicked the door shut. Fuck you, nigga! She thought enraged by Fox's apathetic behavior. She wanted him to be involved in her and their unborn child's lives, but that want would be deferred because, at this point, Fox wasn't with it. He was adamant about LaTicia having an abortion.

****

Antoine stumbled out of the club with, Shawnda, the butter pecan complexioned broad with the perky breast. As he walked into the parking lot Quake was leaning against his Range. He saw from the short distance so he played drunker than what he actually was. This hoe ass nigga 'bout to get his issue fuckin with a real live gangstah! He thought while tugging on the back of Shawnda's dress getting her attention.

That's my Range over there, but don't look, ma. Dude probably gon try to rob us, so act like you carrying me to my car."

"Okay." Shawnda replied timidly. She was scared as hell. What the fuck! This nigga might kill us? She thought as they got closer to Antoine's range Rover, and Quake lifted off the hood.

"Tee!" Quake yelled as if they were friends, and Shawnda continued to cradle him. Antoine had used her body to shield him as he pulled his .45 and hid it behind her back.

"Tee, when you gon come in with them chips, brah?" Quake grabbed Antoine's shoulder thinking he was in a drunken stupor, and Antoine rose up shoving the burner into his mouth.

"I got some of it right here, hoe ass nigga!" Antoine backed him all the way up to his truck. Quake's mouth bled form the teeth that Antoine had knocked out while pushing the four pound down his throat.

"Bitch ass nigga! If you ever roll down on me like that again, I'mma kill you, yo daddy, and yo son offin yo bloodline nigga!" He took the pistol out of his mouth and slapped him across his face. "Whack!" He put it back into his mouth pushing a few more teeth out.

"You get it, brah?!" Antoine snarled and Quake nodded. His eyes were wide when he stared up at Antoine scared that his next breath could be his last.

"No, Tee!" Shawnda said touching his arm. She didn't want to see Antoine catch a prison stint before she got her piece of his ghetto fortune. Antoine chuckled. "Nigga, you should be thanking my home girl for savin your life." He took the pistol out of his mouth again and kicked him in the ass watching him run off in the dark. Antoine was sure that this wouldn't be the last thing he heard from Quake and Erk about Wheat's ten grand, but he didn't give a fuck. Just like the Brick City niggaz, he'd formed himself a small army of killers that were ready to pop off at any given time.

****

Rone lounged around the den reading the New Post and listening to the morning radio show. Him and Sherry were on ends. She'd been upset with him for a few weeks since he told her that they were moving to Houston.

Rone tried to explain, but Sherry wasn't accepting his excuses. He thought he would ultimately be victimized by the same dirt that he once did if he stayed in Detroit after retiring for the game. He'd watched it happen to a lot of gangsters over the years. Pimps who'd let their whore's trick them into using heroin, and murderers who would come home from prison after doin a stretch only kto be smoked by a young nigga who didn't give a fuck about their twenty year old reputation. He'd seen it happen, and refused to let that be his demise.

Sherry walked through the hallway angrily swinging the telephone in her hand. She was tired of LaTicia's late night phone calls, especially since she was no longer running Rone's companies. It was starting to bother her more than it had before and it showed.

"Rone?" Sherry yelled after opening the door to the den. Her face let Rone know that she wasn't pleased about something, but he didn't question her about what was bothering her. Instead he'd let it come out on it's own.

"What's up?" Rone asked and she rolled his eyes at him.

"Telephone!" She rolled her eyes and tossed the phone onto his lap before stomping out the den.

This bitch must be outta her muthafuckin mind! Rone thought while staring at the phone that lay in his lap. He shook his head with disbelief. This hoe gonna try me one too many times. He put the telephone to his ear.

Sherry stood in the kitchen seething. Just knowing Laticia was on the other end of her telephone was driving her crazy.

"I hate that bitch!" Sherry whispered to herself while pouring herself a shot of Grey Goose. She'd noticed LaTicia's ass, tits, and lips getting fatter and wondered if she was pregnant. I know this bitch ain't pregnant by my man! She thought hatefully. She'd seen the pregnant glow of LaTicia's skin a few weeks back, but she hadn't mentioned it, instead she wanted Rone to bring it to her. She'd accused him of enough over the years, and was always wrong, so she wanted to hear it from him because a baby was something that he definitely couldn't hide.

Rone walked into the kitchen as Sherry downed her second shot of Vodka. He was upset when she'd thrown the telephone on his lap, but after hearing LaTicia's voice, he calmed because he understood what was going on. **She KNOW Ticia's pregnant and she think I hooked her and Fox up!** Rone chuckled while walking over to her. He could see, from the evil look that she was giving him, that she wasn't in a laughing mood.

"What's up, cheeks?" Rone asked while wrapping his arms around her waist from the back causing his wife to tense up.

"Nothing! " She lied knowing that she was fuming about what she thought was going on behind her back. And this nigga trying to act like ain't shit goin on! Her thoughts were running and she was trying to hold what she wanted to say back. It was about respect for her husband and respect for the game. She knew what she'd signed up for when she jumped into the bed with a hustler—and infidelity was one of the requirements.

"Nothing?" Rone chuckled again. "Sheeit, something better be wrong. You threw the muhfuckin phone at me." He playfully squeezed her tighter and ground his manhood against her backside.

Sherry's body stiffened as a result. She envisioned him paddling LaTicia from the back. Them sweating her calling his name. Fuck it! She thought. I gotta ask.

"Is she pregnant, Rone?" Sherry asked bluntly.

"What?" Rone chuckled trying to stall his answer. Damn, she gon trip. He thought as she turned to look him directly in the eyes.

"Nigga, you heard me! Is she pregnant?"

"Yeah." Rone replied honestly, although, he wanted to lie to help his mans out. A single tear fell from Sherry's eye and she threw her shot glass to the floor shattering it.

"I can't believe you, Rone!" She screamed vehemently and Rone stared at her like she'd lost her mind.

"That ain't got shit to do with me and you!" Rone replied while thinking, this bitch is overreacting.

Sherry broke his embrace. "Yeah, I knew y'all was fucking and she's the one pregnant, but it still has something to do with us!" She cried and Rone burst into laughter.

"What?" He was taken aback. "You thought she was pregnant by me? Hell nah!" He wrapped his hands back around her waist and pulled her snugly against him chuckling.

"Let me go, Rone!" Sherry wiggled while trying to get loose.

laughed and she stopped wiggling.

Sherry's eyes bulged as she stared up at Rone. She was embarrassed. She dropped her face into his stomach and giggled.

"I look stupid don't I?" She asked knowing damn well she did. She couldn't believe she'd slipped that one after knowing something looked suspicious between LaTicia and Fox.

"Hell yeah, you look stupid!" Rone teased, agreeing with what she'd already admitted. "That's that nigga problem, not mines." Sherry kissed his chest. Damn! I done fucked up! She thought knowing that she'd put her foot into her big ass mouth again. She would have bet her life that Rone and LaTicia were creeping being her back. It was written in every line that they'd spoken to each other, and played in every scene when they were around each other. That dirty bitch was playing me like a two dollar fiddle! She shook her head still ashamed of how LaTicia had gotten beneath her skin.

"I should have seen it though." Rone said trying to bring Sherry back up. She was shit a long time ago, but I didn't think it was important." Sherry softly head butted him in the chest a few times. "Ugh! So you did fuck her?"

"Hell nah!" Rone retorted briskly. "I wouldn't have fucked her and I advised Fox not to, but the bitch is fine!" He shrugged his shoulders and Sherry twisted her lips implying he was lying to her.

"Yeah right you didn't fuck her." She grunted and tried to walk away. She'd heard enough. At least it wasn't his baby, she thought relieved of that.

Rone followed behind her trying to explain what had happened between him and LaTicia. He told her about the night that they'd almost had sex. The night of their first date.

After leaving the restaurant, they were on their way to LaTicia's suite and Rone asked her why she wanted to sleep with him. It was a question that some men asked to boost their egos, but Rone was different. He really was interested in why she wanted to fuck. Laticia turned to him and smiled.

"Because I'm horny and you're here." LaTicia tried to sound cute, but it upset Rone.

Rone felt insulted. He was sure that he had more going on the a stiff piece of meat, and he couldn't sell himself short like that. This bitch trippin! He thought while driving up to her building. Knowing that she had such a shallow attraction to him was a turn off. He popped the locks on the doors.

"Ah'ight then." He said without looking over to her and LaTicia giggled.

"Excuse me?" She asked while laughing because she was sure that Rone was being comedic again. She waited about a mind before she realized he was dead serious. This arrogant motherfucker won't even look at me! She was appalled, but Rone was unfazed by it.

"Bitch, I ain't the type of nigga people pray for." He replied coldly and kept his stare forward looking never making eye contact with her. "Praying for me gon fuck around and make GOD stop answering your calls." She

227

slammed his car door and he drove off not even watching to see that she got into the building safely.

Sherry listened as Rone told his version of the story. I wouldn't have never fucked with you again. Sherry thought while he described how cold he'd acted when dropping Laticia off at her suite. It had to be more to it. She believed that there was something missing. Something that Rone had deliberately left out and she wanted to know. And she was sure that she'd find out.

****

Fox rolled down on Antoine's Range Rover. Antoine was slouched deep into the driver's seat smiling while talking on his cell phone. This nigga done that dumb ass shit and he slippin like this! Fox thought upset that Antoine had caused a beer with the Brick City clique. He wasn't scared. He knew that they couldn't out muscle him because he had killers that would come across country at his call, but he didn't want the trouble. Fox breathed the streets and knew that a hustler couldn't stack his paper if there was beef out there. Like Biggie said, "Beef is when I see you, you guaranteed to be in I.C.U." And the way the hood was talking, they were at war. Fox whipped his Q45 Infinity beside Antoine's truck and honked his horn erratically getting his attention.

Antoine looked up clutching his four nickel. After noticing it was Fox he rolled the window down smiling, but he could see that Fox wasn't amused. Somebody

228

done told this nigga 'fo I could. He thought and sighed while shaking his head. This nigga gone take me to church! He chuckled.

"This shit funny out here, huh?" Fox asked knowing that Antoine was taking the threat that he was getting from Wheat's young gunners lightly.

"Don't even trip." Antoine tried to down play the four missing teeth that he'd slapped out of Quake's mouth.

"Don't trip!" Muhfucka these niggaz ready to coon something!" Fox was getting louder because he was hearing something in Antoine's tone that was too relaxed.

"I'mma push that li'l bread off on the niggaz immediately, my guy. Trust me, I got this." Antoine breathed heavily and grunted. Damn! He thought while busting in a bitches mouth who he'd met a few days ago. After swallowing, she wiped her mouth while raising upright. Fox's eyes got big. "Man, I know you ain't out here like that, brah!" He couldn't believe Antoine was getting capped off outside of his house. Not only did he live there, but so did Kiesha and Jah'lil. This nigga done got outta hand! He thought while watching the broad get out of Antoine's truck and sashay across the street to a beat up Toyota Camry. She was strapped all the way down to her ankles and fine as hell, but there was no way she should be knowing where Antoine stayed. "I gotta bounce, brah!" Antoine said with a fake chuckle. "But I got it! I'mma get at 'em in the next couple days." He assured Fox, but Fox wasn't sure he could count on that alone. Fox nodded and drove off. I'mma put something wit it. He thought a gift could squeeze the animosity that Quake's missing grill had caused. Him and Wheat had a good report so he hoped that he could defuse the bad blood before it escalated into the war that the streets had reported their rift to be.

Antoine pulled up to Zoria's house. Zoria was cold. Thick and chocolate with cat grey eyes. Antoine called her his exotic bitch because she had silky jet black hair that fell to her ass and bowlegged model strut. Fox had told him she was off limits, but getting at her was a line that he had to cross. Fox was his mans and all, but what Zoria carried between her legs could cause a war between nations.

"What's up babygirl." Antoine said and slip his tongue into her mouth. He'd popped a Cialis on the way so he was ready to see Alice, see Suzzane, and Zoria because she always put on an erotic show.

"You and me." Zoria giggled. It was an innocent giggle coming from a not so innocent hoe. "You said you were taking me somewhere, right?" She smiled hoping that the somewhere he was taking her had clothes for sell. Antoine had become a trick like that. He'd even started driving around with a size six pair of Air Max's , in his trunk, for the gutter whores that he messed with.

"No doubt, we gon do somethin wild today." He assured her while walking back to his truck. He looked at the thickness of her thighs as he lifted her into the passenger's seat. They fell from beneath her short cut Coogie dress exposing the holy grail of womanhood, and he'd drunk from that chalice a few times.

"So where are we going?" Zoria asked, hoping that their trip would be as fruitful for her as their last one. She'd came out with the very Jimmy Choo's that she was wearing the last time Antoine had taken her shopping.

"We gon get to the mall or something, but we gotta do what I wanna do first." He answered her bluntly. They had that type of relationship. It was sort of pay as you go, and Antoine didn't mind paying her. He was a baller and would ball out on a bitch at any given time. They pulled to one of his rental properties and Zoria laughed.

"This is where the magic is s'pose to happen?" She asked rudely. She like money as much as Italian's like cannoli's and Mexican's loved guacamole, but she wasn't down with fucking in crack spots.

"It's cool, trust me." He said with a chuckle and parked up on the grass close to the house. Although Antoine had grown arrogant with his paper, he hadn't gotten foolish. He knew that he'd come out on bricks or straight pancaked if he left his truck to far from the house. He was in the hood and hood niggaz tested everyone. Like Peter told Paul, "Hood niggaz try 'em all!"

Zoria's apprehension eased when she walked into the house. It was plush inside. Nice tile and carpet spread throughout the floor and there was a stripper's pole in the middle of the living room. She dropped her purse and playfully swung from the pole like she didn't have any experience. Antoine knew better though. He looked over to her and smiled.

"Let me see what's really up, boo?" He said and popped a suitcase that was laying on the floor in front of him. There were stacks of bills lining it and Zoria's eyes damn near flew from her head. "You're serious?" She said posing it as a question and he nodded. "We gon have a good time then I'mma send you outta here with this li'l bread." He chuckled and crossed his heart because everything that he'd told her was the gospel. He hit the play button on remote and the music came on. "I'm, just a bachelor...." Genuine's My Pony played and Zoria took off. Her swing had suddenly become professional as she gyrated, rolled, and wiggled right out of all of her clothes and underwear. Antoine just sat back intently watching while his devious mind played what he was doing out like a chess game. Zoria lay of the floor cupping and sucking one of her perky tits, while making her thighs and ass cheeks jiggle like Jell-O. Her dark body shimmered beneath the strobe light making the house seem like a strip club. Antoine started taking his clothes off while walking toward her. His erection had rose into a phallic spear and she smiled liking what she saw. "Is this for me?" Zoria sensually asked wile grabbing a hold of his piece. She shoved his dick deep into her mouth showing that she had control of her gag reflexes. It was a talent she'd picked up while she was a virgin, which was only six years ago, but seemed like ages.

"Damn!" Antoine moaned while pushing himself in and out of her mouth. This bitch's head game is the truth! He thought because Kiesha couldn't give a blow job like Zoria. Fucking Kiesha had become like a chore, especially since he had Zoria around.

Zoria watched as Antoine opened the briefcase and spread the money around. Although she had initially been impresses with the look of the paper stacks, her excitement had fizzled. The bills were all singles which turned her fifty thousand dollar dream into about five or ten. Fuck it! She thought because it was too late. She'd already started the show so the show must go on. She took her body and contorted it into a missionary position, putting her legs behind her head, and making her pussy pop outward. If I can get ten this will bring twenty! She giggled and ran her lascivious tongue across her lips. "Damn, bitch!" Antoine yelled with a chuckle of his own. There wasn't much that impressed him when it came to sex because he'd pounded plenty of different types, but what Zoria had just done was sexually moving. He pushed his throbbing manhood into her. Ahh shit! He breathed heavily after feeling her wetness.

"Ooooooh! Yeh…es…yes!" Zoria panted while Antoine rolled pounding deer into her lining. She was dripping wet. This was something she'd always desired, but had never gotten from her man. She'd been around

233

money, so Antoine having bread was just a bonus to go along with his good dick.

They rolled around the floor thirty more minutes riding and grinding against one another's naked anatomy. This was more intense than their last session. Antoine rolled onto his back breathing hard and Zoria lay on her stomach with her ass still quivering form the orgasm that she gotten. Dollar bills were stuck to both of their bodies. Antoine reached over and pulled one from between Zoria's glazed butt cheeks.

"We gotta pack this bread back up." He chuckled.

"Boy, don't play with me." She gave him the evil eye. "I'ont play about my money, brah." She thought while waiting for a smile or indication that he wasn't trying to play her. She'd already heard how he'd short changed Wheat so there was no telling with Antoine. He was gritty and that' the kind of shit that gritty niggaz did.

"Nah, baby!" He laughed knowing that she was going to get the shock of her life. "I said you was leaving outta here with the bread, mami. I didn't say it was yours." Antoine saw the loathsome look spread across Zoria's face. He'd said it plain, but she'd heard what she wanted to hear. Just like a bucket head ass bitch! He laughed not caring that she was upset. He'd spent more than enough money on her, and now it was his turn to use her. "Bitch, you on my time now." Antoine said calmly. "So shut the fuck up." He jumped up. His naked body glistening while the sweat, that their sex had cause, air dried. He scraped the bills off the floor in hand fulls while Zoria watched. She was shocked. This dirty ass nigga! She thought. She couldn't believe he'd played her over something that she would have done for free. She shook her head sadistically. Hell nah, nigga! She was too cutter for this and wouldn't be letting it go unchecked.

"I was gon leave my nigga for you!" She jumped up and scrambled for her clothes slamming her legs into her thongs and angrily pulling her dress over her head.

"I'm yo nigga now and you…" he chuckled, "hoe, you my bitch!" She kicked the briefcase, that he'd just put the money back into, across the floor and Antoine rushed over to her standing centimeters from her face. "Try some dumb shit again bitch." He laughed and walked into the back room. When he came out he was carrying a video disc.

Zoria look as Antoine walked from the back of the house carrying a disc. Ah! Hell nah! She thought. I know he ain't get me like that! She hoped that Antoine hadn't stopped as low as he had.

"No, Antoine!" She pleaded knowing that he'd taped what they'd just done. I let this nigga shoot cum in my mouth. She was ready to cry, but she couldn't. She'd been through too much. The streets had prepared her for some bullshit like this.

"What I gotta do?" She asked knowing that Antoine had some demands before he turned the tape over to her. His smile let her know that it had something to do with Wheat and the Brick City Crew. She'd heard all about their beef, and what Antoine had done to Quake a few nights ago, so whatever she'd have to do would be done as a component of war because the battle field had been laid.

Wheat walked in and slammed the door. He'd just left from seeing Fox and came out ten grand heavier. Fox was a diplomat. He'd assured Wheat that he'd be getting his money before the week was out and to trump it, he'd given him an additional ten. It had been two years, but the wait was worth it, not to mention Fox had enough gun power to tell him to charge it to the game.

"What's up?" Wheat asked while looking around the room. There were about six goons from the Brick city hustlers laying around, including Quake. Quake just nodded because his mouth was still battered from Antoine pushing the four nickel down his throat. Wheat looked over to him not having any sympathy because he'd asked Quake to stay away from his business, but Wheat was his uncle. Quake had always known Wheat was push over because he himself had taken him for a ride before, but he was family and family could get away with things that the streets couldn't. Quake didn't want to let what Antoine had done ride because it was bad for the hustle. "Y'all gon bounce and let me holler at my people." Wheat demanded and all of the left the house. Wheat was like the godfather of their clique, although, he really wasn't affiliated. It was just a respect for the nigga at the top of the food chain. As the crew was leaving Erk was

236

walking in, he had a deranged look on his face. He was carrying a small briefcase that he tossed on the floor. Wheat looked over to him curiously. "What's pullin yo balls, nigga?" Wheat asked. "Ya boy, unk!" Erk threw a disc over to Wheat and told him to pop it into the DVD player.

Wheat put the disc in and his eyes got wide. Dayuuum! He thought, although he wouldn't say it aloud because he knew how Erk felt about Zoria. They'd been together since Erk was a youngster. This young bitch still a freak. And Wheat knew because he had fucked her too, but Erk was to blind to notice what he was working with.

"Damn , nephew!" Wheat said acting shocked although he wasn't. He watched as Antoine shoved pip down her throat and pounded her out on the ten grand. Wheat was sure that Antoine was trying to send a message to him, but he didn't give a fuck as long as he'd gotten his money.

"I'mma coon 'em, unk!" Erk spat out viciously. He'd played the back field while his uncle's beef with Antoine was building. Fox had always been cool with him, but Antoine had crossed the line. It's on! He thought evilly. His blood boiled with rage.

"Nah, nephew." Wheat looked over to Quake who seemed to be enthralled by Zoria's sex video. He snapped his fingers getting his attention because he wanted both of them to hear him.

"Leave it alone." Wheat demanded. "Sometimes you can't win." He meant what he'd said about not being able to win because he knew who Fox's plug was and their organization was more treacherous than Carmillia's cartel, the broad who he'd been connected with for years.

Erk nodded. He loved his uncle and respected what he'd done for him after his mother had passed, but what Antoine had done was over the line. *I'm killin that nigga!* He thought before getting up and walking out on Wheat and Quake. It was a full blown war that he'd been dragged into and had to end himself. *Unk's a hoe, but young Erk ain't havin it!* He jumped into his whip and peeled out.

****

Egypt paced the floor of her living room pissed at herself. *I feel so stupid!* She thought. She was in shambles and couldn't believe she'd been so careless. She didn't expect to get into a situation that she couldn't get out of, especially knowing what type of life style Fox was living. He could bounce out on her at any given moment leaving her stuck with a child, because she was almost positive that she was pregnant. *I know he loves me, but Fox ain't ready for this shit!* She nervously looked at the pregnancy test that lay on the cocktail table. She'd taken it about fifteen minute ago, but was terrified of looking at the results because she already knew what they were. *Ain't this about a bitch!* She saw the two stripes across the indicator letting her know that she was definitely pregnant. She rocked and stared at the test wishing the results would change. She jumped up and rushed to the window after hearing a car pulling up in the driveway. It was Fox.

Fox walked in with a solemn look on his face. He had already cleared things up with Wheat, so he decided to let Egypt know about LaTicia before she found out from someone else. Fuck it! He thought as Egypt walked toward him. She too had a sad look on her face like she already knew or something. I hope that hoe ain't snitched on a nigga.

"E, I need to talk to you." Fox said and sat on the couch. Egypt sat next to him knowing that something was wrong. It was a tell in Fox's eyes.

"What's wrong, baby?" Egypt asked ready to put what she had to tell him aside. He was her man and she loved him, so she was willing to put her shit on pause and let him vent.

Fox could hear the concern in her voice so he quickly tried to ease it.

"Nah, baby. Don't be scared it's cool." Fox slid closer to her and put his arm around her shoulder. This was his boo and he wanted to comfort her and shield her even if it was from him and that she needed to be protected.

239

"I…" Fox paused. "I think it's time for me to clean out my closet, ma."

Egypt snatched away from him. She was cautious and wasn't sure if she was ready to hear what he had to tell her.

"What's in your closet, Fox?" She rolled her neck sassily. "Huh, I hope you're not fixed to tell me you're gay or some bullshit like that!" She pursed her lips waiting on his answer. "Hell nah!" What's wrong with these hoes attacking a niggaz manhood! He thought. "I'm all muhfuckin man! That ain't a issue, but I should've been a better man, E."

"Who is she?" Egypt asked not wasting any time because she knew there had to be another woman involved. "Better yet! Does the bitch know about me?" Her eyes became beet red with anger. Either way Fox answered would be wrong.

"Yeah, she knows about you."

"So what's up?" She grunted. " I know you didn't decide to air your bullshit out on the strength, so what is it?" She stared at him judgingly and Fox dropped his head. He was disappointed in himself.

"She's pregnant." Fox said it. It was hard, but it had finally came out. Egypt leaped off the couch. She was infuriated.

"Hell nah, brah!" Her face was contorted into a hateful grimace. "You mean to tell me that you've been having unprotected sex with those road kills out there in the streets? Fox, you have to be bullshitting me?" Nigga, you better laugh right now! She thought while Fox was shaking his head.

"Nah, E!" It ain't even like that." Fox combated and Egypt wildly threw her hands into the air.

"What then, nigga? The bitch had Immaculate Conception or some shit like that? Because last time I checked monoxinal killed sperm, nigga!"

Fox decided to let it all out. He'd had enough of the arguing. Fuck it! Here we go. He thought.

"I fucked up, Egypt. Ticia is pregnant and I might be the father." He shook his head. "And before you ask, nah she ain't willing to have a abortion."

Tears rose into Egypt's eyes falling across her cheeks. She walked off with her head hung low. She was hurt and wanted to hurt Fox back. She grabbed a fresh pregnancy test and drug herself back into the living room where Fox was. It's gon be a lot of tears around this bitch, pops! She thought while taking off her jeans and panties. Egypt slid the test strip between her legs and pissed on it.

"Looks like we're both pregnant, but I am having an abortion." Egypt tossed the urine soaked testing strip onto Fox's lap and rushed off hurt about what he'd done.

241

"E?" Fox called after and she stopped rushing back over to him.

"Get the fuck out!" She screamed into his face before switching off. Fox left without protest. And Egypt curled into a fetal position until she fell asleep.

****

Rone tried to calm Fox down.

"Alright, brah. I'll see you once you get here." Rone ended the call and put his phone back into his pocket. Sherry snuck up behind him.

"Who was that, baby?" She asked nosily.

"Fox, he's on his way over here." Ron chuckled.

"Is everything okay?"

"I'ont know. I think him and Egypt are having some problems."

"About that home wrecking ass bitch Laticia, huh?"

Rone Laughed. "Yeah, and Egypt is pregnant too."

"Are you serious?"

"Square business. I'ont know the details, but once I find out I'll tell your nosy ass." Rone teased and Sherry playfully punched his arm.

"Shut up, chump." She laughed. "But I do wanna know." She snickered while walking away.

Although they had discussed their problems, Rone was still aware of Sherry's suspicions about his and LaTicia's friendship, especially after the way she'd just questioned him. He shook his head with disbelief after getting out of the shower. I can't believe this broad. He thought with a laugh. A nigga been evading prison for two decades, but being with her for the last few weeks been like OZ. He heard Sherry calling so he walked out into the room.

"What's up cheeks?" He hoped she wasn't going to start bombarding him with questions again.

"Fox is on the patio waiting on you."

"Alright. Let me get my shit together and I'll be out there." Rone continued getting dressed and Sherry walked back out to the patio. Once Rone finished they all kicked it on the patio for a while before him and Fox left.

Fox laughed while him and Rone were being seated. Him and Rone had a restaurant rivalry going on that Rone usually won.

"Carl's is cool, but I'm telling you, brah." Fox said while chuckling and nodding his head. "I know this little steak joking on the east side called Caper's that's rough."

"Nigga, I done ate at the coldest restaurants in the country, but Carl's got the steak game on lock." A waitress walked up to their table flashing a pristine smile.

"My name is Alex." She looked from Fox to Rone. "May I take your order or do you need more time?" She spoke with a subtle French accent, and her body was off the hook. She didn't have typical white girl build. She was thick at the bottom and light at the top like a sister.

"Nah!" Rone snapped at her nastily and gave her a shooing hand gesture while staring into his menu. Alex leaned in pretending to place something on the table. He heavily glossed lips were close to Rone's check.

"You're an asshole." She whispered. "Now order, punk." Rone and Fox burst into laughter. They placed their orders and Fox told Rone about what had happened between him and Egypt while they waited. Fox watched as Rone's expression changed.

"What's up, big brah?" Fox asked. "You cool?"

Rone rubbed his goatee. "Yeah. I was just thinking about some things."

"This me and you, brah. Spill game you know you can talk." He was interested to know what was bothering Rone.

"I've been holding something back from you for a while, but I think you're ready to hear it now."

"Ah'ight. What up doe?" Fox leaned backward into his chair.

"I know you've probably never thought about this, but didn't you find it strange that Tee's pops disappeared around the same time that Fredo got smoked?"

Fox shook his head. "Nah, not really."

"Damn, my nigga. I'mma just come on out with it. Diamond killed your old man, so I laid 'em down." Rone had dropped a bomb on Fox. He casually downed the champagne that was in his glass and leaned back waiting for Fox's response. Unlike him, Fox was an emotional type of nigga. Rone had warned him about wearing his feelings on his sleeve, but there was only so far good game could take a person.

"What?" Fox asked knowing that he'd heard him wrong. He'd been through all kinds of shit and now Rone was dropping this on him. *I know this nigga ain't tryna amp a nigga!* Fox thought hoping he was wrong.

"The nigga Tee." Rone nodded and downed Fox's champagne too. "He's your brother, young trap."

"What's up, dawg? You high or something?" Fox was getting loud. "You on some grime ball shit, nigga?"

"Tee's mom, your mom. Sherry and me were the only ones who knew until now. Why do you think we've always had Tee's back? Even after all the dumb shit he does?"

Fox was shocked he looked at Rone with disbelief, although, he believed every word that he'd said. This shit is fucked up! He thought about what Antoine would say once he found out.

"So Tee don't know either, huh?" Fox asked and Rone shook his head.

"Nah, but he will today because we're going to get him so you can tell him."

The waitress with the accent came back to their table carrying their food. She smiled at Fox and rolled her eyes at Rone. Fox looked from Rone to her and back to Rone. Brah fuckin the white bitch! He thought while watching her twist her wide ass when she walked away.

"You hit that, huh? Fox asked and Rone chuckled.

"Hell nah!" Rone shook his head defiantly while denying what Fox had assumed. "I ain't you, nigga. I'ont be fucking these hoes in the city. If you would've listened, you wouldn't be in the situation you're in now." He laughed while teasing Fox about his baby momma drama.

"Sheeit!" Rone continued. "You're sleep, pimp. Ticia is gonna be drama." He nodded assuring his guy that he was telling the truth.

Fox laughed, but he knew that Rone was telling the truth. He was sure that LaTicia was going to be drama, but he was more concerned about the shit that he'd just learned about. Tee is my brother? He thought because it just wouldn't register to him. He started asking Rone questions because he wanted to make sure Rone knew the real about the beef between Alfredo and Diamond.

Rone explained what had taken place in detail while Fox listened closely. Fox's mouth hung open while hearing about what had really taken place when his father was murdered. After Antoine mother told Alfredo about Antoine being his son, Alfredo gave her an ultimatum. He told her that she could tell Diamond about Antoine or he'd do it. After Diamond found out about Alfredo knocking his broad off, he couldn't accept it. He stumbled upon Alfredo slippin on a humble.

Alfredo was sitting inside of his car waiting on Rone when Diamond took advantage of a grand opportunity. Diamond jumped into the passenger's seat and blew the top of Alfredo's head through the driver's side window. Rone was pulling into the parking lot as the gunshot exploded. He sped in and saw Diamond leap from the car into a full sprint. He could have ran Diamond down, but he drove off in the opposite direction.

Rone explained exactly what had led up to Fox's father's death. Fox was stunned and Rone assured him that he wanted to blaze Diamond at the scene leaving them both there stinking, but he was afraid of being seen and mistaken as the man who had killed Alfredo too.

After detailing the murders, Rone told Fox why they had kept the situation a secret from him until now. Everyone knew that fox had a lot of resentment behind his father's murder, and Rone assured Fox that if they would have told him back then, he wouldn't be the man he is today. They finished dinner and left to pick up Antoine.

The drive was awkward and silent. Fox was nervous about telling Antoine what he'd found out. He knew how much Antoine loved Diamond. That was the man who had raised him. And my niggga thought he was gon see Diamond again. Fox was thinking more about how Antoine would feel about the situation than himself because he'd let it go years ago. Rone tapped his arm when he pulled off the expressway.

"Take Conners, young trap." Rone said. He wanted to check into something that had came by him recently. Playblo, his mans that he'd let go of before bringing Fox into his fold, supposedly popped back up. Niggaz had it rumored that he'd been doing hand to hands on the east side and Rone wanted to see it firsthand. He planned to go check it out by himself, but since he was in the area he decided to blow through.

248

"Ah'ight." Fox nodded and turned down Conners. He was familiar with the area because he'd lived over that way when he was a youngster. He looked at the old dilapidated buildings one of them was a pool hall that he'd worked pushing syringes.

"Right here." Rone pointed. "Make a right."

"This was my hood back in the day." Fox said and Rone laughed.

"What, nigga? Back in the day? Muhfucka, you just came off the porch!" He laughed teasing Fox. He suddenly held his hand up.

"Aye, aye! Pull over, brah!" Rone was frantic. Something had happened and Fox looked over to him wanting to know what.

"What up, nigga?" Fox asked because Rone was acting weird. He'd just dropped a bomb on him earlier and know he was stalking some nigga a short ways down the street that they'd turned onto.

"You see that nigga standing over there?" Rone said pointing to a short slim guy standing near a city dumpster.

"Yeah, I see 'em. He's the only nigga out there." Fox scanned the street to make sure.

"That's him!"

"That's him who, nigga?" He never seen Rone so anxious.

"Remember when I told you my mans wasn't my mans no more." Rone said while watching Playblo's every motion. He was his prey. "Yeah, my nigga. That's him." Rone nodded. "You got them rockers?"

"No question!" Fox popped his stash spot and came out with two pistols. He kept one and tossed the other onto Rone's lap.

"Make a u-turn and park a couple of blocks over." Rone said. He told Fox what they were going to do while they were finding somewhere safe to park his car. Fox was all in. After getting a couple blocks over, they jumped out of the car and walked back to where Playblo was. Rone dipped through the alley and Fox walked down the very block that Playblo was slumping his product on.

Fox's blood boiled as he got closer to Playblo. He watched as he slapped fives with a fiend passing him a couple of stones. Nigga wanna play with fam'ly! He didn't know what had transpired between Playblo and Rone, but he stood on one side whether it was wrong or right. Fox thought about all the shit that was going wrong in his life and he wanted to take it out on someone.

"Whack!" Fox slapped his across the head with his iron causing blood to spurt from his forehead. "Bap!" He slugged him with a straight right hand. "Bitch ass nigga! Jump yo hoe ass in the garbage can!" Fox lifted the lid and Playblo quickly obeyed. He pushed the can to the alley in back of the house where he met up with Rone.

Rone crawled out of a doghouse covered in blood. The dog had been barking signaling the neighbors so he had to slit it's throat. Fido had been doing his job and fell victim as a casualty of war. Rone jumped the gate while his eyes peered around the vicinity. He raised the lid on the can and Playblo's face fell flushed.

"Please, Ron man!" Playblo screamed pleading for his life, but it fell on deaf ears.

"Whack!" Rone slapped him across the gushing forehead gash that Fox had opened up. Blood squirted out. "Please what, hoe ass nigga!"

"Shut the fuck up!" Fox spat through clinched teeth knowing that someone could probably hear Playblo's cries. "Click…Clack!" He cocked his biscuit grinding the steel together, and Playblo burst into a sniffling cry. Tears rose and fell from his eyes and he knew that his death was imminent when Rone gave Fox a head gesture to slug him. Fox pointed the roscoe, putting it close to Playblo's head, but a gunshot didn't follow. Rone gave Fox and angry glance and slapped his burner away from Playblo's head. Rone swung his pistol in.

"Blocca…Blocca!"

Rone planted two slugs deep into the center of Playblo's forehead putting him in his final resting place. Him and Fox ran off into separate direction and met back up at Fox's car. They jumped in and tucked the pistols away before cautiously driving off. They didn't want to bring any attention to themselves. Fox looked over to Rone.

"Where you wanna go?" Fox asked, knowing that he didn't want to stop at Antoine's house who only lived a mile or so away from what they'd done.

"Over Tee's house, scary ass nigga!" Rone sounded upset and Fox became offended.

"What?" Fox asked knowing that Rone didn't just question his gangster. I know this nigga ain't tryna smash down on a nigga! He thought because that was a carnal sin between hustlers. "Ain't shit scary 'bout me, nigga!"

"Why you freeze up on me, nigga?" Rone asked uncertain about Fox's street credibility. Maybe this niggaz a fraud? Rone wondered about the shit that he'd heard about Fox. Sometimes the hood would boast of a nigga being a monster until he was exposed as a sucker.

"Freeze up?!!" Fox shook his head letting Rone know that he was mistaken. He wanted to steal on his guy, but he knew that would cause some problems that he didn't want.

"I ain't freeze up, brah!" Fox was adamant. "The thumper jammed! Fuck's wrong with you, nigga?" Fox drove into Antoine's driveway and dropped his stash box. He took the burner that he'd carried out of the box and threw it onto Rone's lap.

"Check it out, muhfucka!" Fox was fuming and wanted to bring some drama to Rone about respect. Of course, he appreciated everything that Rone had done for him, but he'd muscled the street into letting him eat and a sucker's reputation wouldn't have gotten him to where he was, even if he had a major connect. That's how the streets of Detroit were, if you weren't willing to kill, you couldn't eat.

Rone picked the pistol up noticing that there was a bullet trapped between the chamber and the barrel. He pulled the chamber back and the bullet jumped out. He picked the bullet up seeing that it had dents on both sides of the casing, and he shrugged his shoulders.

"My bad, nigga." Rone apologized. "I thought you froze up." He was real like that. If he'd made the wrong move he'd try to correct it, even if it meant admitting it and that was rare in a game where everyone wanted to be right.

"You ain't the only nigga gotta carry gangstah shit to the grave, brah." Fox said implying that he'd laid a couple of bodies down along the way.

"Yeah, I hear you." Rone tucked the pistol underneath his shirt.

"What up doe, gangstahs?" Antoine asked knowing that they were coming to check him about what he'd done to Erk's bitch Zoria. I told my guy I was gonna pay the nigga. He thought and chuckled.

"Shit." Fox replied and jumped out of the car embracing his brother. Rone tucked the pistols back into the compartment and got out of the car. Him and Antoine had made amends.

"Tee money! What's up, baby?" Rone and Antoine gave each other dap. There was no love so an embrace wasn't necessary for neither of them, instead they just kept it cordial when they were around one another. Rone still had his back on the strength of Alfredo being his father, but that was the extent of it— respect for his bloodline alone.

"I need to use your garage." Fox said to Antoine. He tone was pressing so Antoine didn't hesitate.

"Ah'ight" gangstah. Let me pull the Range out." Antoine walked into the backyard and pulled his truck out of his garage. He was sure that Fox would tell him what was going on later, therefore, he didn't bother to ask. He was just glad that they hadn't came to his crib to talk shit about the moves that he was making. He'd initiated the beef with Wheat by himself and if it escalated he'd end it by himself. Fox drove his Q45 Infinity into the garage and all three of them went into Antoine's pad. Rone looked around the spot with envy.

"Damn, my nigga!" Rone blurted. "You must have a maid around this bitch!" He saw how on point Antoine's house was.

Antoine laughed. "Yeah, something like that. I knocked a fat butt bitch off that works at the Double Tree, baby. She been coming through lookin out." He grabbed his nuts cockily. "Feel me?"

Fox shook his head. This nigga gon get enough of letting these guttah ass bitches slide through the spot like that. He thought after hearing Antoine brag about the housekeeping broad that he was letting clean his crib.

"Kiesha gon smoke yo silly ass nigga!" Fox joked and they all laughed. Antoine nodded strangely agreeing with him.

"I'll die happy though, baby!" Antoine walked behind the bar and grabbed a bottle of Remy Martin. He'd had the bar and the small kitchen built to entertain.

While Antoine was pouring them drinks Fox sat slouched deep in the couch thinking about the reckless murder that Rone had just committed. He wondered why taking Playblo's life was so pressing. That shit could've been done better. He thought knowing that Rone was smoother than what he'd portrayed earlier. He thought about when he'd knocked Que's brains out of his head with a single shot from his .40 caliber. How his eyes stood still and the blood poured from his head in a slow seep. Before his death he'd apologized for his betrayal, so in truth Fox had sent him to his quintessence pure.

255

"Fox?" Antoine pushed a glass over to him then slid on to Rone. "Y'all niggas quiet and shit! What's up?" He wanted to kick it. It wasn't often that Rone slid though his house, so he wanted to gloat a little letting Rone know that he too had made it.

"I got something to tell you, Tee." Fox said knowing that Antoine was going to blow his top. Damn! He thought. This nigga fixin to trip!

"What up?" Antoine asked looking from Fox to Rone and back over to Fox. The nigga Wheat must've put a dollar sign on my head? He wondered. Don't come spookin a nigga and shit." He downed the triple shot that he'd poured himself.

Rone looked over to Fox becoming impatient with his drag. He was ready to skip out to the strip club and watch some ass bounce up and down in his face. HE took his triple shot to the face downing it with on gulp. Fuck it! He thought and rubbed his goatee.

"Tee? You and the nigga Fox are brothers." Rone said flatly. HE didn't try to sugar coat it or dress it up. HE just dropped the truth into Antoine's lap just as he'd done to Fox. He reached over and grabbed Fox's drink downing his too.

"Oh, so y'all finally told him, huh?" Antoine asked causing Fox's head to whip in his direction.

"Ah, hell na!" Fox complained. "You knew too?"

Antoine chuckled while nodding his head. "Yeah, I knew every since I got outta the county."

Rone looked over to Antoine confused. That scandalous ass hoe! He thought knowing that Antoine's mother had spilled the beans to her son. She'd begged Rone not to say anything to either of them only to put it out there herself.

"Who told you and why didn't you tell Fox?" Rone asked wonderin what his excuse was for holding out on his boy.

"Mom dukes told me and she told me not to say shit because it would be best if he heard it from y'all." Antoine gave Rone a judging look before continuing. "She told me about a lot of shit when she got outta rehab."

"Fuck it! I'm glad it's out." Rone poured another shot and downed it.

"What's up with Chocolate City?" He was ready to toss it up.

"I ain't never turned down an invitation to see stripper bitches with cigarette burns on their ass cheeks" Antoine laughed and looked over to Fox.

"Aye, my nigga?" Antoine wanted to lighten the mood. "You may be the last nigga to know, but it's out. Sheeit! We been like brothers our whole life anyway, so now it's official."

Rone poured himself another shot and looked over to Fox chuckling.

"Muthafucka," Rone teased, "it ain't like you gonna get fucked and sucked at the crib tonight, so you better come on and fuck with these bitches at the little shop of whores." They all laughed, even Fox. "Fuck it!" Fox bounced up out his seat and laughed. "Let's get it crackin. And nigga stop drinking my shit!"

"That's what the fuck I'm talking about." Rone said and pushed back another shot. By then he was juiced and ready to go hard. All three of them left out jumping into Antoine's truck and sliding through Chocolate City.

CHAPTER 9

Egypt sashayed into the living room and nestled against Fox as he lay on the sofa. She'd been ignoring him for nearly two weeks and knew that it was wearing on him. She was pissed at him, but she didn't want to push her man too far away where she couldn't reel him back in. She rubbed his chest.

"Baby, I'm not mad at you anymore." She smiled and kissed the part of his check that she'd just ran her palm across.

"I know, but I'm still upset with my damn self." Fox didn't want to have children in two different homes. He thought about what had happened with his father and Diamond over Antoine.

"You don't have to be. Egypt tried to act like it wasn't still bothering her as well. She'd heard about Fox and Antoine being brothers and knew that her man was going through a lot.

"I almost lost you, E. I still have to deal with what I did, you feel me?"

"No you don't." Egypt smiled and rubbed her barely swollen stomach. "I love you and our baby."

"I used to think money would solve a nigga's problems. I would wake up thinking about a couple dollars and wouldn't go to sleep until I had it, but shit changed. I got it, and then I realized it wasn't shit if you ain't got nobody to share it with. I realized that after I almost lost you." He put his hand on top of hers that rested on her stomach. He was smashing game on her and she was loving it. He knew that he had Egypt on lock. She was his woman and would be until he decided different.

Egypt leaned in and kissed his forehead. The kiss said that she'd really forgiven him and believed in him. I love this nigga. She thought while staring at his hand rubbing hers. She knew what it was when she started seeing Fox. All hustlers cheated, but she thought he was smart enough to protect himself against females like LaTicia. What does that bitch have on me? She questioned herself, although, she was certain that the answer didn't have shit to do with her. The most sexually skillful woman couldn't make a man commit if he wasn't willing to.

Egypt was raised by a hustler and knew that the only thing that could tame a man was life. Fox had to learn from his experience. Tragedies had changed the direction of her life and she hoped that the situation that Fox was in with LaTicia would make him think about changing his.

Fox looked over to Egypt noticing the calm in her eyes. This is what I do! He thought knowing that he'd touched her with his words. He rubbed her thick chocolate thigh bringing her out of her haze.

"What's up, ma? Whatchu thinking about?"

"About us. I wonder how these kids are going to affect our life styles, you know?"

Fox chuckled. He thought about something that Rone had said to him a few days ago.

"Yeah, me and Rone were poppin it about that type of shit the other day." He shook his head still giggling about their talk.

"About it how?" Egypt asked curiously. She knew how Rone could get philosophical about the most trivial shit so she wanted to know what he'd said.

"He was basically tellin me to get some education. You know how the nigga is." Fox waved it off because he didn't want to get into it with Egypt.

"Yes I do know how he is." She laughed knowing that Rone could be overbearing sometimes, especially when he thought he was right about something.

"He got to really tripin though." Fox nodded and Egypt got confused.

"How?" She asked wanting to know why was Fox was trying to withhold what Rone had said form her. She was getting nervous and hoped it wan't anything bad.

"E was talking about niggaz who be getting money hustling and shit s'psose to stop they grind while their bitch is pregnant. Talkin about street niggaz get took out the game when their hoe's are pregnant." Egypt's face turned up. She looked afraid about what Fox had said.

261

"What?"

"The nigga told me to fall back for the first five years of the baby's life 'cause a niggaz usually blazed out or locked up before or soon after the seed drop."

Egypt was flaming. How could he say some bullshit like that?! She thought and wonder why Fox would actually sit around and listen to that shit.

"Where in the fuck does he get that shit from? I hate when he says shit like that!" She knew that Fox was trying to keep something from her, but she would have never figured. Why would he wish some hoe shit like that on my man? She wondered and Fox chuckled as if he wasn't bother by what Rone had told him.

"You know that nigga just talkin shit tryna get me back in school. Feel me" Fox laughed. "Don't even trip."

Egypt shook her head in disagreement with Fox. She'd been around Rone almost her whole life and she knew that he peeped a lot of things out. Things that other people didn't see. She knew about Rone's childhood and his life, and his experience is what gave him and edge on life.

"No, Fox!" Egypt was serious about what she was telling Fox. "I'm telling you. That nigga has a gift or something! He knows shit." She nodded and Fox laughed shaking his head.

"Yeah, brah brah is the truth, but…." He shook his head, "that on is a hustlers folktale!" He tried to convince Egypt further, but she wasn't buying what he was selling. HE finally gave up and sprawled around the bed feeling defeated. He started thinking about the four gets and it was time for him to get out before he got killed.

It was time for Fox to make his transition. He'd stacked his paper to the ceiling so money problems wan't one of his. Furthermore, he knew a couple of cats who had smoked their last blunt before seeing their child born. There was always a flip side to the game and Fox wasn't trying to let it become his fate. He would break away before he became a statistic.

"Ooooh, shit! I miss this dick…..oh!" Kiesha whined erotically pushing her voluptuous ass back meeting Jackson's pipe. He pounded her with hard and long strokes testosterone.

Jackson gripped her waist while savagely thrusting into Kiesha from the back.

"Bitch! Who's' pussy is dis?" Saliva flew from Jackson's mouth.

Keisha panted nastily replying, "It's yours. It always has been and always will be." She pushed back against him and Jackson slowed his rhythm into a sensual grind.

263

He continued his stiff slow thrust causing Kiesha to cry earthly moans.

"Oh!" She yelped when he sped up pushing his thick pole deeper into her wet pulsating pussy. "Ah…aaah.ah! Puh…leez!" She begged with passion.

"Ahhshit!" Jackson bust an explosion of cum inside of her and fell back onto Antoine's bed. It was the deceit that made the sex between him and Kiesha so good. Kiesha submissively nestled against Jackson putting her hand on his chest.

Kiesha lay nest to Jackson confused. After she'd gotten pregnant by him, she swore to herself that she wouldn't be gullible enough to fall into the same situation, but she had. She'd allowed Jackson to take off the condom earlier because she was already pregnant, so the damage was done. She rubbed Jackson's chest and smile weakly.

"Baby, I have something to tell you."

"What's up, shawty?"

"I'm pregnant." She said bluntly. She didn't want to get into the theatrics with Jackson like she'd done last time so she just kept it simple.

"I'mma tell him and I'll have an abortion." She quickly promised Jackson because she didn't want to lose him again. They decided that they were going to be together, especially since he didn't run with Antoine and Fox anymore.

After what Fox did to Jackson, their friendship never recovered. Fox tried to reach out to him, but Jackson said, "fuck it", and let go because he knew that he'd always be an outsider to them.

"Nah, shawty!" Jackson chuckled. "We havin it! Fuck Tee. Dis our life." He assured her that he didn't give a fuck about Antoine or what he thought. You my hoe! He thought while slipping his pants on. He couldn't lounge around another man's house all day.

Kiesha was thrown off by Jackson's maturity. She was positive that he was going to flip out her like he'd done when she told him about Jah'lil. I just wish this one was his too. She thought knowing that she was pregnant by Antoine. Her was a love triangle that didn't start with love at ll. Kiesha prided herself in being a second generation sack chaser. She lived to use niggaz for money and Antoine wasn't an exception to that. Jackson, on the other hand, she loved which confused her. She'd became accustomed to being spoiled by a baller. Antoine gave her whatever she desired, but Jackson had her heart. It was a battle, but her heart had won. She was going to be with Jackson.

Fox walked out of the barber shop laughing. He'd just knocked off a red bone with an ass like a mule. She had green eyes and some titties made for a stippers body.

265

Ordinarily he'd listen to Rone's theory about local pussy, but this hoe was exceptional and he was sure that no straight man could walk away for her. I'm fucking the shit outta girlly tonight! He thought and laughed while crossing the street to his Chevy.

Fox didn't like riding around in his old school whips. They were his show cars, but he'd sent the Infinity off and had to drive something until he went to the lost. Who the fuck it that? He saw someone sittin on the trunk of his car. He'd spent a mint gettin the paint on his Classic right, so what homeboy was doing would be costin him and ass whipping.

"Aye, brah!" Fox called out while jogging across the street. He was ready to pull his biscuit out and let something hot fly through the air. This nigga must be outta his shit!

"Aye brah?" Fox repeated after gettin closer and the nigga sittin on his Caprice turned around. It was Quake. He smiled showing Fox his missing grill. It looked like he'd been eating bricks because his front teeth were gone and the rest were chipped up.

"S'up, Fox?" Quake slid off the hood still flashing his beat up grill.

Fox slowed his stride looking around as he approached his whip. I know this nigga don't wanna do this! Fox thought knowing that he had seventeen shots lining the waist of his jeans.

"Brah, get the fuck up off my slab!" Fox demanded still keeping his distance and letting his eyes roam the streets. He saw Zoria's mustang parked across the street near a conney island restaurant. Erk was inside waitin on Fox to make his move. These niggaz for real! Fox stopped and back pedaled into the middle of the street. He had a choice—he could pull his strap and mail slugs through the streets, or run back into the barbershop. HE saw Erk getting out of the Mustang brandishing a Calico.

"Bwah...bwah bwah….bwah!"

Fox upped his strap and sent two slugs whistling through Quake's chest while running over to his Chevy. When Quake fell, Fox sent two more shots into Erk's direction and Erk responded.

"Blah..tah..tah..tah!"

Erk's automatic let off the sound of war while firing at Fox. He'd seen Fox lay his cousin down with tow chest shots. I'm killin this bitch ass nigga! Erk thought while sprinting across the busy street dodging fox's gun fire.

"Bwah…bwah bwah!"

Fox slung three more shots at Erk and jumped into the Caprice Classic letting his big block 454 howl.

Blah..tah..tah..tha!"

267

Erk spit rapidly at Fox as he drove off. Sparks flew from the metal that deflected the 9mm Calico slugs.

"I'm killin you nigga!" Erk yelled after Fox's car and let off some phantom shots that were aimed into the air. He rushed back over to his cousin. Quake was breathing. He'd took two bullets, but only one was serious. He mumbled something and coughed up a glob of clotted blood. He wanted to tell his cousin something, but the blood was suffocating him muffling his words. Erk got Zoria's car and put Quake in before rushing him to the hospital. Damn! He thought while speeding trying to get Quake to St. Johns trauma center. Li'l cuz can't die like this! He knew that he'd been playing in a game that he couldn't win, but he'd tried anyways starting a real war with some brothers that are heavy hitters.

****

Antoine sat on the edge of his bed seething. He'd seen the signs, but now it was undeniable. The evidence was right in front of him..There was a Magnum condom wrapper beneath his bed.

"I'mma kill this bitch! He yelled furiously. He'd been everything to her taking her to places in life that a lame ass bitch like her would have never gone without him. Now, he heard his mother's voice, "ant, are you sure that's my grand baby?" She'd asked on several occasions and he'd assured her that Jah'lil was certified. His mother had played that game and gotten caught up, but Antoine ever thought Kiesha would mess around on him. Yeah, he'd knocked off plenty broads, but in life there were double standards, especially about ballers and their hoes.

"It's cool." He laughed out loud. It was an insidious laugh. I got this hoe! He thought while nodding his head and pulled out his cell phone.

"Lexie?" Antoine said after gettin her on the phone. She was the hoe who had given him head in front of the house and cleaned every weekend. She was his project bitch who didn't want to do nothing, but fuck and was now officially in the running to take Kiesha's place.

****

Fox was heated. "Why these hoe ass niggaz wanna try me?" He shouted while reaching for his chopper. He'd rallied up and arsenal over the years and now it was time to use it. He'd given Wheat his paper and this was the thanks that he'd gotten. Hell nah! He thought vehemently. "I ain't having it!" Fox angrily said and threw a couple of pistols on the bed before sitting down. "Niggaz be getting knocked off around the time they seeds drop." He heard Rone's voice in his mind. Rone had been right about everything he'd told him concerning

269

the game. Niggaz tried to hit me! He couldn't believe a bitch like Erk had tried to pull rank on him. He'a hoe!

"I'mma kill Wheat, then I'mma kill the rest of them niggaz." He said to himself in a calm whisper. I'm burying anything got to do with Brick City!

Fox knew that Erk had put Quake up to what they'd tried because Quake wasn't smart enough to come up with getting at him on his own. Fox hated Quake over the years until he found out that Quake was slow— retarded slow and took orders from Erk. Now, he killed Quake because of Erk's ignorance and to think he thought Wheat was a real businessman. Fox looked up to Wheat while growing up. Wheat was about ten years older than Fox and kept the hood flooded with heroin back in the day. At fourteen, Fox thought Wheat was the coldest nigga in the game, next to Rone, but in truth Wheat was just a visionary with no heart. HE didn't have the muscle to support his hustle so he tried to keep some young guns around her. Erk and Quake included, but Fox was popping their corks first thinking he'd already started with Quake. HE walked to the bedroom and say Egypt laying across the bed looking evil. She looked up and saw him before he could walk back out of the room. "What up, E?" Fox asked and flashed a counterfeit smile at her. She jumped up and stared at Fox with hatred steaming from her face.

"So LaTicia's having a boy, huh Fox?" Her hands were on her spreading pregnant hips and she bounced angrily.

"Yeah." Fox answered flatly and tried to walk away, but she was right on his heels.

"I found the ultra sound on the dresser! Why didn't you tell me?" She asked hatefully because she wanted to have his first son. Fox waved her off and kept walking.

"Because I didn't!" He suddenly stopped scaring Egypt into a rigid stance. "Bitch, I'm tired of kissing your muthafucking ass and tiptoeing the crib like a broad and shit. You my hoe! I'mma do whatever the fuck I wanna do and you gon bow down."

"Kissing my ass? You should be kissing my ass! Ya lying motherfucker!" She stared at him and he laughed a sinister laugh.

"Only muhfucka Fox lying to is a muhfucka he scared of." He spoke about himself in third person while putting Egypt back into her place. "And I ain't scared of no nigga or bitch!" Now go ahead hoe! He thought while giving her a warning stare. He was already on a mission to fuck something up and, at the at point, it could have been easily started at home. Egypt smacked her lips and stepped back staring at Fox challengingly.

"You scared of Rone!" Egypt spat out taunting him. Now, bitch! She thought while keeping an eye on him in case he tried to hit her because she knew that she'd crossed the line and said something that could her ass whipped. Fuck him because an ass whipping wouldn't hurts as much as this hoe having his son is!

271

Everybody trying to test me! Fox thought and walked up on her. He wanted to at least give her a proper pimp slap sending her to the floor, but she was pregnant and losing the baby would hurt more than what she'd said to crush his ego. This bitch gon cause me to pump that eye up! He shook his head and grabbed her shoulders forcefully backing her up to the wall in the hallway.

"Hoe...." He paused while shaking his head trying to resist the temptation to smack her across the face. He'd seen Alfredo put plenty of illicit hood beatings on his mother, so he knew how to put his woman in her place because he'd inherited the game.

"Hoe, you better get somewhere before I do something to your simple ass!" Fox pushed her off toward the room. This bitch just don't know! He thought while going back into the spare bedroom and putting the pistols that he'd thrown on the bed into a duffle bag. Egypt bared in.

"I'm college educated, nigga!" She blurted sadily. "That's more tha I can about.." She stopped an looked over to the chopper that was leaning against the wall. She rushed over to him seeing him tuck the pistols into the bag.

"Where are you going, Fox" Egypt asked using her body to block him from leaving the room. "What are you doing with those gun, Fox?" She was worried. She'd forgotten what she'd been upset with him about because this was more serious. She'd never seen Fox look so deranged. While they were arguing she'd noticed how loose he was talking to her, but that's how Fox got from time to time and what'd said to him warranted is reaction.

Fox pushed her out of the way and walked past her. Not the bitch see how real this shit done got! He thought while walking toward the door with Egypt trailing behind him. Bitch better be lucky I ain't guttah enough to snatch one of these pistols outta this bag and go upside her muhfuckin head! He grunted loudly. I'm scared of Rone! And Fox meant that because the law he lived by said fear no man.

Egypt watched as Fox jumped into the bullet riddled Caprice and peeled out.

Antoine put Lexie's legs over his shoulders wile pounding her. Damn! He thought with closed eyes sliding deep into Lexie's hot pocket. This pussy wet as Sea World! Her libido was intense spurting vaginal juices down her thick thighs, and she had squirting orgasms.

Antoine meet her at the hotel where she worked. He'd been creeping off with Zoria to the hotel for weeks and Lexie had caught on to what they were doing. She gave Antoine a suggestive look while he was checking in, but Antoine played naïve sticking to what he was doing.

Dayum! He thought while smiling at Lexie. This freak is stacked up! HE admired her round rump and protruding nipples. They shot through her blouse like sun dried plums. He'd peeped her flirting the last couple of times he'd been to the Double tree, but he was on another mission. Zoria was one of the most exotic broads that he'd ever seen and he couldn't get enough of her. Although he'd part with a loaf of bread every time they met up, the money paled in comparison to the pleasure she provided. She was a freaky Scorpio who drove him crazy.

"Is it for two?" Lexie asked with a sexy tone. Ooooh! She thought while giving Antoine an inviting stare. I will fuck and suck the shit outta this nigga! She gave him a once over and her smile brightened. "I know he gota big ass dick!" She said to herself.

"Yeah." He replied and she grunted.

"Hmmph!" She passed him the room hey card and looked across the waiting lounge to Zoria. "If that's what you're in to." She walked off switching what had to be fifteen pounds of firm ass.

Antoine left heading to his room and dusting Zoria's fine ass off, but he slid back through the front desk and got Lexie's number. There was no way that a freak like him could let her slip through the cracks. He had to have her and had been having her every since.

Now, Antoine paddled her from the back while waiting on Kiesha to get home. He'd called her about twenty mines ago and was sure that she'd be walking in any minute.

"Yeah, bitch!" Antoine barked at Lexie while thinking of Kiesha's reaction to what he was doing. Pussy is deadly! He thought while thinking about what he'd done to Erk's ego by banging Zoria's spine out on the money that he owed Wheat. The real disrespect came from him sending her to deliver the money along with a copy of the sex disc. And now he was plotting on Kiesha. Trifling ass bitch! He pounded Lexie harder after hearing Kiesha calling him from the living room.

"Oh!" Lexie moaned. "Geh…geh..get this pussy, baby!" She screamed louder.

Kiesha walked into the room and was shocked. This nigga is crazy! She dropped her purse and rushed over to the bed swinging an arsenal of punches. Antoine was fucking Lexie doggie style letting her drippin wet pussy salivate onto Kiesha's clothes that he'd spread all over the bed. Once she got to the bed, Antoine grabbed her by her ponytail and puller her into a vicious slap.

"Whack!" The force of his swing left a palm print across her cheek. She lay on the bed holding her cheek and staring up at him.

"Aw, bitch!" He laughed evilly. "You wanna fuck niggaz in my spot while I'm out there trappin?" He saw the fear in her eyes as he leaned in closer to her. Lexie had disappeared into the closet.

"I ain't done shit!" Kiesha yelled while holding her face. Damn! She thought while looking for the woman who Antoine had been bangin when she walked in. How

275

did he find out? She wondered if Jackson had told him out of spite because of her pregnancy.

"Bitch" Antoine yelled and swung his hand back like he was going to slap her again. I got this hoe! He laughed and dropped his hand after seeing the fear that overwhelmed Kiesha.

This nigga was just fucking a bitch in my bed and wanna trip on me? Kiesha thought upset about how Antoine had flipped everything around making her look like the bad guy. She'd been putting up with his shit for years! Fuck him!

"Hi, Kiesha." Lexie smiled after coming out of the closet.

"Uhn uhn, bitch!" Kiesha screamed as Lexie walked toward her with a strap on that sprouted at least sixteen inches and was think as a Louisville slugger. Antoine tore her pants away from her body while she screamed.

"No, Tee!" Kiesha begged while wrestling with him, but he'd made up his mind and snatched her thong off exposing her naked body.

Um! Antoine thought to himself while pinning Kiesha to the bed. This hoe still got it! He stared at her thick pussy lips.

"You wanna fuck, don't you?" Antoine asked wickedly. H E noticed a look of disbelief in Kiesha's eyes. He recognized the look because he had it earlier when he found the condom wrapper by his bed. Now the bitch wanna explain. He laughed and spread her legs not hearing her pleas.

"Antoine!" Kiesha yelled frantically while fighting him off. "Please, I'm pregnant Antoine stopped and stared at her.

"Tramp bitch!" What she'd said had enraged him further. Now, there was a second baby that probably wasn't his either. I should kill this bitch!

"Lexie, gon ahead and get this pussy." Antoine said and held Kiesha down letting Lexie mount her with colossal strap on. Kiesha screamed and begged for hers and her child's life.

"Please!" Kiesha cried out. The paint from the dildo tearing the lining of her vaginal walls was excruciating. She couldn't believe what Antoine was doing to her. Blood trickled down her legs as Lexie rode her like mechanic bull. It was inside of her stomach.

"Bitch!" Lexie growled sadistically. "You wanna play my nigga!" She humped her viciously pushing the whole foot and a half inside of her. Kiesha had fainted from the pain.

Antoine still held Kiesha's arms down while Lexie tortured her with thrust of the huge phallic plastic. Bet this hoe don't wanna fuck no more!

****

Fox sat outside of Wheat's house waiting for him. Life wasn't promised to anyone, but Wheat's wasn't promised passed the moment Fox saw him. I'mma body this nigga! He thought knowing that today could be his last on the streets. This was a situation that couldn't be solved civilly. His cell phone rang.

"What's up, brah?" Antoine asked. He'd just left from dropping Lexie off and wanted to holler at his brother. They hadn't kicked it since they'd tossed it up and Chocolate City.

"Nigga! I'm burying them Brick City clowns! Fox spat vehemently. He'd been so caught up into sniffing Wheat and his goons out that he'd forgotten to put Antoine up on what happened.

"What's poppin? Antoine asked knowing that it had something to do with what he'd done to Erk. Damn! He felt bad about causing Fox any trouble.

"Dawg, them bitch ass niggaz tried to roll on me!" Fox told Antoine about what had happened and Antoine was on his way. He'd known that it could get ugly for himself, but they'd made the wrong move by targeting his brother. The streets were about to run red with Brick City blood starting with the first nigga who they ran across.

Fox leaned back still waiting because the first sign of Wheat or anything affiliated with him would be getting it. I should snatch up his baby momma!

Fox thought angrily, although, he want' that type of hitter. Instead, he preferred to keep gangster shit in the streets because GOD forbid a nigga smashing down on Egypt of LaTicia about a beef that he caused.

"This shit real out here." Fox whispered to himself while checking the chamber of his .40 making sure it was clear to rock. He'd seen the .50 caliber that Antoine had picked up and planned to get a hold of two for himself once he threw the .40 away after offing a few Brick City cats. He nodded and let a bullet slide into the chamber. This one's for you, Wheat! He thought with a diabolical smile. All of the admiration that Fox had once carried for Wheat, was now hate.

****

Antoine pulled up next to Fox and rolled his window down. He saw the look on his brother's face and was sure that he was thinking in a blind rage. He couldn't let Fox go out like that.

"Brah, follow me." Antoine said and drove off looking in his rearview making sure Fox was following. They drove back to his bachelors pad. The one he'd made the tape with Zoria at. After getting inside Antoine decided to tell Fox about what had initiated the beef.

"What?" Fox was furious and couldn't believe Antoine had done something like that without giving him a head up. This nigga done put my life on the crap table! He thought while giving his brother a hateful stare.

"Chill, brah!" Antoine said calmly trying to act like it wasn't as serious as it was.

"Chill? NIgga, you ain't the nigga almost got slumped out there!" Fox explained angrily while thinking about what he wanted to do to Erk. Although the rift had been caused because of Wheat's paper, Fox still thought Erk was the one who had amplified it. Wheat was usually laid back and would shit on a niggaz name if they had an outstanding debt, but what had happened to Antoine at the club and him while coming out of the barbershop wasn't Wheat's style. He was too much of a coward and wouldn't dare cross Fox because of Rone's status, on the streets, alone.

All of the veteran dope boys knew what type of juice Rone carried so they stayed stray of Fox. It was an unspoken rule that no one violated until now.

"Nah, Fox." Antoine said. "We at 'em, but niggaz aint' tryna do a bid fo this shit." He wanted to get at the Brick City clique just as bad as Fox, but he wasn't ready to lay his life down for it. Prison wasn't an attractive option after living the life style that he'd been living. Antoine glanced over to Fox and laughed.

"Nigga, you wanna see the tape?" Antoine asked Fox and although Fox was still upset, he couldn't resist wanted to see Zoria's naked body.

Fox had been wanting to fuck Zoria for years, but he didn't want to cross Erk. He'd liked Erk until recently. Now, he despised him and wanted to make him one with the earth.

"Hell yeah, mu fucka!" Fox nodded. Fuck's wrong with this nigga? He wondered. "What the fuck you think? I almost caught some hot shit behind this muthafucka, so I gotta take a look at it."

Antoine laughed and popped the disc into the DVD player. Fox's eyes widened after seeing Zoria wiggle out of her panties.

"Damn!" Fox said amazed by Zoria's talent. How in the fuck did the bitch do that? He wondered while keeping an attentive eye on the television screen. He watched her contort her body into a missionary position that was unmatched. Egypt can't even do that! Dayum!

They watched the disc before deciding what they were going to do. Fox's anger had settled, but he hadn't changed his mind. He was ready to go right then. They'd tried to take his life so he was left to defend it. The war had been initiated and Antoine trapped their queen using the hoe against them. Now, it was Fox's turn to take the helm.

Fox's cell phone rang. "Hello?" He answered and it was Egypt.

"Fox? Where are you?" Egypt asked fearfully. She was panicking and almost called Rone. She was sure that putting Rone into Fox's business would have pissed him off, so she quickly thought against it.

"Why? What's up?" Fox asked instead of answering her question. *Fuck this hoe think she is? He thought while holding the phone. Questioning me?*

"Someone named Wheat keeps calling her asking for you." Egypt said and Fox looked over to Antoine.

"What? What the fuck he say?' Fox wanted to know. *I hope this nigga ain't take this shit to my muhfuckin hoe!* Fox thought and his temper began to boil again.

"He left his number." Egypt gave Fox the number.

"Ah'ight then, E." Fox hung up. He looked over to Antoine and shook his head.

"What happened?" Antoine asked hoping Wheat hadn't sent anyone at Egypt.

"Shit yet, but the nigga Wheat wants me to call him." Fox shrugged shoulders and Antoine gave him a a curious look.

"Call 'em." Antoine said and Fox dialed the number. Antoine wanted to know what Wheat had to say. He thought that Erk was behind the whole move, but they all claimed Brick City so they all had to go. Niggaz tried to body big brah? He shook his head feeling sorry for what they'd hate to suffer by his hands.

"What's up, nigga?" Fox asked after getting Wheat on the telephone. "How the funeral arrangements going?" He asked thinking Quake had met an untimely death from his gunshot wounds.

"Funeral arrangements?" Wheat asked shakily. "Fox, I ain't tryna do this, my nigga." His voice was non combative.

"It's done, nigga! You sent your people at me, so it's done!" Fox yelled into the telephone his voice spit like he was breathing fire, and Antoine nodded assuring Fox that he was telling Wheat was right.

"Damn straight it's on, baby!" Antoine yelled out loud hoping Wheat caught on to his voice. He was on it and wanted it to be known. I'mma choke the nigga to death! HE thought cockily. Antoine had became an animal not giving a fuck about anyone who wasn't with him.. The game had a way of corrupting people, especially when you're ego is involved.

"Fox, I ain't have shit to do with that." Wheat explained. He assured Fox that he was willing to do whatever it took to live.

"I must look like a fool, nigga!" Fox laughed evilly. "Bring them niggaz to me then!"

"What?" Wheat asked hoping Fox hadn't asked him to cross his nephews to have his own life spared.

"You heard me, bitch ass nigga! Bring 'em to me!" He demanded again causing Antoine to grin.

Antoine sat in the corner chuckling. That's my nigga! He thought while hearing Fox pull rank on Wheat. He'd never seen Fox so callused. Usually Fox was a pushover, but what Erk had done brought the gangster shit out of him. Yeah, brah might be on it! Antoine was putting a play together in his head while Fox negotiated Wheat's cost for his own life.

"Alright," Wheat finally agreed, "But I ain't bringing Quake, Fox." His voice turned solemn and Fox understood why he didn't want to involve Quake any further.

"Ah'ight, so it was all Erk, huh?" Fox asked Wheat. I knew it was that bitch ass niggaz idea! Fox thought while clinching his teeth angrily.

"You know it was him, Fox! Quake can't think like that and me......you know I ain't tryna come at you." He sounded defeated, although, in truth he hadn't even been involved in the war.

****

Later on in the week, Wheat invited Erk to a whore house on the east side. He pulled up to Erk's house. Damn, nephew! He thought while watching Erk strutting to the car. It's either me or you, and you caused this shit! He was taking his family to be slaughtered.

"What's up, unk?" Erk greeted Wheat with a pound after getting into the car with him. He was sure that Wheat knew about everything he'd done because Quake couldn't keep his mouth shut. I know Quake's fat ass snitched! He thought and tilted his seat back lounging Wheat's DTS.

"Shit, what it do, nephew?" Wheat asked him with a fake chuckle. He should have felt horrible inside, but he didn't. He was a coward and would trade his mother's life for his own.

"These bitches better be freaks too, unk!" Erk laughed hoping his uncle wasn't pump faking with him on some bust down bitches. Nigga better have some trump pussy waitin on a nigga! He thought with a chuckle. Erk was slipping out of town later on this weekend. He was sure that his days in Detroit were numbered after what he'd tried to pull on Fox, so he had to bounce. I'mma hate to leave Quake like that. He sighed. Quake was his nigga, but the responsibility that came along with carrying him was too much. Erk had been carrying Quake for years, but this was the end of the road. Once Quake got out the hospital, Erk would be gone.

"This muthafucka is raggedly as hell!" Erk said and laughed at the shabby looking spot. I know these some drunk pussy hoes in this bitch! He thought and followed Wheat inside. There was one lonely broad swinging from the pole to a rhythm that didn't exist because there wasn't any music on.

"What's up with this shit, unk?" Erk laughed and pointed to the bowlegged hunnie who was swinging from the pole and gyrating her ass cheeks. They sat down and the music came on. This some real live bootleg shit! He thought and chuckled not wanting to shit on his uncle's hangout.

Lexie swayed off the stage swing her butter pecan hips all the way to where Wheat and Erk was sitting. Her ass rubbed against Erk's shoulder and she dropped bending over and wiggling her ripe tits in his face. Her hands canvassed his body checking him for a burner. Here it is! She thought after rubbing her hands across the pistol that was tucked into his belt line.

Fox crept up behind Erk with his .40 caliber already drawn. I got that ass now, bitch ass nigga! He thought while drawing his hand back.

"Whack!" Fox's thumper slapped into Erk's cranium. The sound of the metal crashing against bone was thunderous. Lexie held her hand on Erk's pistol when he tried to reach for it. This bitch down!

"Whack!" Fox landed another blow with his pistol. This time blood squirted from his head in a beeline, and

286

Erk fell to the floor. His eyes bulged from his head. He looked form Fox to his uncle, and Wheat shrugged his shoulders.

"It was you or me nephew." Wheat said coldly not caring that Erk was breathing his last breaths. Lexie pulled Erk's pistol out of his pants and left while Fox chained Erk to the stripper's pole. Wheat tried to get up and Fox swung his clapper into Wheat's direction.

"Coward!" Fox yelled through clinched teeth. "Sit your bitch ass down!" Wheat through his hands into the air and sat back into the chair. Shortly after Erk was chained to the pole and Wheat was chained to the chair, Antoine and Lexie came out. Lexie was strapped with the sixteen inch hoe handler. Erk's eyes moistened.

"Please, Fox man!" Erk begged and Wheat's mouth hung open. "Tee, come on y'all!" He pleaded, but his cries didn't have any merit. He'd initiated this beef.

"I'mma step out." Fox laughed as he walked out of the room. Lexie just became fam'ly. Fox thought knowing what she'd been brought into do.

She slowly and sensually stripped Erk down to his bare skin. His balls had tightened into small sack from fright. He looked at Lexie, although she was beautiful, he saw a monster. She ain't gon do it! He rationalized with himself, but he came up short because Lexie ran up in him with no Vaseline.

Wheat tried to hide his eyes from seeing what was happening to his nephew. I'm next! He thought scared that his assumption would become is reality. These niggaz wrong! He'd seen a lot of killing throughout his length in the game, but nothing as diabolical as what was happening to Erk. Blood oozed from his rectum and he'd thrown up repeatedly. This bitch is Satan! He thought while looking at the pleasure that she was getting from sticking the strap on inside of Erk. The music came back on and Fox reappeared. Everyone was silent and Fox walked over to Wheat handing him a small handgun.

Antoine walked him, at gunpoint, over to the pole where Erk was and nodded. Wheat raised the pistol to his nephew's head.

"Pap.....pap!"

Wheat put two into his forehead killing Erk instantly. It was something that came along with the territory of being a coward. And the death that he'd died from selling his own family out.

Fox spared Wheat. Antoine wanted to off him too and warned Fox that letting him live would come back to haunt them on day, but Fox had given him his word. They had taped the killing for insurance just in case Wheat ever got out of line or they needed him for something. Fox gave Antoine dap and slapped Lexie across her heart slapped and voluptuous ass.

288

"We up!" Fox said nodding to Lexie letting her know that she'd just became part of the team. Antoine winked at her.

This hoe might be the female me. Antoine thought while watching her get dressed before they left. Lexie walked between them smiling silently. She'd found herself a home with some thorough ass niggaz.

Chapter 10

Antoine pulled into Shawnda's driveway and honked. It had been months since he'd seen Kiesha. After finding out that Jah'lil wasn't his son, he called it quits. He wanted to lay her ass down, but Fox had talked him out of it. Now he was living the good life. Papered up and single. Every hoe in Motor City was at him, but he'd became interested in Shawnda, the hunnie that he'd met at the club when he had to check Quake. He smiled liking what he saw when Shawnda walked outside She was built like a fantasy. Her golden brown breast bounced sensually with every step she took toward Antoine's truck. She got in and smiled him.

"Hey!" Shawnda always seemed exited to see him when they got together. Antoine's eyes traveled up and down her curvy body.

"I hope someone from yo job sees you." He laughed while staring at the way her thighs hung from her short skirt. She pursed her lips.

"Whatever, Antoine." Shawnda answered sassily. "I have a life. They don't run me." She finally giggled.

"I hear you, but what if doctor was to see you samsing through the theater looking like a prostitute?" He gave her a once over again hoping she took notice to what he was talking about. Antoine liked what he saw himself, but if she was trying to maintain a professional swagger, she'd lost it today.

290

"Fuck doctor!" Shawnda retorted letting Antoine know that she was her own woman. Antoine like that about her and that was on the reason he'd been spending so much time with her. Lexie found something strange in Shawnda, but Antoine believe it was just jealousy.

"I'm grown, Antoine." Shawnda snickered. "And I'm professional when I'm at the clinic. What I do on my time is personal." She pulled down the sun visor mirror and checked her lip gloss. It's on point! She thought and smiled.

"You're right!" Antoine chuckled and glanced over to her giving her a cynical look. "You look like a professional on your personal time too." He teased implying that she looked like a whore. Shawnda shot Antoine a evil look.

"Boy!" She replied quickly. "You better stop playing with me because I swing back." She gave him a warning look letting him know that she was serious.

"I apologize, boo. I was just teasin." He laughed and gave her a suggestive look letting him know that she was serious.

"I apologize, boo. I was just teasin." He laughed and gave her a suggestive look. "You definitely lookin good." He assured her with a nod. Antoine felt Shawnda. She'd bossed up with it was time to and he lied that about hood bitches. They'd stand up when a hustler mans stood down. Yeah. He thought with a nod. You certified.

"You better recognize how good I look." Shawnda smiled impressing Antoine with the way her gloss spread across her mouth.

"I do recognize. Look under the seat. I brought something for you." Shawnda reached beneath the seat and pulled out a gift wrapped box. She smiled brightly.

"You bought me something, Antoine?" She tore the rapper away from the bos.

"Damn straight I bought you somethin!" He chuckled lightly hoping she'd like what was inside. Antoine had been with sack chasing ass Kiesha for years so he had picked up an edge for gift shopping. She pulled a perfume bottle from inside and smelled the lid.

"What is it?" Shawnda asked wanting to know what kind of perfume it was, and Antoine laughed.

"It's perfume." He teased knowing that she wanted to know what kind. She pushed him playfully.

"you know what I mean!' What kind is it?" She laughed and smelled the lid again.

"Good life for women."

"Thank you, Antoine. It smells good too."

"I got on the men's version." Antoine said confidently and Shawnda leaned in smelling his neck. She nodded.

"Mmhmm, you always smell good." She smiled. Even your dick smells good! She thought while looking

292

over to him.. "Especially that night we met at the club." She laughed and Antoine joined in.

"Yeah, that night was crazy too. My brother was gonna slap the shit outta yo girl Kizzie!" He laughed remembering how he had to stop Fox from hand checking Kizzie. Brah was gonna put hand on the hoe! He thought while laughing.

"Oooh, she is infatuated with him too!" Shawnda nodded while puttin her girls business out there. "I think she into getting checked. She keeps asking me his name. Is he really gay?"

"Hell muthafuckin naw my brother ain't gay! Zerven Fox is a wealthy real estate investor and a true to life hood nigga! He just ain't into slimy ass hoes like Kizzie." Antoine laughed. "Now me, I would've fucked the shit outta her!"

"Don't play, nigga." Shawnda gave him an evil look. You and all that money you got belongs to me." She thought.

"Nah I was bullshittin, but Fox a player reformed. This nigga got two babies on the way by different bitches! Now, how pimpish is that?"

"Yeah, I guess you're right, but tonight is our night. Forget about them. It's us tonight, baby." Shawnda smiled letting Antoine know that she had something planned for him once they got back from the movies.

293

"seems like every night this week been our night."

Shawnda smiled. "It doesn't have to be just this week. We can make it official."

"What I do to deserve you exclusively?" Antoine asked jokingly, although, he really was shocked by her forwardness.

"First of all you're sweet and you bought me perfume."

"Perfume? Is that all it takes?" HE tease, and Shawnda shook her head letting him know that it wasn't that easy.

"Nope!" She replied cutely. "Let me rephrase myself. Men usually give woman money as gifts. If a man spends an ounce of time shopping for a woman it's impressive because it shows he has real interest in her."

Antoine nodded while driving into the theater parking lot. He understood exactly where she was coming from, although, he'd never looked at it that way himself. This bitch be poppin boss game at a nigga. He thought after glancing over to her. He saw that confidence within Shawnda. It was something that a lot fo women that he'd been with lacked.

"I feel that, boo." Antoine answered genuinely ageing with her. Maybe I did shop because I feel the hoe? He considered what she said. "I gotta fun in here and grab the tickets for the show tonight." He opened the door, but Shawnda stopped him before he got out of the truck.

"Okay, but you didn't answer me." Shawnda said and smiled letting him know that she expected to hear something and wasn't going to let him change the subject. She let his arm go and he walked off.

Shawnda was serious about her commitments to everything, especially her men. She'd been abused since she was a child. Man after man had taken advantage of her physically, verbally, and mentally. Whether it was relatives or boyfriends they'd done something abusive during the course of her relationship with them. Her passion had caused her to accept the abuse during those times in her life, but she overcame her compulsive need for a man and has been steam rolling them every since.

Shawnda looked over to the theater noticing crowds of people running from inside. They were pushing and screaming even trampling one another. She got nervous because he meal ticket was inside. I hope my baby is okay! She hoped while her eyes roamed though the crowd. Okay then. She saw Antoine ascend from the crowd and rush over to his truck. He jumped in and immediately drove off.

****

LaTicia's phone rang and she answered. "Crawford's law offices. LaTicia Crawford speaking. How may I help you."

"Ticia," Antoine's voice spewed into her ear through the telephone. "I'm in a situation. I need to see you as soon as possible."

"I can meet you now." LaTicia replied after hearing the urgency in Antoine's voice, and he gave her direction to where he wanted her to meet him.

"I'm on my way." LaTicia assured him and slowly lifted herself from behind her desk.

Being seven months pregnant didn't agree with LaTicia. She'd gained thirty pounds which caused her to have serous mobility problems. She snatched her car keys from her desk and rushed out of her office. She called Rone from her car and gave him the address that she'd gotten from Antoine so he could meet them there also.

LaTicia had a good idea what the situation was about, but this time she wasn't going to be available to help him the way that he'd need her to. She was two months from giving birth to her first child and didn't have the drive or desire to take on any serious cases. Her time was limited and precious. She didn't want to make any adjustments, but she was sure that she would have to because Antoine was family to her.

As Laticia came off the freeway, she saw Rone's Mercedes SL600 Roadster crossing the intersection so she jumped behind him trailing him to the address that Antoine had given her.

"What happened?" Rone asked as they walked up to the house. He looked concerned because he knew how carless Antoine could be at times. He'd been hearing a lot of ill shit about him lately and wondered if he'd let his bankroll black his vision of reality.

"I don't' know!" LaTicia replied and rand the doorbell. Antoine quickly came to the door letting them in. Rone gave him a straightforward stare.

"What the fuck happened?" Ron eased angrily. I'm tired of this stupid ass young nigga! He thought. He'd heard about what Antoine had done to Kiesha and knew that it was only matter of time before hood karma caught up with him.

"I fucked up, big Rone." Antoine replied elusively and began pacing the floor hysterically. He wanted to tell them what happened, but he couldn't remember.

"How, Antoine?" Laticia asked and sat on the couch. She was sure that it was another murder because Antoine was too shaken. Antoine stopped his pacing and hung his lead low.

297

"I stanked the nigga Jackson." Antoine finally came clean with what he'd done. He'd killed his guy, but at the moment it was between life and earth. Although he couldn't remember the details of what happened, he was sure that Jackson had upped his cannon first causing him to throw a couple of hot rounds to his chest.

Rone's face curled into an angry grimace. You's a dumb ass nigga! He thought while backing up toward the door. His loyalty to Antoine had ran out. There wasn't a doubt in Rone's mind if Antoine was going down because e was and Rone refused to let him drag him along for the ride. Fuck this nigga! He waved Antoine off while standing by the door.

"Nigga!" Rone said with rigor. "I'm out! You're on your own with this one, pimp!"

"Hold up, Rone." Antoine wanted to explain his side of the story. That nigga was Jah'lil's father, brah!" He voice cracked when he said that because he loved Jah'lil.

"Annnnnnnd action!" Rone pointed letting him know that his bullshit was real theatrical. "Nigga, where are the muthafuckin camera became you a comedian? What the fuck you mean he was Jah'lil's dad?" He stare was contemptuous and all that hate for Antoine, that he let go of years ago, had suddenly came back.

"Big Rone. The nigga was at the theater with Kiesha and the baby. I don't really remember what happened after that." Antoine hung his head with grief

298

again. "I know he dead though." He looked contrite, although, he was only sorry that it had happened in the way it did because he'd done what he saw fit. The nigga crossed me and got crossed out. HE though while still looking sorry for what had happened.

"Ticia," Rone said while opening the door that he'd came in. "Leave me out of this one because I'm though with his nigga." He walked out turning his back on Antoine and the promise that he'd made to Alfredo. Antoine shook his head knowing Rone was serious.

"I can't even blame him, Ticia. I really fucked up this time. I was just feelin betrayed." He clinched his fist wanted to use them. He was frustrated and knew that the world would look different from behind prison walls.

"Not only about Kiesha!" He explained. "But that hoe ass nigga ran and left me when I smoked them two cats in the corridors."

LaTicia sat on the couch staring at him. She understood his pain because she too was being abandoned by someone she loved. She got up and touched his back trying to comfort him.

"But Antoine?"

"Yeah, I know because I regret it already." He lied because the only thing he regretted was his fate which was prison time for what he'd done. LaTicia looked around.

"Who's house is this?" She asked knowing that it wasn't on Antoine's properties.

"My girl's. She said I could stay her until whenever. She owns a few house and shit too."

"Good because the law is probably at your front door looking for you as we speak."

"Yeah." He nodded. "They just left. I got Lexie squatting over there for me."

"Don't call there, Antoine!" LaTicia warned him. She was sure that they had someone monitoring the calls goin in and out and following whoever stopped by there.

"If you send someone over there, don't let them come directly back to you either. And do not tell anyone where you're at! No one!" She demanded sternly knowing that his arrest could become someone's come up.

"Shawnda already knows. This is her pad and she was with me when it happened."

"Well make sure she doesn't tell anyone and don't send her to your house. I'll bring you groceries tomorrow, but I have to leave right now." She walked to the door and Antoine followed behind her.

"Ah'ight then, Ticia. Thanks. I appreciate your support." Antoine said sincerely and LaTicia smiled weakly.

"It's going to cost you more than a thanks this time, Antoine." She walked out and Antoine closed the door behind her. I know he didn't say his bitch es with him? She wondered knowing that that was exactly what he'd said.

"He was with a hoe and killed a guy for being with his baby's mother?" She asked herself, trying to make sense of what he'd said, while getting into her car. LaTicia couldn't believe he'd been so niggardly. She was sure that he was in trouble on a grander scale than he was after his last murder and it bothered her. She'd became attached to Rone, Fox, Antoine, and even Sherry because she didn't have any family of her own. So knowing that Antoine was most likely going to be behind prison bars for a while upset her.

LaTicia grew up in the foster care system. Growing up she bounced around going back and forth between orphanages and foster homes, because her parents died in a car accident when she was six years old. Although her parent were wealthy, she couldn't enjoy her inheritance until she was emancipated from the state. After graduating from high school she went straight to college where she met Raymond. Until then her life had been lonely. Now she had a family.

LaTicia teared up. She knew that Rone was upset with Antoine about him being so hotheaded, but she was certain that it would pass because Rone had eternal love for family.

Fox rushed to the telephone. "Hello?" He answered winded from the short jog that he made to the phone. It was Rone calling.

"What's up, young trap?" Rone asked. "I just left your simple ass brother. You ain't gonna believe what this nigga done did this time."

Bullshit! Fox thought. I know he's capable of any muhfuckin thing! He envisioned what Antoine had commissioned Lexie to do to Erk. Although he didn't watch, the raw sounds of Erk's pleading still haunted him. He was used to a simple kill, but Antoine had gotten diabolical with it.

"What the hell he do, brah?" Fox was sure that It was serious for Rone to call because he wasn't the type to sweep gossip around.

"He done killed ya mans Jackson!" Rone told him flatly.

Fox nearly dropped the telephone He knew that it was coming, but he didn't want to believe it. Muthacuka! He thought Fox had known about Kiesha fucking Jackson for years. After hearing her in the background a few times he finally caught on to who she was, but he stayed out of it. He knew how niggaz were. They'd tell you that they would want to know, but would flip out once you told them, so he stayed clear of their ghetto love triangle.

"Quit bullshittin, dawg!" Fox said, although, he knew Rone was as serious as colon cancer.

"I play bitches! I don't play my niggaz." Rone replied letting him know that it was truth that he spoke.

"Damn, where at? Did he call Ticia?"

"Fox, man don't even trip! Fuck that stupid ass nigga. You know why he did it?"

"Probably over Kiesha's scandalous ass!"

"Boon! How in the fuck did you know? Rone asked. I hope this nigga ain't know he was gonna do it and didn't stop him? Rone wondered hope that Fox hadn't turned his head to something that ignorant.

"Brah, you can look at Jah'lil and see that's Jackson's seed. Not only that, but I heard her in the background a few times when I was talking to Jackson on the phone."

"You knew and didn't say shit?"

"Hell naw!" Fox snapped in reply. "It wasn't my business. I got shit of my own jumpin off. I can't baby sit a grown ass nigga and his bitch, brah."

"You've got a strange way of showing love for your niggaz because I would have told you. Believe that, brah."

"I feel you, but I don't get involved in niggaz personals, especially about they bitches. That's the quickest way to lose a friend."

"Teach then, nigga." Rone laughed after realizing Fox was right. "I feel that, but keeping it moving. I 'm on my way to the steak joint that you turned me on to. What do you want me to order for you, so it'll be ready by the time you get here." That was Rone's way of telling Fox he wanted to talk to him.

"New York strip platter. I gotta make moves with Egypt so give me a half hour."

"Bet it up. How is Egypt anyway?"

"Mean!" Fox replied and laughed. "She mad at you too, muhfucka."

"Why?"

"For telling me these hoe ass hustlers folk tales, nigga."

"Man, fuck what y'all talking about! That shit is gospel! I've seen it first hand, my nigga. You'd better take heed of this good game, li'l hard head ass nigga. I should put it in a book!" He boasted.

"Whatevah, nigga! I'll be there though." Fox hung up the phone and shook his head again hoping Antoine would be able to squeeze out of this one too. This some bullshit. He thought about seeing his brother behind bars for the rest of his life. Growing up, older people in the

304

hood would tell him, "boy, you got it good right now, but wait until get a a hold of you." He didn't understand what they were talking about during those juvenile days, but now he has experiencing what they were talking about first hand. Life had gotten a hold of him and it was constricting.

Fox pretended to be uncovered about what Rone had told him, but he'd taken heed. He was making preparation to back away from the game for awhile. His hustling season was coming to an end before it came to the end.

****

Shawnda walked into the house that she'd allowed Antoine to hide out in until he figured out his next move.

"Antoine." Shawnda called for him as she walked into the living room. Antoine came out of the bathroom naked.

"What up?" he asked while Shawnda lustfully stared at his hanging game.

"You can stay here forever if this is what I have to come back to." She giggled and Antoine waved her off.

"Nah, boo. I got too much respect for myself. I'll fuck that pussy 'til its beet red daily, but I ain't runnin 'round butt ass naked and shit."

305

"Shut up, boy!" Shawnda said and laughed. "I was just playing with you." She took another look at his fat dick and smiled suggestively. "Unless." She teased him some more and he walked back into the bathroom.

"I ain't on it, baby girl." Antoine came back out wrapped in a bath towel.

Shawnda walked over to him. *I'm getting this nigga.* She thought while smiling happily. She was sure that he had something for her and she wanted it.

"Stop being man, Antoine." She said and touched his arm. "We're going to get through this." She smiled and leaned in kissing his bare chest.

"Whatchu mean we?" Antoine asked bothered by the way she'd just included herself into his situation. *Bitch, you'll be bouncing at the first sign of a bid!* He thought while giving her a look that assured her that he was offended.

"You did say that you were my man, right?"

"Yeah, no doubt, but that was before I caught that body." He laughed although his situation wasn't funny. "Shit done changed now, boo."

"Antoine, I'm serious about everything that I commit to." She nodded "Everything."

"I'm sure you are and that's some raw shit, but I'mma have to bounce or turn myself in sooner or later. What happens then?" He said staring at her knowing she didn't have a loving answer for that one. Who this bitch think she's playin? He wondered because he was sure that it wouldn't be him.

"I have good intentions, Antoine. It ain't shit out here in these streets. These niggaz either come to take something or give a bitch something that she doesn't want. Sheeeit!"

"I feel you, but a nigga with a life bid ain't gon benefit you either!"

Damn! Shawnda thought while looking defeat and out of comebacks. This nigga is good! Antoine wasn't budging making it hard on a gold digger, so Shawnda had to do what she thought was necessary. Fuck it! I gotta go desperate! She pushed her voluptuous body against his wrapping her arms round his shoulder and making sure her soft tits massaged his chest.

"I don't want any benefits! I want you. I deserve you." She pleaded convincingly."Why? Sheeit, why you need me so much?" Antoine asked apprehensively. This hoe might be psychotic! He thought while watching her. He watched her because she was staring to act like fatal attraction.

"I didn't say I needed you, Antoine. I don't need shit. I said I wanted you and I deserve you."

"Why? I care about you and wanna be with you too, but I'm in a fucked up spot right now." Antoine had heard stories about cats doing time with their woman

307

hanging on in peril and he was trying to avoid that. Sheeit, the less weight the easier the haul, baby. He thought as Shawnda grabbed his hand leading him into the living room. They both sat on the couch and she looked over to hm.

"I want to tell you something, Antoine."

"Spit." Antoine replied giving her an opportunity to run whatever game she had on him. I wouldn't give a fuck what you say. He thought while staring at her in an attentive manner.

"I was in an abusive relationship for six years…." She was saying when Antoine rudely cut her off.

"You're only twenty four so cut the bullshit out." Antoine was blunt. Trifling ass hoe wanna play game?" He wondered hoping that this wan't the route that she wanted to take. Lexie's a telephone call away, bitch! Shawnda nodded.

"Right, I was fourteen when I lost my virginity and he was twenty two, so basically he manipulated me into doing it. HE abused me mentally, physically, emotionally, and any other way someone could be abused, he did it to me." She teared up while telling Antoine her truth. She'd survived what most would have buckled under, but it hadn't came without any bumps or bruises.

"I left him when I was nineteen and ended up in another abusive relationship for a year. After that I was so messed up, I had to get counseling." She giggled and wiped tears from her wet cheeks. "I even went to etiquette classes, man."

Antoine was stunned by what Shawnda had told him, but his life hadn't been a walk in the park either so he wasn't as empathetic as she expected. *Bitch, I got a muthafuckin story of my own! He thought.*

"I hear you, and. . ." Antoine said before getting cut off by Shawnda flailing her hands.

"Nope, don't be sorry for me because all that shit brought me to you." She smiled and wiped the rest of her tears away. "Yep, I'm ready for you. I'm stronger and smarter. I have my nursing degree and my real estate license."

Antoine smiled thankful that she'd cut him off before he had a chance to say what he really wanted to say, and it wasn't sympathetic to say the least. *This hoe might be real wit it? He thought giving her the benefit of the doubt.*

"Why were you cryin then?" Antoine asked taking on last shot at catching her slipping.

"Because I went through all that t get to you and you don't want me." She pushed him playfully. *Got 'em! She thought knowing that she'd finally broken through his barriers.* This was what Shawnda did. She recycled the game that had been ran on her, and pushed it off on other men.

"Boo, you just don't how much I want you." Antoine had finally dropped his guard. He was being sincere with her. "I just don't wanna take you through this shit."

"Let me decide when enough is enough." Shawnda said and leaned over kissing him.

Yeah, hoe! Antoine thought while Shawnda capped him off. We'll see what it do. He palmed the crown of her head and guided her strokes as she slurped. He wanted to believe her, but something made him apprehensive. Kiesha's treachery had scared him and, although, he was in a situation where he had to trust someone, he was hesitant to trust a bitch.

****

Fox walked in the bathroom catching Egypt checking her panty liner for blood. His heart dropped when he saw the red bloodstained pad being pulled from between her legs. Fox hung his tie across his shoulder and rushed over to her. I hope E ain't lost the baby! He prayed. He'd had enough bad shit happen in his circle and didn't know how he would react if something was wrong with his unborn child. What the fuck did I do to reap this type of karma?

"E, what was that about?" Fox asked while pointed to the soiled pad that Egypt tried to discreetly wrap in a paper towel. He was sure that something was wrong because what other reason would she have to hide what she was doing.

"Fox, I've been spotting." Egypt said solemnly. She'd been having blood discharge throughout the past few weeks and had already been to get checked out. Her and the baby were fine so she didn't tell Fox about her bleeding. She knew that he'd already been through a lot with Antoine killing Jackson, and more bad news would have devastated him so she held it from him. Fox sat on the edge of the bathtub with her. He was fucked up inside, but he didn't show it because he had to be strong for his girl.

"So let's go get checked out." He offered wanting to skip Jackson's funeral to see what was up with his seed. I've been fucking up, but a nigga back in his lane." He thought knowing that some of the decisions he'd made could have cost him more than his freedom. Now, he was taking a closer look at what Rone had told him. Egypt smiled and that lighted his load.

"I'm fine and the baby is fine." Egypt replied not wanting to tell fox that she'd went to get a check up without him.

"We have the best of both worlds too." Egypt smile got brighter because she knew Fox was going to be happy about what she had to say next. "Were having a girl." She nodded. Fox lifted her off the tub and walked her back into their bedroom. He laid her across the bed propping two pillows behind her.

"Fuck it!" Fox blurted with a smile. "After I get back from the funeral let's go to Vegas and get married?" He saw Egypt's disinterest in his idea in her defiant head shake.

"Nope!" She said swiftly while shaking her head. "You know I wanna do it big! What's wrong with you? Are you crazy, man? She laughed after letting fox know that she refused to settle for less than what she deserved. Fox shrugged his shoulders.

"Well let's just go anyway. Just to chill out for a few weeks or something?" He suggested while Egypt tied his tie. She and her hand down his chest.

"Fuck it, I need a vacation, but we can't have sex." She pointed to the bloody panty liner that was wrapped in the paper towel letting Fox know that sex was off limits, and he nodded.

"I'm cool with that. I haven't been with no bitch since that shit happened with LaTicia." He lied with a straight face, and Egypt rubbed his face.

"I know." She smiled believing in her man. "I can tell."

"I love you, E." He kissed her neck and shoulder. "I ain't fuckin this up. I Just need you to believe in me."

Egypt smiled.   I do and always have.   She thought knowing that she had a soldier that would ride with her and for her She was certain that she was where she wanted to be.

****

This is some awkward shit right here! Sherry thought and shook her head while tying Rone's tie. She refused to go to Jackson's funeral and wanted to know what possessed Rone and Fox to attend.   Uhn uhn!   Ain't no motherfucking way!

She couldn't do it. She'd always liked Jackson and under ordinary circumstances she would have encouraged Rone to pay for his funeral, but he'd been killed by her brother.   She was aware of the conflicting interest of her showing up at the funeral. The same people that would be there to support his family at the funeral would also be at the courthouse to support the prosecution against Antoine.

"Nope!" She said to herself and patted Rone's flat chest after finishing his Windsor knot.

"Is Fox coming to get you, babe?" Sherry asked because he wanted to talk to him before they left.

"No, he's still waiting on the insurance check, for the Q45, to clear." Rone said while fidgeting with his diamond studded cuff links. Sherry smiled and rubbed her hands across his shoulders.

"You're looking good." She chuckled.

"Thanks, cheeks!" Rone replied sarcastically because he knew that she wanted to crack on him. "I appreciate the compliment, and once again you've complete the look" He praised her tying skills glibly and Sherry smiled.

"I can't let you leave up out of her looking any kind of way. I have an image to uphold, pimp." She giggled and sassily placed her hands on her hips like a diva. Rone smiled to show kindness before he put her back into her lane.

"I've told you about images. They're fake and we're genuine. Be you and do you, but most of all make sure it's for you." He nodded and playfully slapped her across her ass. "Fuck what someone else thinks."

"Check me then daddy!" Sherry sang playfully while holding her backside.

"You're crazy." He chuckled. "Come walk me to the door." He took her hand and led the way. They shared a few words while they were standing near the doorway.

Things had been peaceful between them lately. Sherry had finally accepted the fact they would be leaving Detroit. She was still against the move, but over the years she'd learned how to support her husband's decisions regardless if she liked them or not, because she loved him and believed in him.

Rone was looking forward to starting a family of his own. He hadn't discussed it with Sherry, but he was sure that she would be elated with the decision. She'd wanted to have children for years, but he was against it. He was convinced that pregnancies and hustling didn't mix, but now that he was retired from the game he was all in.

Fox walked up to Rone's car looking debonair in his grey Brooks Brothers with soft power blue pinstripes. He looked like a young executive leaving home for the office, but instead he was a young entrepreneur leaving for a friend's funeral. After talking to Egypt earlier, Fox sat around thinking about the decision he'd made not to tell Antoine. He couldn't decide whether he'd made the right decision or not. And the thought about what he'd don't to Jackson after the robbery at the 70west building. His mind had gotten cloudy and he started really questioning himself.

"What's up, big brah?" Fox greeted Rone with a pound after getting in the car.

"Funeral time, my nigga." Rone replied and nodded. He'd been there.

"This that part of the game niggaz don't like."

"You ain't bullshittin either, brah!" Fox shook his head. "I almost didn't get outta the muthafuckin bed for that reason."

"Yeah, I know how it is. I had to bury all of my niggaz, including Playblo and your pops."

"Nah, brah brah. I'm cool on that. I just feel like I'm betrayin Tee by going to this funeral, but at the same time. I wouldn't feel honorable as a man, if I didn't pay my last respects to Jackson. Feel me?"

Rone nodded knowing exactly where Fox was coming from. Although he was familiar with game and all that came along with it.

He knew that a nigga had to be willing to die for everything around him to die in that life style, that's why he always kept it light because at that time he was willing to make the necessary adjustments no matter who it was.

"Hell yeah, I feel you." Rone said. "life had a strange way of making a nigga question his integrity. Sometimes a nigga has to make decisions that go against his code of morality. Gangster code, my nigga."

Fox shook his head. "But my conscience." He nervously rubbed is pants legs.

"One thing you can be on, trap. You can's beat your conscience. If you're wrong, your conscience will let you know." Rone rubbed his goatee and cleared his throat.

"Dig, my nigga." Rone continued. "The thing is, you have to make a decision and stand on it. That's the only way your conscience will let you rest."

"Yeah." Fox replied. "I feel that. Definitely." He turned the radio up and reclined in his seat. Fox admired Rone's wisdom. He had a way with words and regardless of arena, Rone seemed to say the perfect thing at the right time. Rone kept talking during the drive. He was sure that fox was confused because this was the first time that someone from his crew had been on the slug receiving side. They'd laid a lot of niggaz down over the years, but this was the first of many for them. And he was caught in the middle of a murder that could have been avoided if he would have told Antoine about Kiesha and Jackson. Rone was sure that whatever Fox's decision was, would probably be questionable and he'd regret it, but it was a decision that he was going to have to make despite the circumstances.

When they drove up Fox saw Jackson's parents greeting everyone as they entered the church. He hadn't been to many funerals, but he thought that was odd. Damn, they must be really grieving. He thought seeing the sadness in their faces. Rone looked over to him once they parked.

"What's up?" Rone asked. This is it, baby. What is it going to be? He thought while looking at his guy. "I hope you've made your decision because once we leave this car you have to stand on it."

"Let's bounce." Fox said and shook his head. "I can't do it. Plus, I know Kiesha's trifling ass is in there and I don't wanna act up at my man's funeral."

Rone's face tightened. Hell nah! He thought disappointed in Fox trying to take the cowardly way out. This nigga 'bout to man up!

"Nigga, this ain't about Kiesha or Tee. It's about you paying your last respects to a lifelong friend. You don't need no excuses. If that's your decision, we out." He started the car back up and pulled off.

"You think I made the wrong decision?" Fox asked wanting to know what Rone thought about him not going to the funeral.

"Hell nah! I was wondering why we were here in the first muthafuckin place! I just wanted you to make the decision on your own."

Fox laughed as they pulled out of the church parking lot. This nigga is a animal. Fox thought knowing that one day he'd probably have to kill Rone or vice versa, Rone would try to send him on that stairway to hell.

"Rone, you's a cold hearted ass nigga, brah." He shook his head. "I just couldn't do it, dawg. I laid on that shit all night, but I couldn't make a decision until now."

"Sheeit, family comes first. That nigga knew how Tee felt about that tramp. He could have told him he was popping that hoe years ago, but he choose to be underhanded and got what his hand called for."

"So why you mad at Tee then, nigga?" Fox was curious because Rone sounded like he was saying he would have done the same thing if he were in that situation. Rone laughed.

"That nigga is six feet, dark skinned, with dimples and long paper. He could have found another Kiesha at any club in the city. He should have been dropped the bitch and upgraded." Rone chuckled. "The hoe have him a clean exit, but he let his heart beat his brain. That's why I'm mad at that simple ass nigga."

Fox nodded. Although he himself wasn't as upset with Antoine as Rone was, he had to admit that Rone had made some good points because Antoine could have done a lot better than Kiesha.

"I feel you, brah brah, but love is a muthafucka."

"I'm going to be real with you. I love Sherry, but I don't love her enough to stop loving myself."

"I don't get it?" Fox asked. He as puzzled by what Rone had just said. He knew how Rone felt about his sister, but he didn't understand what that had to do with him loving himself.

"Any nigga that will smoke a cat in a crowded movie theater doesn't give a fuck about their self. That's what I'm saying."

319

Fox pointed to Egypt's car as they drove up to Rone's house. It was parked in the driveway.

"Ain't that Egypt's whip?" Fox asked knowing that it was and wondering why she'd driven to Rone's house and she was on medical bed rest.

Rone shrugged his shoulders and started laughing. "I guess so! You should know, nigga! You bought it!"

"Fuck you. Silly ass nigga. I wonder why she's over here though?

"She came to see big brah, muhfucka!" They both laughed and got out out of the car.

Rone and Fox saw the tension in Sherry's and Egypt's faces when they walked into the house. Rone locked the door and turned to them.

"What's going on?" Rone asked them knowing that something had happened. "Sherry?" He started walking towards her and flinched after hearing the door crashing down. He spun and saw dozens of policemen flooding into his house.

"Down! Down! Down!" The cops demanded pointing their assault rifles in every direction.

They cuffed everyone in the house immediately after the search. A large white trooper knelt beside Fox. Fox smelt his breath his face was so close to his.

"Zerben Fox?" The officer asked knowing who Fox was.

Fox looked him directly in the eye wanting to spit in his face. Bitch ass fed! He thought and arrogantly sucked his teeth showing the policeman disrespect.

"Are you Zerben Fox?" The cop asked again angrily. He moved closer to Fox his lips nearly touching his face.

Fuck this nigga think he fuckin wit? Fox wondered because he wasn't getting anything out of him. I'ont talk to the law, bitch!

"Okay!" The officer said, fed up with Fox's attitude. He looked around the room and snapped his thick dirty fingers. "Fuck it! Arrest everyone, including the lying ass pregnant bitch! Since the motherfucker doesn't wanna answer me."

Fox lay on the floor handcuffed watching the police harass everyone else. One of the cops grabbed Rone by the cuffs and snatched him to his feet causing the metal to grind against his bare flesh. As he rose the trooper sweep kicked his feet sending him crashing to the floor. Rone cursed and belittled them furiously.

"Y'all some bitches and ya mothers are bitches!" Rone spat at them seething about what they were doing. I'll stank one of y'all bitches! Kill ya seeds! He thought while grimly staring at each of them.

Another badge approached Egypt sending Fox's heart into a hard hitting pound. *I hope these hoes don't try my baby!* He started hoping the cop would have better judgment. The cop knelt next to her and glanced over to Fox making eye contact with him implying that he'd fuck over Egypt if Fox didn't answer him.

Fox dropped his head conceding. *Damn!* He thought knowing that his arms were tired. *Punk ass cop got me!*

"Yeah, I'm Zerben." Fox admitted and the white man wasted no time letting him know who was in charge.

"You have the right to remain silent." The cop said and looked around. "Other than that, you don't have any motherfucking rights!" He shot a swift uppercut to Fox's nuts sending him crashing to the ceramic.

"Ooush!" Fox let out a deafing gasp, and Sherry and Egypt burst into tears. Two badges carried Fox from the house by his hands and feet like an animal.

Rone lay across the floor in a silent rage. He wanted to even shit up. *These bitches gon pay!* Rone thought vehemently. He watched as the police leaving the house pushing the door, that loosely swung from its hinges, all the way off. Rone followed behind them.

"Y'all some hoes! Pig bitches!" He yelled as they drove away with Fox. *Fuck it! I'm moving!* He thought because there was no way that he could stay there after the police had been inside of his home. It was against the code that he lived by. Them punk bitches! Rone was furious. They'd violated his privacy and took his family away in cuffs. He paced the floor steaming.

"What happened?" Rone asked knowing that something had occurred prior to him and Fox getting there. The looks on Egypt's and Sherry's face had warned him, but the door came crashing down before they could let him know what was going on.

"They already raided my house." Egypt replied still crying about fox being taken away in cuffs. Rone shouldn't have said that shit! She thought about the hustlers folk talks that he'd told Fox and her crying intensified. She wanted to slap Rone across his face, but she knew that it wouldn't help.

"You knew better!" Rone yelled. "They must have followed you here! Why didn't you call me?"

Sherry pointed to his cell phone that sat on the table. "You left your phone at home, Rone." She said calmly although she too was still teary eyed behind what was happening to her brother.

"Sherry wanted me to come her so we could get you. When we were on our way out, you and Fox were coming in. And the police came in behind y'all." Egypt whimpered.

"Egypt, did they tear up your house or take anything?" Rone asked curious about what they'd taken Fox in on.

They didn't tear up the house, but they took our plane ticket receipts. We were going to Vegas tomorrow."

"Damn!" Rone pounded the wall. "Sherry, you and Egypt gotta get on a plane to Georgia immediately. Don't even pack. Once you get there don't call. I'll be there as soon as I wrap shit up around here." He snatched his car keys from the floor, where the police had slammed him, and darted out of the house. Sherry and Egypt left shortly after he did. They all knew shit had hit the fan because they all were smelling it. Life had gotten a hold of them.

CHAPTER 11

LaTicia rang the doorbell of Antoine's safe haven. She was in a frenzy. Her world had come crumbling down and Fox was the ceiling. Antoine opened the door looking startled. He looked around cautiously before stepping aside letting her come in.

"You scared the shit outta me, Ticia." Antoine sighed relieved that it was his attorney on the other side of the door, instead of the law. He'd been hiding for a week know and was sure that the police would be applying pressure to the hunt for him soon

"Tee." LaTicia's eyes swelled with tears. She'd been crying every since she'd gotten the news about Fox's arrest. He was her unborn child's father and the only man that she'd ever loved. Antoine sat her onto the couch after seeing the panic in her.

"What's up, Ticia?" He was curious about what was bothering her. This was the first time that he'd seen her so ruffled and it was starting to worry him.

The police just raided Fox's and Rone's homes about an hour ago." She whined and whipped tears away from her face at the same time.

"I've been feeling fucked up all day too! I thought it was because of Jackson's funeral though. Did they take anybody?" Please don't say they done snatched my nigga up! He prayed knowing, from LaTicia's saddened stare, his prayers were falling on deaf ears.

325

"Yes." LaTicia nodded. "They took Fox on murder charges."

Ain't this a bitch! He thought knowing that they were trying to use Fox as a bargaining tool for him to turn himself in.

"So they're tryna put Jackson's blood on his hands, huh? Antoine asked ready to take out for his and set his brother free. Bitch! He thought. Life in prison didn't seem livable, but how could he look in the mirror living fee knowing his brother was carrying his load. Nah, I can't allow that! He shook his head with frustration because the end had came sooner that he thought.

"No, Tee." LaTicia said while shaking her head. The tears that had fell were drying and she looked aged. "They've charged him with the murder of that guy named Playblo.

"You talkin 'bout that nigga they found in the alley 'bout eight or nine months ago?" He asked puzzled about what Fox could possibly have to do with that.

"Yes, remember. It was all on the news because they were more concerned about the dog who's throat had been slit than him."

"You know damn well Fox ain't killed shit." He said trying to ease LaTicia's worries, although, he as sure that Fox had laid a few niggaz to rest, including Que. Although they'd never spoken on it, it was known that

Fox had laid Que and his henchmen down at the West apartments.

"They're just tryna harass him to bring me out." Antoine said knowing that Fox was more calculating that to do something as ignorant as he'd done himself. Nah, not brah. He thought hoping Fox hadn't been that careless.

"Antoine, you can't turn yourself in now. I have to focus on Fox's charges since he's already locked up."

"That's cool. I don't even know if I'mma do it now anyway."

"Antoine?" LaTicia gave him a stern look emphasizing her seriousness. "If the police catch you they're going to kill you."

Antoine chuckled arrogantly. "Fuck it, I'll take my chances. I'm more concerned with them fuckin with my nigga, right now." He turned as the door opened. Shawnda walked in carrying groceries. She'd been holding him down like a veteran, every since the shooting happened, and he was starting to catch feelings. Feeling that Lexie and everyone else had warned him against.

"What's up, boo?" Antoine helped her with the grocery bags.

"Hey, baby." Shawnda replied and kissed his cheek. "I see you have company." She waved at LaTicia.

She is fine! She thought while walking over to her. "Let me rub your stomach, Ticia?"

"Be gentle because I'm stressed out, girlfriend." LaTicia replied while Shawnda gently rubbed her stomach.

"What's wrong, girl?" Shawnda asked and sat next to her. They'd became cordial during Antoine's stay and Shawnda was playing her role to a fault. She rubbed LaTicia's shoulders showing support. She'd been around a lot of pregnant woman and knew how much they craved comfort.

"Fox was arrested today." LaTicia sighed almost falling back into tears. She was still in disbelief. This wasn't what we planned! She thought. Knowing that Fox's roll was suppose to be without with any obstacles. Rone had set the path form him and it was clear through the finish line.

Shawnda covered her mouth with her hands. She looked shocked. Another child born into this world without a father! She thought feeling bad about what Laticia was going to go through alone.

"For what?" Shawnda asked, and Antoine grunted angrily.

"They're tryna put that body on Conners on 'em." Antoine replied still trying to figure out the police's angle. These whities scandalous! He thought while rubbing his head.

328

"Who?" Shawnda asked looking confused. "Are you talking about Playblo?" She slipped letting them know that she knew him. Fuck it! She thought. He should have been dead! Playblo was another one of the men who'd abused her over the years so she didn't hold an ounce of sympathy in her cold heart for him.

"Yeah." Antoine replied while giving her a suspicious look. "That's the nigga. How'd you know who he was?"

"That sleazy ass nigga lived across the street from one of my girls." Shawnda retorted swiftly noticing Antoine's curiousness. I hope he don't think I was fucking him! She thought while giving him a warning look not to ask.

"Oh." Antoine stared at Shawnda with disbelief. I swear her friend better not be Kizzie! He hoped he hadn't stumbled across a woman's scorn that could cost his brother a life sentence in prison.

"I have to leave." LaTicia glanced over to Shawnda. "Are you coming Friday because I'm leaving early?" She asked her.

"Yeah, I'll be there." Shawnda replied while walking her to the door. Shawnda was taking care of all of Antoine business and needed money so she was suppose to meet LaTicia every Friday. Antoine had became close to Shawnda, but what she'd just told him made him weary. He was question her loyalty and her intentions.

329

This nigga is trippin! Shawnda thought noticing the way Antoine was staring at her. There was tension in the air and it came at the mention of knowing Playblo. My relationships are personal. She thought about what she'd say if he questioned her about Playblo.

"Antoine?" She finally said because she was getting nervous about the way his eyes were following her. "Why are you staring at me like that?"

"Please tell me yo girl that lives across the street from his ain't Kizzie?" Antoine asked already predicting the answer.

"Yeah, why?" Shawnda replied with a question of her own.

"Shawn! Did you tell her about me staying here?" He dismissed her question and went into a panic. They could be coming right now! He thought knowing that Shawnda had told Kizzie everything. That flaky ass bitch!

"No!" Shawnda replied flatly. She hadn't told anyone about him hiding out at her house. That would make her an accomplice and she wasn't about doing time for a man's crime. "What's wrong because you're scaring me, Antoine?" She was getting nervous and wondered what Antoine was insinuating.

"Put it together, boo! That scandalous ass hoe asked you all those questions so she could set my nigga up for that body!" Antoine's face darkened with anger. I'mma slaughter the rat bitch! He thought.

"I can't believe her!" Shawnda was shocked.

Antoine touched Shawnda's face. "Do you love me?" He asked her.

"Yes." She lied without pause. Nigga I barely know you and look what I'm into. She thought wanting to bail out right then. Her come up didn't look too attractive at that point, at least, not at the expense of a friend's life because she was sure what Antoine would be asking her next.

"I need you to do something for me."

Shawnda nodded. She'd already known what he was coming with. Fuck it! She thought. In for a penny in for a pound! She listened as Antoine detailed what he needed her to do.

Antoine knew that his brother was facing some trumped up charges and he was going to come through for Fox just as Fox had always came through for him.

"I gotchu, my nigga!" Antoine said after walking away from Shawnda. He was sure that what he'd put together would work. All bitched like that cake! He thought knowing that money made everyone sing a different tune.

****

Fox sat quietly in a dark holding cell in the homicide division. He'd always known about the consequences of what he'd done, but he never expected to get caught up on a charge that belonged to someone else. This some fucked up shit! He thought wanting to scream it out loud, but knowing that everything he said was being heard even if he was speaking to the darkness. The punishment for taking a life was giving a life and Fox wasn't about to give his laying down. I'mma fight this shit! He looked around the murky cell knowing that life had taken him down a dark path.

He watched as insects and rodents devoured scraps of food that were scattered across the floor of the cell. It was the battle of the fittest on the lowest level. The walls that surrounding him were riddled with tales of urban life "Rest in peace Lil Man", "Rock was here", "Fuck the police", and "Y.B.I 4Life" were some of the tags that aligned the walls.

"Ghetto Murals." Fox whispered as his eyes canvassed the wall. Suddenly his body stiffened. It was as if he'd seen a ghost.

"Wait until life gets a hold of U!" He read what had been carved into the masonry brick above his head. What the fuck? He thought while staring at the words. It was like his conscience had sent him a forewarning of his fate. A premonition of sorts. He'd experienced a lot

332

during the last month and those words had preceded all that he'd encountered.

"Fox!" An officer cracked his door and yelled startling him. He'd already been beaten during his ride to the precinct so there was no telling what he had coming next. "Step out!" The turn key took Fox on a short walk to the clergy room.

Fox's face lit up with he saw Raymond standing behind a small wooden desk waiting on him. Seeing him was relieving Fox shook his hand.

"Mr. Hinselton. Good to see you." They both sat.

"Yes, the feeling is mutual, except for the circumstances." They kept it very formal, although, the two of them were like family.

"So how are you holding up?" Raymond asked knowing that Fox hadn't been under that type of pressure before.

"I'm good considering. How's my family?"

"They're worried. The prosecution has an eyewitness placing you at the scene."

"They're lyin! Sheeit, I don't know why, but they're lyin like a muthfucka!" Fox replied confidently because the body that they'd put on him wasn't his. Somebody a dirty muhfucka for this one! He thought.

"You don't know, huh? Have they placed you in a lineup yet?"

"Yeah, and they keep pulling me out of my cell asking me all kinds of dumb shit." Fox wanted to tell him about the beating that he'd gotten during his ride in the squad van yesterday , but he didn't think it would do him any good other that making him look like a bitch.

Raymond cleared his throat trying to find the right words because Fox was in a delicate position and he didn't want to make him feel alienated.

"What type of things have they been asking you?" Raymond asked while giving Fox an examining stare.

"Nothing about me. They've been asking about a friend of mines." HE nodded.

What friend and did you tell them what they wanted to know?" Raymond struck him quick with that question. He didn't want to give him any warning seeing if he could see a weakness in him.

Fox's stomach churned. He couldn't believe what Raymond had just asked him. Is this nigga asking if I threw up? He wondered angrily.

"Antoine, and hell nah I ain't tell them shit!" He spat furiously. I ain't no lawman muthafucka! He thought wanting to lean across the table on Raymond, but he needed him to fight his case.

"I'm Teflon, brah!" Fox said knowing Raymond understood where he was coming from. No bend! No fold, pimp! He thought while giving Raymond a reassuring stare.

"I'm taking your case." Raymond said. "Your arraignment is Monday so you won't be moving to the county jail until then." He stood and shook Fox's hand. Now that his fears, about Fox flipping, were gone, he could focus on getting him out of the jam that Rone and Egypt had gotten him into. He pulled Fox close whispering in his ear. "Don't leave your cell. Don't speak to anyone. Don't even talk to the walls." He demanded in a hushed tone.

Fox went back to his cell knowing that he was good. Although he was faced with serious charges, he saw light because Raymond was defending him.

****

Things had been distant between Rone and Egypt. She was still upset with Rone for telling Fox those hustler's tales, and Rone was still pissed about Egypt leading the police to his house. Sherry was caught in the tension between the two of them and tried to stay neutral. Rone wouldn't let either of them go back to Detroit until he was sure that they were safe. He was certain that the district attorney would jump at the chance to destroy a happy black family by trying to flip one of them.

Egypt walked onto the patio into beautiful weather. Ordinarily she would have jumped at the chance to take a dip in the pool, but Fox's absence was hurting. It had been nearly three weeks since Fox's arrest and he hadn't been back to court since his arraignment. That haunted Egypt and she wanted to know what was going on with her man. She saw Rone and gave him an ice grill. Punk ass bitch! She thought wanting to cal him that to his face, but she had too much respect for him. She wasn't scared of him. She wasn't scared of him unlike most of the people that he dealt with.

Rone lay across the chaise lounge reading the news paper. He saw Egypt walk pass him with an evil look on her face. That's my girl. He thought knowing that Egypt was upset with him. Mean as hell. He wanted to laugh at her tough act, but he chose not to. He knew what type of shit she was facing and didn't want to compound it. Rone folded his newspaper and put it on his lounge.

"You look good pregnant." Rone said civilly knowing that a compliment would ease the tension between them so he could talk to her.

"Thank you." Egypt spat nastily knowing what Rone was trying to do. He'd been doing it her whole life, but this time she wasn't letting him in. She tried to go back into the house.

"Hold up. Don't go because I need to talk to you." Rone waved her over to him and she reluctantly walked over.

"I'm mad at you, Rone." She said and rolled her eyes at him.

"I know." Rone said nodding his head. "Fox told me a few days before he was arrested, but this ain't the time for that."

"I miss him." Egypt's face softened. She wanted to cry, but she was sure that Rone would tell her to man up. "I'm six months pregnant and I don't want to do this alone."

"Egypt, you know you're not alone. That's something that you don't have worry about as long as I have breath in my body. " Rone assured her.

"I Know, but I want him here."

Rone nodded. "Me and you both, but we know the chances of that happening are none. I spoke to ray, and he says the prosecution has an eyewitness placing Fox at the scene of the crime.

Egypt's face curled. "Kill him then! Shit! Do something!" Egypt yelled furiously. "Fuck it! Where the nigga at? I'll smoke him."

Rone chuckled lightly because he knew that Egypt was serious. "This ain't TV, Egypt. Shit doesn't work that way." Rone shrugged his shoulders. "We still don't know if he did it anyway."

"Rone, please! You must have forgot! I met Playblo and I remember what he did, so put a cap on the bullshit!"

"I did it." Rone confessed holding his head high showing confidence. It was something that he didn't want to say, but she needed to hear it. "Fox went with me, but I did it."

"So he can beat it then. Can't he?" She perked up believing that there was chance for him.

"How?" Rone asked with a dark sunken stare. I know she don't want me to take out! He wondered staring at her. This little bitch done lost her muhfuckin mind!

I'm not turning myself in!" Rone said stiffly hoping she understood him. "Sheeit! We can fight this shit tooth and nail, but I can't go out like that!" he shook his head defiantly. That shit was a roll of the dice! He thought knowing it could have been him who got identified, instead of Fox..

Egypt shook her head. "No, Rone. I'm not saying anything like that. Hell no! I'm talking about reasonable doubt. Some O.J type of shit." She suggested desperately.

Rone signed. "My nigga was on trial in eighty-nine for a body that he didn't commit. We copped him a Jew lawyer out of Cali to represent him. He was the coldest trial attorney in the country, but he lost and my nigga hot a life sentence."

"How did he lose?" Egypt asked curiously, although, she didn't understand what his situation had to do with Fox's. "He was innocent and he had a good lawyer."

"That's the crazy part." Rone chuckled although the situation wasn't funny.

"He knew my guy was gonna lose before he even took the case, and he warned us. He'd been a prosecutor in Florida for ten years before he became a defense attorney. H e said he'd never lost a case where he used a snitch while he was a prosecutor, and he'd never won a case where a snitch was used against him as a defense attorney." Rone shook his head felling bad about what Fox was going through, especially since it was his body.

"So basically." Rone continued. "That's thirty years in the legal game and he's never seen the prosecution lose with a snitch on their team."

"Well we have to do something." Egypt insisted, although, she didn't know what else there was to do.

"You're right. That's what I need to talk to you about…." Rone paused. He knew what he was about to tell her would hurt, but he had to say it.

"Fuck it." He continued. I'm going to be real with you. Fox is going to prison. For life, no way, but ten or twenty years look inevitable."

Tears rose and fell from Egypt's eyes profusely. "Rone, please don't say that!" She cried knowing that he'd given he the real.

"E, you have some decisions to make because your life is going to change completely."

"My life has already changed." She replied in a solemn tone.

"You have to do whatever you think is best for you. Are you ready to raise your child with its father? Are you ready to be faithful to a man that many never hit the bricks again? Better yet! Are you coldhearted enough to say fuck a nigga who's been your rock?"

"Why are you asking me this shit?" Hs screamed. "I don't feel like this shit today!" Her tears flew from her eyes.

I'm trying to prepare you because this is the shit that you need to be asking yourself." Rone stood and walked away leaving her to think about what life was gin to be like without Fox.

Egypt put her face between her legs and cried violently. Why does he do that shit? She wondered because what Rone had said to her was torturous. She loved her man thoroughly which made him being locked up for something that she could have avoided more hurtful.   Egypt was Playblo's contact in Atlanta. Wherever he visited for business, she would be his dope boy concierge service book him rooms, renting cars and escorting him into party of Georgia that he wasn't familiar with.   Rone had warned Egypt not to get to familiar with Playblo, but she rebelled against what he'd told her.

Egypt hooked me up with Playblo on a personal level.   He was cool and Egypt wanted to kick it. Although she didn't' want to be romantic with him, he'd came with lustful intentions of his own.

"Come on, mami." Playblo pleaded trying to get into Egypt's pants. He wasn't giving up easily.

"No, Blo" Egypt laughed while pushing him off. She knew he was feeling her, but it wasn't mutual. I don't even know why I came. She thought still dodging his advance.

"Yeah, mami." He reached for her belt. Yeah, bitch! He thought while wrestling with her. I'mma get this young pussy! He slapped Egypt across her face sending her to the floor at the foot of the bed.

Egypt tried to run for the door, but she was too fast. He snatched her by the hair pulling her into a vicious choke hold. He is going to rape me and kill me! She thought while being choked and stripped at the same time. Playblo raped and sodomized Egypt.   He disappeared after his savage act of sexual deciation, and

341

wasn't seen until the day Rone and Fox tracked him down and killed him.

After Egypt's rape, Rone promised her that he would find Playblo and murder him. Egypt had helped him to that promise and was relieved after hearing about his death on the news. She'd craved that vengeance for year, but would never imagined what it would cost her. She'd traded Fox's freedom for Playblo's life, and that was a barter that she would regret for years to come.

****

Fox paced the holding cell awaiting his bond hearing. He thought about Egypt and his unborn children. It was month since his arrest and he was still unable to have contact with the world the turn key opened the door letting Raymond in.

"What's up, ray? How was your weekend in the Motor City?" Fox asked

"It was a blur. I was busy working on getting you a bond." Raymond replied an sat on the cement bench next to Fox.

"So how's it looking for me?" Fox braced himself for bad news.

"It's hard to say right now, but whatever the end may be there will be some light." He patted Fox's back.

"So basically, I'm going to prison, huh?" Fox asked, although, he already knew the answer.

"Most likely that will be the case. Hopefully we can spread some of that big paper you've got around. Try to shave some years off." He stood and signaled the turnkey that he was ready to leave. He looked around the small cell sorry that his young guy had to go through what he was gong through.

Fox entered the court room escorted by two sheriff deputies. He scanned the room for some familiar faces only seeing his mother. Everyone stood as the bailiff introduced the judges' entrance. The judge immediately asked the defense attorney and the prosecution to approach the bench.

Fox noticed Raymond's face contorting into a grimace. He looked puzzled. What the fuck's going on now? He wondered hoping Raymond wasn't hearing more bad news. The judge kept cutting his racist eyes into Fox's direction. After Raymond came back to the table, the judge kept his stare on Fox. It was intimidating, especially to some whose life was in his hands. Fox wouldn't make eye contact with him, instead he kept his eyes on some papers that lay on the defense table.

"Defendant is remanded without bail.!" The judge said swiftly hit the gavel. Raymond turned to Fox.

"Fox?" Raymond said, sliding close to him so no one else couild heaqr him. "Don't say a word. Not even your name. Most of all, don't talk to anyone in your cell

343

block." He gave Fox a look signaling his seriousness. "Not even idle chitchat."

Fox nodded devastated by what had happened and he didn't even know what was going on. Another body done caught up with me! He thought while being escorted back to his holding cell. He felt defeated and the fight hadn't even started.

Antoine stretched across the bed breathing heavy and tired from pounding Shawnda's back out. He was sure that she was the woman for him. She was a freak and she'd given up a lot to protect him from the law. His gratitude was without bounds. He nudged her side.

"Boo?" Antoine rubbed the nape of her back causing her ass to quiver.

"You're ready again?" Shawnda asked still winded from their first round. "Boy, you're an animal!" She teased and they both laughed.

"Nah, that ain't what I want."

"What's up, babe?" She giggled. "Uhn, uhn!" She shook her head. "You ain't putting that us my ass!"

"Nah, boo!" He laughed knowing that she'd do whatever he asked her to. "You serious about going through this wit me, so let's go all the way. Fuck it! Let's get married?"

"When? Now? I think that'll be hard with you on house arrest."

"Is that an excuse? I'm serious. I wanna get married to you, so what's up?" He asked again not wanting to give up. Bitch! He thought while flashing her a fake smile. You ain't tellin on me, hoe! He knew that she wouldn't be able to testify on him if they were married.

"Yes, but…" She started before Antoine cut her off.

"I hollered at LaTicia. She gon give you a cashier's check. And Lexie gon give you some bread that I stashed at my house."

"No, Antoine." Shawnda replied. Checkmate, nigga! She thought. "I don't want your money. I just want you. I'm cool on that other shit." She shook her head refusing the money, but hoping that he'd insist she took it. In for a penny, in for a pound! She was putting it all on red and letting it roll because her new fiancé had bank, and wanted to break bread with her.

"That comes along with me. Sheeit! Besides, it ain't my money. It's ours, boo. You gon be my wife!" He said excitedly while intently watching Shawnda's reaction He'd thrown the money out as an incentive, but her fate was sealed weeks ago. Either she jumped the broom or lay down because there was a sneakiness about her, that everyone around Antoine saw, makin him want something more concrete than a good fuck and a place to hide out. The passion was there, the emotion was there, but the trust was lacking.

"I wonder what everybody see in this hoe that I'm missing?" Antoine asked himself while he lay on the bed next to Shawnda. Lexie had taken one look at her and swore by Shawnda's deceitfulness. Him and Lexie were sitting on the enclosed back porch of his safe haven bouncing game back and forth. He'd just gotten head and she was amped up from what he'd shot down her throat. She jumped up looking ruffled.

"I'm telling you, Ant!" Lexie said agitated by what she saw in Shawnda. "This skank is gutter!"

Antoine looked at her wondering where the sudden attack on Shawnda's character came from. I know this hoe don't think we're together. He wondered hoping Lexie hadn't gotten the wrong idea about their relationship. He felt her and made sure she was taken care of, but she was the bottom bitch and Shawnda was wife material. This bitch jealous!

"Bitch! You worry 'bout this dick and doing what the fuck I tell you to do!" Antoine lashed out at her. He knew that he had to keep a hoe like Lexie in her place because if she got out of line it could be trouble for everyone.

After that, Lexie went silent. Antoine had questioned a lot of shit in his life, including Shawnda's intentions, but he just couldn't see what everyone else saw.

****

A loud crashing sound startled Egypt, as she rested in the sitting room, waking her out of her sleep. She went to see what was going on. Rone and Sherry must be thumping! She thought because everyone in the house had been on the edge lately. She found Rone leaning over the desk in his den. His eyes were filled with pure malice and the telephone was beneath the desk banged up.

"What's wrong , Rone?" Egypt asked afraid to hear what had upset him so much.

"I'm sorry for waking you up, Egypt. I got some bad news and didn't handle it the right way." He nodded towards the shattered telephone, although, she already noticed it.

Egypt walked over and rubbed his back. Damn she thought. She felt bad seeing Rone like he'd been since Fox had gotten Locke up. He wasn't his usual laid back self and his new look wasn't appealing.

"Talk to me, Rone." She smiled trying to lighten the mood in the room.

Rone shook his head sure that Egypt wasn't ready to hear what he had to say, because heat was bothering him would be devastating to her. The worst case scenario had became reality. Damn! He thought knowing that she was going to be crushed.

"Ray said ten years was the best sentence that he could get for Fox."

Egypt' smiled changed quickly. A wail of tears fell down her cheeks and she hugged Rone. Her tears were of sadness and relief. She was saddened because she would be without her man and, on the other hand, she was relieved because the sentence could have been worse. She'd been questioning whether she could still love Fox unconditionally despite him being away for years.

Now that she had confirmed what she was up against, Egypt was certain that she could maintain her relationship because she loved her man. Rone rubbed the tears from her eyes.

"Fox is being sentenced next week, so you have to get on a plane tomorrow. I'm sure he'll want to see you there."
Egypt's loving manner changed. She threw her hands onto her wide spread pregnant waist staring at Rone enraged. I hope this nigga ain't trying to leave my man out there without support? She wondered.

"What?" Egypt asked nastily. "You're not going to be there to support him?" She held her sassy pose.

"To support him?" He answered her question that he really didn't want an answer to. "You're tripping, E." He brushed her sudden filthiness off. "I've been supporting him from the jump. Fox hasn't spent a dime throughout this. Ray's my guy, no question, but he ain't cheap." He tried to keep a cool head, although, Egypt was being too flip.

"Money doesn't have shit to do with this, Rone. You said we were a family. So what? You're going to let family go through this shit alone?" She pursed her lips.

"No." Rone replied bluntly. "That's why you're going. Me…" He pointed to himself with his thumbs. "I'm never going back to Detroit. Not even to visit."

"Why? Are you scared or something?" she asked knowing that questioning a gangster's G was as insulting s you could be. She stared at him with raised eyebrows. I know, nigga. She thought not afraid of him. I know how to hurt people's feelings too!

Rone chuckled evilly. He knew what Egypt was trying to do. Nah, li'l girl. He thought showing her no emotion. He'd raised her and she knew how to get a rise out of him. But this time he wasn't buying what she was selling because he'd already been duped with that game a few times before. He shrugged his shoulders still chuckling.

"I don't know?"

"What do you mean…you don't know?" She was upset with the way he'd answered her so vaguely.

"Egypt, listen." He replied demanding her attention because he wanted her to understand him. "I don't even know what fear feels like. I've never been afraid of shit." He pounded his chest roughly. "I'm the muthafuckin Boogie Man! So how in the fuck can I tell you about feeling some shit that I've never experienced?" His tone and his stare had became detached. He'd isolated himself from his presence. Becoming numb. This was how Rone got when rage overtook him, but he wouldn't go to his usual extremes with his baby girl. Egypt was the only blood relative that he had left living.

"Is Sherry going?" Egypt asked changing the subject because she knew that she'd gone too far, furthermore, she knew that she couldn't beat Rone with words.

"Hell yeah, she's going. She's coming right back afterwards though. We're posted until we close on our new spot in Houston."

"So I have to come back too?"

Rone shrugged his shoulders. "Sheeit, that depends on you. If you're going to stand by Fox, no. If you're not, I think you should come with us to Texas." He was direct about his feelings, although, he was sure that Egypt would walk through hell with Fox.

The tears reappeared in Egypt's eyes. Rone was tormenting her and she didn't know why. This man is the devil! She thought.

"How can I stop loving a nigga who showed me how to love?" Egypt asked. Because you make loving someone hard! She thought.

"Egypt, this is a helluvah predicament! I know, but it ain't got a muthafuckin thing to do with how much you love Fox. Sheeit! I know how you feel about him. I'm the nigga who showed you hot to knock him." Rone smiled arrogantly. Yeah! He thought. I did that! He'd set the tone and the path of their relationship.

"This…" Rone paused knowing he had to get rough with Egypt because she was too high strung. "This shit here is about a process and your willingness to complete it."

Egypt nodded. "I thought about it, Rone." She said knowing he wouldn't like the answer because it was evident to her that Rone was trying to make her jump ship on him.

"Well, while you were thinking about it. Who'd muthafuckin life did you consider more import? His or yours?" Rone appeared to be upset, but he wasn't. He was just giving her the game uncut like real niggaz did because she was going to need it.

"Ours together! Why would you even ask me some shit like that?" Egypt was seething at that point. I should slap this nigga! She thought angrily. Rone was being brutal to her feelings and she didn't know what had brought it on. Maybe he's taking this shit worse than me?

Rone laughed sadistically. "Y'alls together?" He asked and continued his diabolical chuckle. "You sound stupid as hell! If you plan on standing by a nigga in the joint for ten year, that'll subsisting for both y'all! And

351

trust me, it won't be together." He calmed and shook his head letting her know that what he was dropping on her was the gospel. He'd seen the best of bitches break under the type of pressure a ten year prison sentence brought.

"What the fuck is wrong with you?" Rone continued grilling her while she cried. He knew that she was soaking it up because she hadn't tried to run off yet. "You've been to college! You know about evolution. The process of change for all living entities. He's going to change and you're going to change." He shrugged his shoulders. "How…is yet to be seen, but the certainty is reality."

Egypt cried violently. "Alright! Fuck it! It's deeper than love. The way I feel about him is…" Damn! She thought not being able to find a word for how she felt. "Fuck it! I can't find a word!" She chuckled knowing how silly she'd just sounded. "But it exist! Why..do..you..want me to leave him so bad?"

Rone threw his hands up defensively. Nah! He thought because that was the furthest from what he was trying to do and she had misunderstood his tough love.

"Hold up, E! I never said that. Sheeit, I don't want you to leave him. That's my li'l nigga and my brother-in-law. Trust me, I want to support your decisions, but it seems like you want to be there for him…just for his sake. It shouldn't be like that, baby girl. Be there for him because you want to for you. If you would have told me that loving him makes you a better person, or some poetic shit like that , you would have had me, but you didn't. He wrapped his arms around Egypt hugging her.

"E, I'm drilling you because I want you to be sure that this is what you want to do. As long as it's for you and you can handle it, you have my support." He used the back of his hands to wipe tears away from her face. "Think about it though." He walked away relieved that his job was over. This was a conversation that he didn't want to have, but knew it was necessary.

Although Egypt had started off confused about what Rone was trying to do, she'd finally caught on. He'd laced her with boss game over the years and questioning a situation before diving into it head first, was one more to add t the list.

****

Everything that Fox had experienced over the last few years blew through his mind while he sat quietly inside the holding cell of the courthouse. His hustling season had been brief, but he'd made it through. Sheeit! He thought looking at the bright side of the situation. At least the hustler out lasted the hustle! He'd seen a lot of ballers get taken out of the game before the clock expired. Some by his hands and others by their own ignorance. Some of the things in his life were concluded, but there were something's that were still unanswered.

Fox thought about the robbery at the 70west building. It was something that haunted Fox.

"I'm sorry! I didn't know!" Visions of Que pleaded for his life flashed in and out like the flicker of the light in the interrogation room, but it was in his head.

"Blocca..!" He heard the single shot that he'd fired leaving a hollowness to Que's forehead.

Jackson was dead, but he believed him. He's a coward and was too afraid to mention anything about the shooting to anyone. So how in the fuck did Rone find out so quick? He wondered know that there was something missing. Antoine was in police custody and couldn't contact anyone and Que didn't know Rone. Fox rubbed his goatee while in deep thought.

"What was Rone's purpose for sending me to Atlanta?" He whispered questioning himself about Rone's loyalty. It was evident that Rone was trying to create distance between Antoine and Fox, but Fox didn't want to believe Rone was capable of that type of treachery.

Fox remembered a conversation that him and Rone had. He was trying to convince Rone that Antoine was trustworthy and loyal, but Rone wasn't with it.

"I couldn't have known someone since birth and known them to be an honest person, but I still wouldn't trust them." Fox heard Rone's voice replaying what he'd said to him.

Was that a hint? Fox wondered had Rone been that arrogant to warn him before sending some hitters at his brother? His mind was everywhere and nowhere at the same time. He was sure that seven months in a cell alone would play tricks on anyone's mind. He'd even pondered over the supposed eyewitness testimony in his murder case.

The witness had claimed to have seen Fox force Playblo into the dumpster and kill him. She swore to the grand jury, that she'd been alarmed by the dog in the next yard barking so she peeked out the window witnessing Fox slit the dog's throat, stopping it from barking, before shooting the victim.

He was sure that the woman was probably there because she had some details in place, but the majority of her testimony was fabricated. Fox wasn't the shooter, nor did he slit the dog's throat which left holes in her testimony the size of the one he'd sent through Que's forehead. He could have fought the case, but it was useless, especially knowing it could have made the witness remember the real details of the story—Rone. Rone had done too much for him and his family, so what he was doin was payment of sorts. They cell door opened disturbing his reminiscent state. He stood knowing that he was taking the first steps into a ten year bid.

Fox entered the courtroom and his comfort level took off. This was the first time he'd seen his family since the arrest at Rone's house. Seeing all of the women in his family supporting him meant everything. Laticia and Egypt were sitting side by side. He had undeniable love for Egypt , but his respect for her was what drove their relationship.

Fox knew that the potential of losing Egypt was prevalent He wasn't naïve to the game. He knew that some niggaz lost their hoes right after they got the cuffs slapped on, but he had faith in Egypt's loyalty to him despite his shortcomings. And the look of love that she'd given him when he walked into the courtroom assured him that her commitment was still alive. She made eye contact with him and moved her hand over clasping LaTicia's . Egypt wanted to show him they were a united front and he'd caught on to her message.

Although Fox knew that he was being railroaded by a faulty court system, who used a counterfeit witness, she stood in court with his head high. He'd played by rules that some hustler's had forgotten. He took one for the team and was sentenced to ten year, in state prison, while his family looked on.

****

Egypt helped Sherry pack the last of her and Rone's things. They talked about the life altering situation that Fox's incarceration would bring. While they talked, Sherry abruptly burst into laughter.

"Egypt!" Sherry laughed hysterically trying to catch her breath. "You're good!" She teased while still laughing.

356

"What?" Egypt asked not knowing what Sherry was talking about. They were packing to leave a place that had been her and Rone's home, and she didn't know what was so funny about that. Just being in that house reminded Egypt of the day that Fox had been arrested.

"I comment you." Sherry said. "Ain't no way I could have sat next to LaTicia!"

"Yeah, it was hard." Egypt replied and smiled weakly. She'd done that to show her man how much she loved him. It didn't have anything to do with LaTicia.

"I'm telling you, E!" Sherry balled her fist waving them. "I would have been on trial tomorrow for smacking that hoe into next week!" They both burst into laughter after what Sherry had said.

Egypt waved her hand. "I'm over it, girl. I have to let it go because our children will be brother and sister." She chuckled trying to take the high road, but knowing she wanted to whip LaTicia's ass!

Sherry threw her hands onto her hips and stared at Egypt jokingly. She smiled after seeing what she knew was Egypt all along—hate for LaTicia. She changed the subject out of respect, but she wanted to talk about next wasn't too inviting either.

"So are you going to do right by my brother?" Sherry asked seriously hoping Egypt answered her question the right way. "You know I can fight." She put her fist back up playfully.

Egypt sighed. "My intentions are in the right place , but Sherry. A lot of things change in ten years, even people." She'd thought about what Rone told her realizing that making a decision like that would take time and experience.

Sherry nodded agreeing with what Egypt had said. She was sure about Egypt, especially knowing that she'd put up with Fox having a bitch on the side. LaTicia had nearly killed her and Rone's marriage and Rone wasn't even having sex with her.

"I can only imagine, but I'm sure the change won't affect how much y'all two love each other." She giggled. "Fox is a muthfucka, but he's one of the few that has a heart of platinum."

Egypt smiled thinking about Fox. "You're right! He's a motherfucker, but he's my motherfucker." She flashed her engagement ring at Sherry and they laughed.

"So when are you doing to see him because I have something I want you to tell him."

"Thursday." Egypt answered.

"Do you remember the bitch Kiesha?" Sherry's face tightened at the mention of her name she hated her so much.

"Yeah, she's the one who started all that stuff between Tee and their other friend." Egypt didn't like to say Jackson's name.

"Yeah, that's the tramp. I ran into her while I was at the cleaners. Do you know the hoodie rat had enough nerves to tell me she was eight months pregnant with Tee's baby!"

"Quit playing!" Egypt replied shocked that she would even show her face around Antoine's family after what she'd done.

"I'm not playing! The bitch fucked me up with that one, E!" they both laughed.

"What did you say?" Egypt kept laughing. "I know your ass said something."

Sherry nodded. "Hell yes, I said something. I told her to go jump in the grave with her dead ass nigga! Then I walked away."

"You're crazy! You said that shit for real?"

"Ummhmm." She nodded. "I was wrong and I hope Jesus forgives me, but I most certainly did."

The two of them kept talking while they packed. Egypt felt a strong emptiness without her man. She was also saddened about Rone and Sherry moving away. Being part of a strong family structure was a new experience for Egypt, and now it was all being taken away from her.

****

LaTicia reluctantly passed Shawnda a cashier's check for one hundred thousand dollars. She'd tried to talk Antoine out of it a few times, but it was his money so she fell back. Laticia didn't understand why he needed to give her such a large amount, but he insisted on it. Laticia had been around the game for over a decade camping out with some of the coldest paper chasing hoes in the game, but none of them were as vigorous as Shawnda.

That bitch is about her scratch! Laticia thought while walking out of her office. She was sure that a women as beautiful, successful, and intelligent as Shawnda was would never settle for someone like Antoine unless she was after something. Her undying support for a fugitive thug was too much for LaTicia to believe in.

LaTicia had even supported his decision to marry the broad, but giving her that type of money didn't seem logical. He's a sucker! She thought giggling knowing that Shawnda had ran boss game down his throat separating him and his paper. She too was a fool for love, but she wasn't a fool about her scrilla.

After leaving the office she rushed out to see Fox. She was nervous during the court proceedings. LaTicia wanted to apologize to Egypt for betraying her, but Sherry's hawking stare warned her not to say a word. Although she never got the opportunity to say what she wanted to say, her and Egypt shared a moment when

Egypt grabbed her hand. It represented the beginning of a long healing process, and she was ready and willing to complete   it.

LaTicia walked into the county jail and saw Egypt standing in the visitation line. She wanted to skip out, but Egypt say her and waved her over. She approached Egypt cautiously. Although they held hand in the courtroom, there was no telling how Egypt felt.

"Hey, girl." Egypt said with inviting eyes. She could tell that LaTicia was frightened, but she'd dropped her resentment off and forgiven her.

"So how are you doing?" LaTicia asked nervously not knowing how to talk to her. She'd watched Egypt grow up and now they held ill feelings towards one another over a man.

"I'm doing terrible to be honest." She grabbed LaTicia's hand. "Come on, let's grab a bench and sit down."

"Egypt, I'm sorry for everything I did." LaTicia said sincerely.

"I know. I already let it go, but to be straight up with you. I don't want to be friends or no shit like that. Not right now, but we can be civil. Our kids will be brother and sister. As far as that goes, we're cool. They say time heals all wounds, so let's let time do its work." She smiled politely hoping wht she said would could actually be possible. LaTicia pointed toward the sheriff.

"He's calling you." LaTicia said.

"I'm going to be a while, so you go up first." She smiled . Don't start bitch! Egypt thought. I've already let you slide once! She watched as LaTicia disappeared into the elevator. She wanted to keep track of how much time her and Fox visited.

After getting onto the elevator a feeling of shame overcame LaTicia. She realized what a mess he'd made of her life. She now understood why Fox loved Egypt the way he did. She saw the heroine qualities that Egypt possessed and knew tha she was worth of being lived completely.

"Hey, Fox." LaTicia said as he sat. Her eyes wailed with tears from seeing him after so long.

Fox smiled. "Stop it. Don't even start that crying shit." He chuckled staying upbeat, although he was defeated as well. "I've done enough of that for both of us, sheeit."

She wiped her face trying to clean up the tears. "I'm sorry. How have you been?" She smiled happy to see him despite the circumstances.

"I'm good. How have you and the baby been? That's more important." He looked at her stomach knowing she could drop his seed at any moment. She rubbed her swollen stomach.

"We've been fine. I've missed you. I wanted to come see you before, but Rone advised me not to." Her voice was apologetic because she felt bad about not visiting him.

"Yeah, he advised you right then. This whole case is some bullshit!"

His face darkened with anger about being railroaded.

"What do you mean?" She asked looking confused about what he was insinuating.

"Sheeit, some hoe lied on me! Now I'm spitting ten bars. That's the bullshit I'm talking 'bout!" He snarled.

"You must have forgotten who you are talking to?" She reminded him, with a look , that she knew what had happened.

"Nah, ma! Don't get it twisted. It is what it is, but the hoe was their only witness and she lied about what happened. The bitch said I cut the dog, jumped the gate, and smoked a nigga all at the same time. Sheeit! Superman can't even do that!" He chuckled about being shafted, but LaTicia didn't find what he was saying amusing.

I knew I was better than Ray! She thought knowing that she should have taken Fox's case instead of letting Raymond handle it. Shit! She pulled out a paper pad.

"Was she a witness or an informant because that shit sounds coerced?'

"A witness. A lying ass witness!"

"How did she look?"

"Shit, I'ont know. We didn't get that far, so I never saw her. Her name was on the transcripts though. It was Porter, Roshaunda Porter, if I'm not mistaken."

LaTicia's neck snapped whipping her face away from the paper pad and into Fox's direction. She was stunned. Not able to talk or anything. Scandalous ass bitch! She thought and tossed her tablet to the floor rushing back to the elevator while Fox looked on.

"Boom, boom, boom!" Fox banged the window wondering what he'd done to run her off.

∎∎∎

LaTicia dialed Antoine's number while rushing pass Egypt and out of the jail. No one answered so she kept redialing and redialing. Antoine always answered his calls because he was usually looking for company to come around. Dirty trifling bitch! She knew something wasn't right. She jumped into her car and peeled out of the lot. She was still in shock an wondered how anyone could have slipped it.

"Shawnda..Roshaunda?"   She question herself catching it, but she knew that logic was subjective. She'd known something was off about the way she'd taken Antoine in after such a short time of knowing him. I thought she wanted the money! LaTicia thought upset at herself for letting Shawnda out think her.

She'd became suspicious after Shawnda told them that she knew Playblo, but she thought they'd just had a thing before or something like that. Never did she think she was the eyewitness in Fox's murder case. Antoine had brought a rat into their fold confirming everything Rone had thought about him. Now Fox was on his way to prison and Antoine was sleeping with enemy.

Laticia thought seeing her parents killed in that car accident was the worst moment that she'd ever experience, but as she turned the corner seen gall the police lights, she realized she could be approaching something worse. Helicopters hovered about the house where Antoine was hidden. She was sure that he was ignorant enough to let off a few rounds at the law. Callousness was in his bloodline. Damn! She thought while waiting to see the outcome praying that he conceded without a war.

"Pssh." She sighed letting out a wind of relief after seeing Antoine being escorted from the house in cuffs. Although every step he took was piercing to her heart, she was relieved that he wasn't being carried out in a body bag.